# THE DREAM FEAST

# THE DREAM HEIST

## THE DREAMSCAPE SERIES BOOK 1

CHRISTINA FARLEY

EVERBOUND PRESS

The Dream Hunt

The Immortal Secret

The Immortal Legend

Gilded

Silvern

Brazen

The Princess and the Page

*For my boys, Caleb and Luke Farley. To past and future adventures.*

My hands shake as I check the final calculations and enter them into my sleep pod. If only I could ignore the hollow dread that has locked itself into the pit of my stomach.

I want to chalk it up to nerves. After all, entering people's dreams is cutting-edge science, and though Dad and I have been working on the Dreamscape for the last four years, I'm always hoping that this time we will make a breakthrough. Or perhaps it's because with every Dream Walk, we get that much closer to saving the lives and memories of our patients.

No, I sigh. If I'm being honest, this is all about saving Grams' memories and her mind. Ever since she came down with dementia, and now watching it worsen, I'm determined to do whatever it takes to retrieve or at least save as many memories of hers as I can. Maybe that's selfish. Maybe my love for her is getting in the way of everything. But right now I don't care. I just want results.

"You look green, Aria." Tony chuckles at me from where he preps his sleep pod. "Or maybe purple. It's hard to tell in this lab's crappy light."

"Mornings and I don't get along," I grumble, smoothing down my forest-green scrubs. They hang on me, wrinkled and disheveled like they hate mornings, too. "Especially before I've had breakfast. Can't wait to go back to sleep."

"Sleeping on the job," Tony says. "The ultimate career choice."

I grin. We're the only team members at MaxLife who are interns and still seniors in high school. But the whole experience has really pushed us to the limit, and it's totally been worth the lack of sleep. Sure, we might have to get to work at 4:30 a.m., but what high schooler gets a chance to enter people's dreams for a job?

"Buenos días, team," Javier, our team leader, says as he strides into the room. He checks the Dreamscape board on the wall, reviewing the clients scheduled throughout the day. "Looks like today's going to be a busy one. Tony and Aria, you're just here for our first session, correct?"

"Unfortunately, high school calls," I mutter.

"Right," Javier says, distractedly still staring at the board. "Looks like for this morning's patient, our number one goal is to detect any unusual brain functions. Of course, I wouldn't be too upset if we found that infamous Vault we've been looking for."

"Dude. It doesn't exist." Tony adjusts his long dreads so they don't get tangled in the heart monitor cords. "Your Vault of Memories is as real as a pink-striped unicorn."

"I refuse to believe that." I tap in my MaxLife employee code into the sleep pod. "We just need more time and I know we can find it."

Sun pads into the sleeping lab in red cashmere slippers while reading her tablet. Knowing her, she's doing one final check on the brain's data before we enter the patient's dream. Sometimes it's annoying how over-the-top thorough she is, but then that's why Dad hired her as our fourth team member.

"Patient 145's brain appears perfectly healthy." She drums her manicured nails on the edge of the tablet. "No sign of decomposing or atrophy. Don't you find that strange?"

"What about this patient hasn't been strange?" I say. "I can't remember a time when we weren't given a patient's medical history before a mission. Something's up."

I glance over at my dad—well, *Dr. Hale* while we're working—and adjust my scrubs for the tenth time. He's in the adjoining room with our technicians. They're partitioned off by a glass wall, studying the wall full of computer screens, each one that hoists our brain waves and images our brain sends in from the Dreamscape.

MaxLife's number one rule is complete patient

privacy. It prevents us from knowing the patient's name or getting personally involved due to the intrusive nature of the procedure. But Dad's never withheld a patient's medical history from us before.

"Every case is different." Javier shrugs, but lines form along his forehead. "Maybe since this client is so different, we'll finally get our breakthrough. Stay focused on the job and make this mission a success."

"You are traveling through another dimension," Tony calls out in his best Rod Serling voice. "One of dreams and imagination!"

He hums the Twilight Zone music as his clear sleep pod lid encloses his body. "See you kids in the Twilight Zone."

"Keep it professional in there," Javier orders before Tony's lid clamps shut.

"Twilight Zone." Sun huffs. "How are we supposed to make progress when no one takes our missions seriously?"

Chuckling, I climb into my own pod, glad Tony is with us. He always knows how to calm my nerves. My body sinks onto the soft, padded contours. These sleek white pods are specifically designed for each team member with swooping upward sides in case we thrash about during the dream, protecting us.

And yet, as I strap on my pulse tracker and attach the patches to my heart monitor, my eyes seek my dad. Could he be hiding something?

"You might be right about this Vault." Sun sets down

her tablet and narrows her eyes at me. "Just don't do anything stupid, Aria. Got it?"

"Stupid?" I put on my most innocent face. "I never do anything stupid."

She lifts her eyebrows, shooting me an I-totally-don't-believe-you look. I cringe, remembering our argument after the Dream Walk last week when I decided to not follow Javier's orders. She doesn't understand that Grams doesn't have time to wait around for protocols and orders because every day she loses more memories.

Which is why time is so important.

"Okay, maybe the elevator wasn't the best choice," I concede. "Next time, we can borrow your brother's jet. Then we could've kept up with the Dreamer for sure."

Her lips quirk. "Behave yourself, Aria, and I'll consider asking him."

"Deal." I blow her a kiss as my pod's cover rises over me.

I slip my Neuro-Read sleep mask, strapping it around the back of my head so it can read a complete assessment of my brain waves. Between the sleep mask and my heart monitor, the techs can read my EEG's, EOG's, and ECG's to measure my brain waves, eye movements, and heart. It transfers my thought processes into the Dreamscape Network and converts them into visuals. Dad calls it our brain connector.

Once I'm in a dream state, the technicians will connect my brain waves and the three others on my team into our client's dreams. Basically, it inserts our team's consciousness into the dreamer's consciousness. We can't read each other's thoughts, but we're able to interact and think just like a normal dream.

As if any dream is normal.

"Sleep induction enacted, Ms. Hale," a woman's melodic voice vibrates through the pod. Javier named her Celeste. "Sweet dreams."

Within moments, the Sound Oasis kicks in, emitting the cry of seagulls and crash of waves to my ears. Beneath these noises, a thrumming hum trickles through. It's this noise that will induce my brain waves into sleep mode. I count down, waiting for sleep to come.

10, 9, 8, 7…

TWO

INTO THE DREAMSCAPE

The first seconds are the hardest, standing between worlds of dreams and waking. I anchor my body onto the ground, focusing on the shifting floor that appears more like waves than carpet. With a concentrated effort, I breathe in deeply, touching the papered wall, willing my stomach to settle. The room shifts and buckles as if it can't quite remember what its form is.

I double-check to make sure the gray scarf covering my red hair is in place. I program myself to wear a scarf since sometimes my hair color attracts unwanted attention. Our job is to watch, observe, and guide the dreamers through their dream to reach their Vault of Memories.

I blink to focus my vision. Soon I make out four adults sitting at a long rectangular table eating dinner inside a house. Now to figure out which one is our dreamer.

"You need to concentrate on college and your future,"

a woman is saying. She's wearing a constricting black dress and her white hair is yanked back into a tight bun. "Not playing games. Bringing shame to the family is the only thing *that* will bring."

"I'm sick of this," a light-haired guy says. His back is to me so it's hard to get a read on him. "This is my life we're talking about, remember? None of these classes are preparing me for what I want."

"Such nonsense." The woman picks up her fluted glass and takes a delicate sip. "Dreams are for fools. Besides, how often do they last before you come crawling back to us? Do I ever know about *that*."

Her chin dips and eyes narrow pointedly at the man to her right. It's then that Tony swaggers into the room, marching over to me and jerking his hand into a quick salute. "Dreamscape entry success," he says.

I take in his bright yellow shirt and flamingo shorts. "What are you wearing?" I whisper harshly as he moves to my side.

"I was hoping for a beach day." He shoots me a slow it's-totally-going-to-work smile. "Subliminal messaging. I've been reading up on it."

"You better hope the dreamer doesn't notice you and realize you're not from his mind. If you wake him up, our mission is a failure before we've even begun."

"When I win the Nobel Prize, I'm going to make sure you're in the front seat to watch, Aria. It's going to be epic."

"Shut up." But then he gives me his puppy dog look so I say, "Just make sure you say my name in your speech."

He chuckles and saunters over to the table. I gasp as he picks up a serving spoon and starts loading food onto a plate.

"What *is* he doing?" Sun appears beside me. Her pixie haircut is askew and her cheeks are flushed. She must have had a tough time acclimating. "Someone has to stop him. He's going to ruin everything."

"Sorry I'm late." Javier sidles up to the two of us. "Took me longer than expected to fall asleep."

Suddenly the blond guy stands, turning just enough that I can see the profile of his face. He's younger than I had expected, probably my age.

There's something about him that niggles at the corner of my mind. "I think he's our dreamer."

"Too young," Javier says.

Which is probably right since all our patients have dementia, so they've all been older.

"I'm out." The guy slaps his cloth napkin on the table. "Don't ask me to attend any more of your stupid Sunday brunches again."

"Uh, oh." Sun presses two fingers to her forehead. "I hate it when we shift right away."

The guy storms out of the room, throwing the Dreamscape out of whack. The walls begin to crumble into nothingness. The moment a dreamer transitions to the next phase of their dream, everything vanishes since the dreamer's consciousness has moved on.

Including us. If we don't move fast enough, we'll be kicked out.

"It's him," I say. "He's our dreamer."

Now that he's left, there's no reason to maintain our wallpaper pretense. I bolt across the room, jumping onto the table and scattering plates and glasses before dropping back to the ground and beeline for the door before it vanishes. The people within the room don't even look at me, instead, their bodies morph into nothingness along with the furniture.

Our target marches out the front door and seconds before it shuts, I stick my foot out, kicking it open. My team and I manage to stumble out seconds before the entire house dissolves.

My vision blurs briefly as the world around us changes. As my eyes refocus, I discover we're now standing on a beach. A wind kicks up, swirling sand around us.

"This isn't good," Sun says. Her usual perfectly ironed pants and chic designer shirt whip against her thin body like a flag braving a windstorm. "The conditions are going to get us kicked out of the dream."

"Stay on mission," Javier orders, "and stick close to our guy."

We take off after the dreamer as he heads toward the

ocean. A buzzing sound cuts the air. A helicopter swoops down from above, landing beside our dreamer.

Inwardly, I groan. I hate it when these dreams get out of control.

"He's going airborne," I warn.

Gritting my teeth, I pump my arms, focusing all my thoughts on getting within ten feet of our guy. Before I can reach him, the dreamer steps into the chopper and it lifts into the air.

We've lost him. We're going to be kicked out of the dream.

Or will we?

I push myself faster and leap for the lower bars of the chopper. My hands grasp the cold bars of the helicopter, and I gasp as my body is lifted into the air, the wind whipping me back and forth beneath the belly of the helicopter. It's a stupid, reckless move that could kick me out of the dream, but solutions don't come without risks, right?

My hair untangles itself from the scarf and slaps against my face. My muscles scream in pain. I'm not sure how much longer I can hold on when a hand pulls me up, helping me clamber into the chopper. I belly over the side, my whole body shaking as I take in the height.

It's just a dream, I remind myself.

Below my team is staring up at me and I manage a half-hearted wave. Tony holds both hands up like a football referee calling out a touchdown. "You go, Air Girl!" he yells.

Then they all fade, consumed by the nothingness. As long as they remember they are in a dream and haven't accepted the dream as reality, they will be fine and wake up back in their sleep pods, completely safe.

Still, a pit forms in my stomach. I'm alone now so the responsibility of the mission lies with me. I swallow down my fear and face our dreamer.

But one look at him and my heart dives.

That sharp jawline. Those loose blond strands hanging over piercing eyes, deep blue like a summer storm.

I know this guy. It's Jake Sutherland from my high school.

# THREE

# THE DREAMER

"Aria?" Jake asks in a voice that sounds as confused as I am.

*Crap.* He recognizes me. Quickly, I look away, hoping I'm fast enough before the video feed stemming from my brain picks up the visual of him saying my name. Everything I see transfers into the Dreamscape and forms a soundless video of the dream back at MaxLife. The thing is, if they realize I know our dreamer, they'll try to wake me up.

We aren't supposed to know our patients personally.

"Hey, Jake." I lick my lips, unsure what to say.

He reaches out, hesitant at first, as if to touch a strand of my hair, but stops himself. Crap, my hair color is going to ruin everything.

My face burns as he studies me.

In the real world, we barely talk to each other. He

hangs out with the computer nerds while I hang with the science nerds. But here, in this land of dreams, anything is possible. My heart beats faster. Which is silly. I'm a professional here in the Dreamscape. Not some swooning eighteen-year-old in high school.

"Let me come with you," I say.

"You can't." He backs away, inching too close to the other side of the helicopter. He looks out the other side of the chopper like he's going to jump. Which is bad. I've never dream-jumped before. In the past, I've always faded rather than taken the risk.

He turns around, already forgetting about me. I can't allow that to happen. I need to stay with him. The way he's dreaming is different from our other patients. He could be the difference in finding how a brain makes its connection to the Vault of Memories. For Grams sake, I have to try.

"Jake." And I grab his hand.

His fingers, warm and strong, intertwine with mine, and heat floods up my arm, sending goosebumps over my body. Is this what it would be like to touch him in real life? Or is this just a sensation I'm making up in my mind?

Touching him is totally against the rules and holding hands is *definitely* against the rules. How many times has Dad told our team we are only observers and guides, leading our dreamers to find their memories?

Ignoring protocol, I go with my gut and squeeze Jake's hand. "Let me come with you."

He nods and then steps to the edge of the doorway. The wind roars around us, whipping against my clothes and face. I look down to find mist curling around jagged mountain peaks and ocean waves raging against sharp, hundred-foot cliffs. I think about Dad's theory that you can't die in a dream unless your mind thinks it's real.

This is just a dream, I tell myself. *It's not real.*

Jake smiles at me and then his hand slips from mine as he leaps. The moment he's gone, the helicopter begins to disappear, piece by piece.

"Now or never," I say.

Sucking in a shaking breath, I jump.

I fall and scream in absolute terror. And yet somehow, it's as if I'm flying, soaring through an unknown sky over a strange world. I stretch my arms out, mimicking Jake, and mentally urge myself closer to him. Even as terror is streaking through my veins, I can't deny the thrill somersaulting inside me.

"Wait up!" I call out to Jake.

He glances back and frowns. Seeing me has got him confused all over again. The world shifts and the ground rushes up at an alarming speed. With a whoosh, we're suddenly both standing on a dirt road, purple flowers blooming around us. My knees buckle and my stomach churns. I sink to the ground, trying to pull myself together.

Jake leans down and touches my shoulders. "I have to go. There's something I need to do."

Then he takes off toward an ancient temple-like building. Vines curl up along its sides and crumbled pillars are scattered about the ground.

"Wait up." I try to stand, but my knees buckle. These quick dream sequences are too much on my body.

He turns around. "No one is allowed. Not even you."

My pulse kicks up a notch. I should be upset, but I'm not. I can't prove it at this point, but something tells me this temple could be what our team has been searching for all year. The Vault of Memories. One of our theories is the Vault stores a mind's memories. Theoretically, if we knew where the dementia patient's memories were stored, we could reconnect the path to their memories so they could retrieve them.

Jake takes off again and I stumble after him. We pass by a small hut filled with computers. Strange creatures are sitting at tables playing video games and eating hot dogs. One of them has green skin and a large eye in the center of its head.

"Dude," I mutter. "Your dreams are weird."

"They sure are," someone near the hut says.

It's Tony, leaning against the side of the shack. Beside him, Javier is throwing up in the bushes while Sun is sitting on the ground cross-legged, hands massaging her temples.

"You got back in," I exclaim. "Except you three don't look so good."

"Yeah." Javier wipes his mouth. "Reentry is a beast."

"See that temple." I point to where Jake is headed. "I think it's a Vault."

"Good work," Javier says. "Let's check it out."

Except we must have let too much space grow between us and Jake as large chunks of ground start vanishing around us.

"Come on," I urge, and then break into a sprint. "We have seconds at most from fading."

"I can't—" Sun gasps, running alongside me. "I can't —keep up."

A chunk of the hill to our right vanishes. A rooster runs across our path squawking, only to fall into between two land masses.

"A rooster?" Javier asks.

"Not as weird as that flying teacup from last week," Tony points out.

"Be careful of the gaps," Javier warns. "They open up into the Void. If you don't think you can make it, step away from the dreamer's consciousness zone and revert to fade."

My heart skips. Not much scares me in dreams, but the Void is something entirely unpredictable. Basically, it's nothingness. Dad's theory is it's the subconscious of the dreamer's mind so when we fall into it, we could get lost in that subconscious.

When Dream Walkers fall into it, sometimes it takes longer for us to wake up or we've gotten severe headaches that lasted the rest of the day.

My thoughts are yanked to the present when I'm

forced to jump over a gap onto another land mass. Meanwhile, Jake has reached the double doors of the temple and is staring at etched symbols moving across the door's surface. What do those symbols mean? I have to get to him.

"This is becoming too risky," Sun says. "The gaps are too wide."

"Sun's right," Javier says. "We need to fade."

"I can't let this opportunity pass," I argue. "We're so close to making a breakthrough."

And it could be the breakthrough we need to heal Grams' dementia. If I can keep my mind focused and remember this is a dream, I'll be fine. After all, didn't I just jump out of a helicopter for the first time?

"You promised you wouldn't do anything stupid," Sun warns.

"Sometimes science is about taking risks," I reason. "I'm going to see if this Vault concept exists. No more theories. No more conjectures."

"Like hell you are," Javier says. "I'm the lead for this mission. You're still an intern. Your father will kill me if anything should happen to you. The order is revert to fade."

"It's not worth it," Sun adds. "We'll have another chance."

"Will we?" I ask. "When? This is the first time we've come so close."

What I'm really thinking about is Grams. How many

of her memories are already lost because we are too slow to find answers?

"I'm with you, Aria," Tony says. "Let's do this."

The ground shifts and wobbles. Dirt crumbles off the sides of these tiny islands, spilling into the black nothingness below us. I nod to Tony and take off in a full sprint and leap through the air, pin-wheeling my arms to propel me to the next land mass.

It's all in your mind, I tell myself.

For a moment, I'm running on air, stretching my body to land on the mini island before me. Then my hands sink into dirt. I did it! I scramble onto the mass and nod to Tony. He cracks his knuckles like he does before every exam at school, and with a running start, he jumps.

It's when he's halfway across I realize he won't make it. Thick darkness widens below his feet as if aching to drown him. His eyes widen with the realization he won't make it.

Crap.

I spot a tree root jutting out from the edge of my land mass. I slide down to it and snatch hold of the root, my legs dangling over nothingness. As Tony plummets, I reach for him.

Our hands clasp and I'm overwhelmed with relief. Except the weight of his body is too heavy, and my arm holding the root screams in pain as Tony's body hangs from mine. *This is only a dream.* My fingers on the root begin to slip.

"I'm going to swing you up," I explain.

He nods, the white of his eyes brighter than stars.

*It's all in your mind.* I swing him upward.

Dirt splatters my face as he claws at the earth and scrambles onto the land mass. Sun's and Javier's cheers fill my ears. We did it!

But the dirt my root clings to loosens, shedding from the landmass like an unwanted snakeskin. My heart jams into my throat in horror.

"No," Tony cries.

"Jake!" I yell. If he'll just look at me, he could change the dream's landscape.

Then Jake turns, and his eyes land on mine. "Aria!" He runs, reaching for me.

But I'm already falling.

My arms stretch for him, except it's too late. My body dives deep into the abyss of nothingness.

My eyes blink open to a blurry world of faces leaning over me.

"She's awake!" a voice says. I piece together that familiar cadence, soft and soothing. Sun. "There now, Aria. Everything is going to be fine. Just fine."

I wait as the faces focus into place. I recognize the crew from MaxLife: Javier, Tony, Sun, and my dad.

"There, there." Dad pats my shoulder, which even in my half-zombie-like state, I find myself bristling from. Leave it to Dad to revert to treating me like I'm still eight. "You're coming around just fine."

"I told you it was too dangerous," Javier says. His tone may be sharp and biting, but there's worry in his brown eyes. "Escúchame, hermanita. Next time, stick with the crew."

I smile weakly at his pet name for me.

"But dude, she found the Vault!" Tony says. "She's proven it exists!" Then he picks up my limp hand and slaps my palm with a high-five. "And bonus points for falling into the Void and not dying. That was epic."

"Well," Dad says. "We don't know for sure if it was a Vault, but it was definitely something different than we've yet experienced."

I push myself up, unable to resist letting loose a low groan. My head pounds and my muscles ache like I ran five miles. "The Void part was far worse than I thought it would be," I mutter.

"Oh, no, no, no you don't." Sun pushes me back down onto my sleep pod. "Don't go rushing about, now do you hear me, Aria? And the deal is off."

"Deal?" I'm completely confused.

"You said you'd behave and not do anything stupid." She clamps her hands on her hips. "So forget about getting a ride in my brother's plane."

I lay back down and moan. "Bummer."

"Javier!" Nurse Debbie demands. "Get her some food. Orange juice and how about some of those sliced pears?"

"Donuts," I say, my voice raspy.

Javier tromps off to find food, muttering under his breath in Spanish like he does when angry or worried. Meanwhile, Nurse Debbie pushes everyone aside and checks my blood pressure again.

"I'm fine." But it's impossible to force any enthusiasm or punch into my words. I try to take off the blood pressure wrap, but Debbie wags her fingers at me. "Don't you be messing with my work now, Air Girl." She laughs at that. "I saw you flying on the monitor."

Dad rubs the side of his face like he does when he's keeping something from me. "You did well, Aria," he finally says.

"I did 'well'?" I sit up. "Are you kidding? That was amazing! It was the first time we've come this close to proving that a person's mind holds a Vault with their memories locked inside."

"I'm not saying it wasn't." Dad rubs the gray stubble on his face and sighs. Those bags under his eyes have gotten heavier. "More than any Dream Walker has ever done. But though it looked like it could be a Memory Vault, we don't know for sure. Regardless, I'm pulling you from any more Dreamscape treks until we get you cleared by Nurse Debbie."

"Seriously? I told you I was fine." And actually, I do feel fine after taking a few sips of juice and a bite of the chocolate doughnut Javier passes to me. Except a million questions fill my mind. The foremost is seeing Jake Sutherland in the Dreamscape. "What do my vitals say, Debbie?"

"That you need to give yourself a rest." She gives me a pointed look over her glasses. "Maybe you'll be ready next week for an observation assignment only. No more dream walking for a while."

"By the way, you touched the dreamer," Dad begins once everyone has left, leaving the two of us alone. He takes a swig of his coffee, screws up his face as if he tasted something sour, and then dumps the coffee into the sink. "You know that's against the rules."

I stiffen. If Dad had any clue I knew Jake, he'd pull me from working on Jake's case so fast. I can't let that happen. I don't know why Jake is coming in for memory therapy, but I want to be on the team that goes back in the next time Jake's here. I cross my fingers the video footage doesn't show his lips saying my name.

"He seemed to trust me," I hedge. "I knew it was a risk, but I think that's how I got so far into the memory." I decide to turn the tables. "Why didn't you give us this patient's medical records? And why are you and Dr. Cage acting so strange?"

I swallow the lump in my throat and wait for Dad to justify his actions or give me some type of answer, but he just refills his mug with steaming hot coffee.

"It's complicated and nothing for you to worry about." He shuffles to the work panel and reviews our visual footage of the mission. "Things should get back to normal tomorrow."

"So something *is* up." I swing my feet to the floor and my knees buckle slightly.

"Make sure you get food in you before logging into your dream account. I'll call your school and tell them you're sick. I'm writing you a doctor's note right now."

I decide not to argue the point that he's more of a Doctor of Science than a practitioner. "You're avoiding the question," I huff. "Besides, I'm fine. I'm going to school today."

I hold up my finger to Dad's lips when he spins to argue with me. This usually makes him laugh, and he teases me about being stubborn like Mom. But not today.

"Don't tell your mom about the dream incident." His jaw clenches and he won't look at me, which unnerves me even more. "If she knew, she'd insist you work with her instead."

"Trust me, I won't."

"Good." Dad nods distractedly and despite the cool AC pumping through the lab, a line of sweat trickles down the sides of his face. "Now go get some rest."

Inwardly, I stiffen at his quick dismissal. Ever since Grams was diagnosed with dementia, the two of us have worked hand in hand to develop this Dreamscape. I've been just as much a part of this as he has. So why is he shutting me out now? I could stay and argue over this, but my mind is drawn to the door at the far end of the lab. The door that leads to the room where Patient 145 is.

Usually coming out of a Dreamscape can be rough on the body. There's disorientation, dizziness, nausea, hunger, and sometimes prolonged headaches. I've always been the lucky one. Unlike the others on my team, I have minimal side effects other than being ravenous for a good breakfast as if I've been sleeping all night rather than entering a short NREM or REM sleep cycle of another person's dream.

But as I shuffle down the corridor, the dizziness and aches remind me why we have the rule to steer clear of the Void. When I felt them pulling me out of the dream, it was as if I'd been smashed against a brick wall. Maybe Sun was right. I was more stupid than brave today.

Glancing around to make sure no one is watching, I crack Patient 145's door open and peek through the narrow slit.

Cheryl and Craig, our two technicians, are working at their computers, probably entering their report, but the sleep pod is empty. The dreamer has already left.

Disappointed, I head to my debrief terminal when Tony slides open the glass door to his station, and tipping back his chair, winks at me as he continues his monologue of our mission. "Then that Aria went and leaped out of the chopper, paddling her arms and legs like she was swimming for an Olympic tryout. I thought she was going to plummet to her death, but she flew like a bird, a plane—"

Before he can say the rest of his line, I push his chair upright and slam the glass door, shutting him inside his room. This makes Tony laugh even harder. I can't hear him between the sound-proof glass, but he's pointing at me, mouth open and head back, mimicking a dead fish. I roll my eyes.

"Hilarious," I say. But as I slip inside my terminal, I recall jumping out of the helicopter with Jake and that exhilarating feeling of flying and falling.

After we leave the Dreamscape, we're supposed to watch the footage of the dream the computer pieces together from our brain waves. Once we make an audio commentary of the footage, it goes into our client's files, which are then passed over to the psychiatric department for review. Their job is to figure out the best ways to reroute neuron pathways in the patient's brain.

Except recently our Dream Walks discoveries have shifted our goals. Since dreams show the natural process of long-term memories, when a person dreams, it strengthens those memories. So if we could connect these new traces with their stored memories, it's possible to stabilize them so they aren't erased or damaged.

It doesn't take long for me to review the dream into the audio. I pause the footage as Jake's and my fingers intertwine. The memory of the rush that flooded my body surges back to me. I lean in closer to get a better look at him.

"Is that really you, Jake?" I whisper. "And if so, why are you losing your memories when you're so young?"

Or maybe it isn't Jake from my school. It's not like we hang out. Ever. Maybe this dreamer looked a lot like Jake when he was young. Or perhaps it was Jake's grandfather.

That would make a lot of sense. Except for the fact that he knew my name.

Or what if Jake is a part of an experiment even I'm not aware of?

I nibble on the corner of my thumb, knowing exactly what I need to do.

# FIVE
## WHO IS JAKE SUTHERLAND?

"Hey!" Tony calls after me as I slide into my convertible. "Do you think you can give me a lift to school on your way home?"

"Sure, hop in." I slip on my sunglasses and tie my long hair back. "But only if you promise yourself to secrecy."

"Secrecy?" Tony plops into the passenger seat and grins. "Oooo, juicy. I'm in. Wait. Don't tell me. Let Tony, the master, guess. You're in love with Javier."

"Eww." I scrunch up my nose. "No way. He's like fifteen years older than me."

"You actually died in the dream, came back to life, and now you're a zombie."

"What?" I pull the car out of the office parking lot and into traffic. "Have you been watching those reruns of Hunting the Dead? Because you need to stop."

"Those are life-changing! I'll never see the world the same after that series."

We debate on whether the world will truly be overrun by a zombie apocalypse until I pull into Lake Nona High School's parking lot and slip the car into my numbered spot.

"Wait." Tony stares at me. "What are you doing? You're going to school today?"

"Yep."

"But your dad. Didn't he say you couldn't?"

"Shouldn't," I point out as I sling my backpack over my shoulder and head toward the front office. "I can't miss my classes. I have assignments due in Psychology and physics. Missing school would totally interfere with my GPA and future plans. After all, you can't sit around waiting for success. You have to pound on success' door."

"Not with the quotes again," Tony mutters.

The truth is I'm desperate to go to class and see if this Jake guy is really the same one from the dream. Although, I'm technically not lying about my GPA obsession. I'm determined to be the youngest scientist in the field of Consciousness and Transformative Studies. It's totally cutting edge and the possibilities are endless.

Possibilities to make a difference in Grams' life.

As I stride down the crowded hallway of my high school, I glance down at the emerald ring on my right hand. Even in the drab hallway, it shimmers under the lights, and I'm reminded of Grams and the day she gave me this ring.

It was twilight, that time between times. Grams lounged on one of the pool deck chairs while I sat cross-legged in the other. We were waiting for the neighborhood's Fourth of July fireworks to start. Classical music played from the stereo system and inside Mom was humming as she prepped the lemonade. Dad was cleaning up the last of the plates from our dinner, but from his distant expression, I could tell he was brainstorming another idea for the memory company that would someday become MaxLife.

"I want you to have this," she said, holding out her fist, fingers tightly closed. I hated how her hand shook as if just holding it was too much effort. "Hold out your hand."

She dropped a glistening emerald ring into my palm. I knew this ring. In fact, I don't remember a time when Grams didn't wear it.

"I can't."

"It was my mother's, and her mother's before that. I don't know how much longer I have until I don't remember how special this was to me. I wanted to give it to you while I still knew what it meant."

"Thanks, Grams. I'll remember you with it. Always." Tears crept into the corner of my eyes as I slipped the cool stone over my finger.

Thinking back to that moment unsettles me, but I can't allow myself to lose sight of what I'm doing. Not now when everything Dad and I have worked for these past few years is about to explode into making scientific history. What I need to do is focus on Patient 145.

This Jake guy could be the key to it and healing Grams.

"You know what's almost as bizarre as zombies overtaking the world?" Tony asks as we step into the classroom. "That guy from the dream. He looked familiar. I just can't place the dude though."

"Yeah, that's strange," I say, vaguely.

My heart beats against my ribcage. Tony hadn't considered the idea that Jake Sutherland from our class could be the dreamer because all our clients have always been ancient. The thing that has me all wound tight is in a few minutes we're both going to find out the truth. Because Jake is in our psych class.

Tony heads to the back corner of the room where he always sits. I pause for a moment, scanning the room for Jake. He's not here.

A mix of relief and disappointment floods me as I settle into a seat, front row of course, and pull out my paper on brain development that's due today. I'm scanning over the contents one last time, double-checking that I put my name and date on the paper when the door to the classroom flies open a minute after the bell rings. My heart flutters.

*Jake.*

Seeing him again in real life, I've no doubt it's the

same guy from the dream. He's wearing different clothes, jeans, and a navy T-shirt that has some gamer design on it, and his hair isn't quite as neat as it was in the dream. The blond strands hang over his eyes and he has to flip his head to be able to make eye contact with Mr. Kores. There's an ease to his stride, slow and yet confident as if he rules time itself.

I bite the edge of my pencil and peek over my shoulder to see if Tony has noticed Jake, but he's busy talking with Melissa Benson.

What do I know about Jake? Not much. Word around school is he's a total genius and he won some national computer competition. He keeps mostly to himself and the techies. He's pretty hot, too, not that I should care. I'm a career-focused girl. I don't have time for guys.

"Had a doctor's appointment," Jake is saying to Mr. Kores as he hands over a slip of paper.

"No problem," Mr. Kores says. "Find a seat. We're about to get started."

Jake scans the room, but the only empty chairs are the two in the front row beside me. When his eyes land on me, I could swear something flashes through them. Recognition? Realization? My cheeks burn, and I duck my head.

"Okay class, open to page 56 from last night on Freud," Mr. Kores announces as Jake settles into the chair next to mine. "Talk to your partner about the reading for the next five minutes and be prepared to share your collaborative findings. In the meantime, I'll be coming around to collect your papers."

I peek from the corner of my eye, studying Jake. He's pulling his Psychology textbook out of his backpack along with a tablet. As he lifts his head up, those blue eyes catch mine and my heart jumps a little.

"Something wrong?" he asks.

"Err, nope." *Look down! Don't focus on his face!*

"You're Aria, right?" He drums his fingers on the desk. "I'm Jake Sutherland."

"Hey." I look around to find another partner to pair/share with, but everyone else is already paired up.

"Have we met before?" he presses. "Cause you look really familiar."

*No joke. I hung out with someone who looked just like you all morning.* His forehead knits as if he's made some connection. He remembers me from his dream. I'm sure of it.

*Crap.*

In the Dreamscape, I'd just be bold and deal with this head-on, but here in the real world? Nope. It's suddenly way more complicated.

"Um, well we've been in this same class so—" I let my voice trail off. "What do you think of last night's readings? About um—" I sound like a freaking idiot, not Lake Nona's next valedictorian. I open the textbook to find the discussion covering Sigmund Freud's thoughts on why we dream. Inwardly, I groan. Life is completely unfair.

"Freud was an unusual guy, don't you think?" Jake scans his finger down the page. "I mean, this line about how our dreams are actually a secret outlet for our repressed desires."

The memory of how he looked at me in that dream causes me to shift in my seat. It's really time to steer the topic into a safe zone.

"Personally, I think dreams are so much more than that, don't you?" I begin. "I mean, they provide ways for our minds to figure out problems, make connections, and deal with issues."

Mr. Kores wanders by our desks. "I like where this convo is going," he says. "You two will make a great team."

"Team?" Jake and I both say simultaneously.

"You heard me." Mr. Kores writes something down on his notepad. "I'm assigning your team the topic of Dream Interpretations. You'll gather the research, write a two-page essay, and present the topic via PowerPoint on Friday."

Jake leans back and runs his hands through his hair, letting out a long breath. Mr. Kores is a brilliant teacher, so much so that to get into his class, you have to write an essay on why you want to take his course. But right now, this class is the last place I want to be.

"Do continue." Mr. Kores taps the desk with his knuckles before moving on to the next group.

How could I have let this happen? The last thing I want to discuss with Jake is dreams. Sure, I have first-hand experience and I've already got plans to go into the field, but our work at MaxLife is confidential. Dad's clients put their complete trust in our work and discretion. Most people don't even know what we do at MaxLife, which is exactly how Dad likes things. It allows him to try out new ideas without the pressure of the world breathing down his neck.

But maybe I'm making something out of nothing. After all, Jake hasn't seemed to put the connection that reality might have interfered with his dreams. Or maybe he really did have a doctor's appointment and I'm making this all up. Who knows? Maybe we entered the dreams of his grandfather or—gross. Ugh. I need to stop overanalyzing.

"So Friday." Jake gives me a sideways glance as he pulls out his phone, swiping through his calendar. "That gives us three nights to knock this out of the park."

"Right. But I don't want to delay working on it. I *have* to get an A. My GPA can't handle anything lower than that. What are your plans after school today?"

"Wow. Okay. Well, I've got my gamer's club, but I can meet after that."

"Gamer's club?" I can't keep the scorn out of my tone. "As long as it doesn't get in the way of my education."

"Ouch." He slaps his chest like he's been wounded, but the smirk on his face tells me he's anything but offended. "You're one of *those* girls."

"What's that supposed to mean?"

"That you think you're too good and smart to have a little fun."

I narrow my eyes on him. "Is there something wrong about being driven and successful?"

"Driven and successful?" He cocks his head. "That's pretty sexy."

My face, no, my entire body burns like it's on fire. I need to refocus this conversation. Stay on track. "How about 4 p.m. at the library?"

"Works for me." He checks his phone. "But the library closes at five so let's meet at one of our houses. You okay with coming to mine?"

I nod. What have I gotten myself into?

## SIX
## IN OVER MY HEAD

To say I'm worried that Jake will put the pieces together is the understatement of the millennia. I cringe at the thought if he ever found out that I'd been in his dream. Talk about awkward.

A light wind tugs my hair out of my ponytail as I pull into Jake's driveway. My heart drops into the pit of my stomach as I take in the house. I've been here. Not physically, but in Jake's dream. It's the same front door and the same porch, except instead of a beach like in the dream, it's a front yard with trees and flowers and a hedge.

In the past two years of being a part of MaxLife, this has never happened to me or any of the team members for that matter. It's unprecedented. I'm way over my head.

My hands shake as I pull out my phone and call Dad. The phone rings five times before it goes to voicemail and his hologram pops up on my phone. "Greetings. This is

Dr. Dustin Hale, psychologist specializing in dream therapy for dementia patients. I'm unable to speak with you at this time, but please contact my secretary to schedule an appointment."

I tap my foot as I wait for the voicemail. Finally, the beep plays, and I open my mouth to tell Dad everything. Except I can't. I hang up.

I blow out a frustrated breath and stare at the house, fiddling with my phone. It doesn't help that Jake's house is intimidating. Actually, it's more of a Spanish-styled mansion with a rounded tower. A balcony with a wrought-iron fence juts out over the arched wooden front doors. Tall palms border the mansion, waving in the breeze, while ivy clings to the smooth stucco walls. The hedges curve around the house like piped green frosting and flowers dot the landscape in a perfect array of colors.

Everything is so perfectly manicured I doubt there is even a blade of grass out of place here. I'm about to crank the engine and bolt when Jake strolls out the front door, hands in his dark jeans pockets. He knocks lightly on the hood of my car.

"Where are you going?" he asks. "Have I already scared you off?"

"I'm not scared. Just had to make a phone call."

"Is that why you've been sitting in my driveway, staring at my front door?" His lips quiver as if it's taking all his power to hold in a laugh.

He's making fun of me again. *Screw it.* I frown, push

the button to slide the top over the car, and turn the ignition off. If I play this right, he'll never guess it was me in the dream.

"Nice place." I slip out of the car and join him up the stone walkway to the intimidating entrance.

He opens the front door and a gush of cool AC hits me in the face. Mom always insists on keeping our house nearly the same temperature as outside because she says it's a healthier way to adapt to the environment around us. But I think it's just because she's so obsessed with her plants that she wants our house to imitate the jungle where her plants really should be growing.

"It's big," he explains sheepishly as he watches me spin, taking it all in. "A little big for my mom and me."

I expect the inside to be like Jake's dream with the lace tablecloths and that tight-bun-haired lady staring down at me. It's not.

The foyer spans all of the way to the ceiling where a wrought-iron chandelier hangs. In the center of the area, is an ornate fountain. Its rushing water adds a soothing staccato to the air. Persian carpets lap over brown tiles. The walls are painted a dark tan and medieval-styled sconces are set between huge paintings with gilded frames. Twirling Grams' ring on my finger, I follow Jake down a ribbed-arched hallway.

"Jake!" A woman waves at us as she marches down one of the hallways. She's wearing purple running gear and her short blonde hair has been pulled back in a ponytail. Blue eyes that look just like Jake's widen when she spies me. "Oh! And who is this?"

"Mom." Jake nods toward me. "This is Aria Hale. She's here for a school project."

"Hello, Aria," Mrs. Johnson says with a bright smile. "You can call me Katy. I'm so glad you've brought a—" She pauses suddenly as if she was about to say something she shouldn't, and then blurts, "*Study partner*. Well, I'll let you two get right to work. How about I bring up some snacks! That's an idea, isn't it?"

"Great idea," Jake agrees, but as she bustles away, he scrunches his face like he swallowed a package of sour candy. "She can be over-the-top sometimes. Just go with it."

"Your mom seems really nice. Mine never has time to cook. She always gets home from the university so late, or if she is home, she's too wrapped up in her research. And then Dad is hopeless when it comes to cooking. He gets so distracted that you never know what he'll put in the ingredients. Like baking soda instead of salt or a half a cup of butter instead of a cup. Which is why it's always up to me to find us food. Usually, I order from Talini's."

Gosh, what is wrong with me? I'm just rambling like an idiot. Of course, when was the last time I've been at a guy's house other than Tony's? Except Tony and I are like best friends. There's something about being with Jake that feels totally different.

"They've got good food." Jake leads me up a spiral

stairwell. "But I wouldn't say my mom is exactly reliable in the cooking department. She only cooks when she's completely stressed out. She's on the board of trustees for Lake Nona Medical and when things go crazy, she locks herself up in the kitchen and cooks up a meal to feed an army. I can't promise anything she brings up will taste good."

We enter Jake's room and I'm floored by how incredibly neat and organized it is. The walls are painted a soothing gray. He's got a single bed with a gray comforter, not a wrinkle in sight. Two large panels hang from the wall with paintings of skateboarders. A round black mat lies in the center of the room and a metal desk presses against a large bay window overlooking the lake. The desk is completely void of anything other than a computer, pencil holder, and tablet. I think about my desk back home, stacked with journals, M&M packages, and empty water bottles.

"So this is your room." I linger by the door.

"Yeah, I guess you could say it is."

I've always found that entering someone's room is like getting a peek at their personality and history. In the Dreamscape, the rooms we enter usually symbolize the dreamer's mood or desires. Plus, since a Dreamer only dreams of people and places they've seen before, it's a way for us to store those memories for our dementia patients. But this room is sterile and rather disappointing. Jake is already sitting at the computer, pulling up a fresh Word document.

"You like skateboarding." I perch on the edge of his bed, noticing how incredibly fast he types.

"Nope. My mom's choice."

"Doesn't that bother you? That she doesn't let you choose what you want for your room?"

He swivels in his chair to face me. "I've got my games. Which if I remember, you weren't all that impressed with."

There's something about his tone that irks me like it's digging under the surface of my skin. My words tumble out before I can stop them. "So you prefer to live in a fantasy world rather than your own?"

He studies me intently, rubbing his chin. "We should start our research. We've got a lot of ground to cover."

My face burns a little. Again. He definitely has a way of unnerving me, which is unsettling. I like to be in control of situations and today I've felt zero ounces of control. A niggling feeling tells me there's more to him than he's letting on.

Still, he's right. I should be concentrating on nailing that A. That's all that matters. Not figuring Jake out. I fish out my laptop while he begins pulling up various medical journals.

"What's your internet password?" I ask.

"I just logged you in." He shoots me a sheepish grin. "For security sake."

"How do you do that? Get into my computer? That's creepy."

"Creepy? Well, it's all about perspective. I look at it as being convenient."

"Convenient? Seriously?"

We argue over the invasion of privacy until I win, or at least until he gives in, and we begin working on our project. About thirty minutes later his mom pops into the room. Most of her hair has fallen out of her ponytail and strands are stuck to her face from sweat.

"How are my two students doing?" She is holding a platter piled up with food that I'm unable to identify.

"Wow, that looks great Mom. What is it exactly?"

"Hummus and tortillas freshly made!" She beams. "Oh, it's so nice to see you hanging out with a girl." She clears her throat at the dark look Jake shoots her. "Err, I mean friends, girlfriends, boyfriends. Friends!"

"Thanks, Mom." Jake picks up a burnt tortilla. "Really appreciate the snack."

"Okay, then." Her eyes focus on Jake and the tortilla he's holding as if urging him to eat it. "Well, if you get hungry, just let me know."

"Thanks, Ms. Sutherland," I say.

"Katy." She smiles.

Once she heads back into the hall, I pick up a tortilla, but Jake rips it from my hand.

"You seem like a brave person." He pulls out a garbage bag from his drawer and dumps the entire contents of the platter into it. "But trust me, that's not worth it."

"That bad?"

"Why do you think Talini's is still in business?"

I laugh and then accept Jake's offer at a granola bar he's got stashed in his top drawer. As we munch on our snacks, it takes all of my discipline not to analyze his dream this morning. Who was that lady in the dream who told him his gaming was pointless? Was that why my teasing about his gaming irked him? And he had been running from someone, which according to our research, running often means the dreamer is trying to escape something. Then there was that whole part with the weird ogres.

But the biggest thing I don't understand is why he was at MaxLife.

"So you were at the doctor's this morning," I venture. It's a risky move, and maybe I should just stay out of it all, but according to Mom, one of my undying faults is my curiosity. Of course, Dad would always argue it's one of my best attributes.

"I've been having some killer headaches lately. Had some CT scans done, but they weren't able to figure out the causes. I didn't want to get into all of that with the teacher, you know? Next thing everyone will be asking if I'm going to die or something."

"Oh. I'm sorry about your headaches." Huh. I don't know what to think now.

"Here's an interesting theory." Jake points to his screen, changing the subject. "Harvard Medical School research indicates that when the brain dreams, it helps you learn and solve problems."

I press my lips together. Dream interpretation and maneuvering in dreams are some of my strengths. Which is why I can't go into too much detail. So I just say, "For the most part, but usually the dream and its environment symbolize how the dreamer feels or emotions they are dealing with."

"Really?" He peeks at my laptop, so his face is inches from mine. The fresh scent of his soap causes me to lose my focus. "Where does it say that?"

"I just read it somewhere." Actually, it's in a thesis I'm writing based on my work at MaxLife. Definitely not going to tell him that. "I'll look up the source when I get home. In the meantime, just put that information in the presentation."

I've always prided myself on my ability to read people well. Okay, so maybe it's a slight obsession. Not only in real life do I overanalyze people, but in dreams, I take that to the next level. I don't just look at the person, but the environment the dreamer is taking me through. Their reactions. The twitch of the fingers or eye. Which is why I'm feeling slightly off over Jake. I can't get a good read on him. I'm searching for any usual ticks. His clothes, room, really everything about him is such a mystery. It's almost as if he's hiding something.

My phone beeps. I ignore it and keep reviewing articles, but then like a flood, a bunch more texts rattle the silence.

"Your phone is missing you," Jake says, a twinkle in his eyes.

I laugh. "It's probably Sun, my coworker. She's been worried about me." But when I look at my phone and see Mom has sent me a bazillion texts.

"Worried about you? Everything okay?"

*Shut your mouth, Aria.* When did I become such a blabbermouth? "It's my mom actually. I don't know—"

My words are swallowed up with the texts filling up my phone's screen.

*Mom: Come home!*

*Mom: Never mind. Go to the hospital. Lake Nona Medical.*

*Mom: It's your father.*

# SEVEN
## UNCOVERING CLUES

I stand, hands shaking. "I have to go." My words are slurred, panic-stricken.

"What's wrong?"

"My dad." The room blurs slightly and my knees become so weak I'm finding it hard to exit the room. "I don't know. Hospital. I have to go to the hospital."

"Right." Strong hands grip my arms, keeping me from crumbling. "Is your dad okay? Let me take you. You're in no condition to drive."

I want to tell him no. That I'll be fine. That I'm strong enough.

But that's a lie. So I nod and let him direct me downstairs to his car.

"Hurry," I say as I try to call my mom.

"You got it."

The tires squeal against the pavement as we back out of the driveway. Then Jake shifts his car into drive, and we shoot off down the road. Numbly, I realize we're going to get pulled over going this fast. But I don't care. I think back to earlier today. Dad had looked tired this morning, hadn't he? I'd noticed it. I should've said something. Forced him to go and take a rest. Beside me, Jake remains silent, jaw tight in grim determination.

"She's not answering," I say out loud, not expecting an answer.

"Keep trying."

Finally, on the third attempt, Mom picks up.

"Aria!" There's a frantic tone in her voice. She's always been the down-to-earth person in our family. Keeping Dad's and my wild ideas grounded. Calm and soothing, just like the plants she grows.

"Mom, what's going on? Is Dad okay?"

"I—I came home early. Needed to work in the green-house. I found him—" She chokes back a sob. "It was bad. You have to come. Emergency room."

She hangs up and slowly, I lower the phone to my lap.

"Oh, my god," I whisper, my chest tightening.

"We're pulling in now." Jake careens around a corner, driving up over the curb to pull into the emergency room drop-off.

I don't even wait for the car to stop before I open the door and stumble out. When I step inside the emergency room, I spot Mom in the waiting area on the right. She's sitting in one of the chairs, her knees tucked against her chest. Her hair, a lighter shade of red than mine, clings around her face. She's got her cross in her hand, twisting it about, her lips moving in silent prayer. She looks so young, so vulnerable that I almost don't even recognize her.

"Mom?" My feet slow as I grow closer to her.

Her eyes land on me, and instantly she lowers her feet to the floor and straightens. She holds out her hands to me saying, "Aria. You're here."

I hug her, and she wraps her arms around me tight, clinging to me like she might never let me go.

"You're safe," she says. "I was so worried."

"I'm fine. What happened? How is Dad?"

"I came home. The house was ransacked, and your dad... they beat him up..." A strangled cry comes out of her mouth, but she presses her fist to her lips as if to hold it in. Tears well up in her eyes, yet somehow she holds those back, too. "I don't know who they were or what they wanted. The police are looking into it now. Oh, um, hello."

She takes in Jake who is standing not far from us, leaning against the wall, arms crossed over his chest.

"That's Jake Sutherland. He's my study partner. Drove me over here. I was so worried... I couldn't drive."

"I'm so glad you didn't. Smart girl." She pats my cheeks and then drags her red hair out of her face, yanking it back into a makeshift bun. Despite her efforts, strands of her hair flutter about in rebellion. "I appreciate what you've done, Jake. Maybe we can come by sometime and pick her car up? Tomorrow maybe?"

"It's no biggie," Jake says as if he comes by the hospital every other day. "I'm happy to help. I hope your husband will be okay."

Before Mom has a chance to answer, a doctor comes over to us. "Mrs. Hale. Your husband is ready to see you."

"He's awake?" she asks. "Is he okay?"

"He's had a concussion, but his wounds are just superficial. We've got him bandaged up and he'll be bruised and sore for a while, but he's lucky."

I pause at Jake's side before following the doctor. "Thank you. You've got mad driving skills."

"Video games. They're good for something, I guess."

We stand awkwardly for a moment. Behind me, Mom is calling for me to hurry.

"I'll have Mom drop me off tomorrow to pick up my car. That okay with you?"

"Yeah, absolutely. But what else can I do? I feel like a jerk just leaving you here."

The strangest feeling rushes over me. A desperate need to reach up and touch his face. To throw my arms around him in a hug. Perhaps it's that feeling you get when someone comes to your aid and rescues you.

"I won't forget what you did," I choke out the words, tears edging the corners of my eyes.

I step closer and lightly touch his arm. He doesn't flinch or back away. Instead he reaches up as if he is going to touch a loose strand of my hair. But he stops suddenly and jerks backward.

My heart stutters.

Because that was the very same reaction he had in the dream.

I turn and run to my mom, heart pounding.

# EIGHT

# THE ASSAULT

"Dad," I whisper, coming to his bedside. His eyes are closed. I shiver at the cuts along his arms and neck.

A long bandage runs along the side of his face. The left eye is ringed with a dark black circle. His bottom lip is cracked and swollen. Two of his fingers are clamped in a splint. Broken I'm guessing.

"Aria." His eyes open and he smiles at me. "How are you feeling?"

I choke back a sob. He's asking how I'm feeling? But that's Dad, always putting me first. If it wasn't for him believing in me, he'd never have let me work for him at MaxLife.

"Why would anyone do this to you?" I ask as Mom settles down on the other side of the bed. "Mom says someone came into the house and ransacked it."

Dad licks his dried lips and tries to sit up. Mom pushes

him back down telling him to take it easy. There's something unsettling about seeing my dad, once so strong and
capable, lying there on the hospital bed, bruised and
broken. The only other time I saw him look unraveled was
when we first discovered my grams' sickness. Being here
now at the hospital brings back all of those awful
memories.

It had been my twelfth birthday. The piles of presents
were stacked up on the table and I had snuck inside and
been secretly pulling back the tape of each package,
getting an early peek.

Everyone else was outside, cheering over the magician
Mom had hired. But Grams had wandered into the living
room and caught me in the act.

"Oh!" I exclaimed, clamping the wrapping paper back
into place, tucking my hands behind my back. "I was um ...
just checking out the presents."

"Who are you?" Grams frowned at me. "You're not
supposed to be in here."

I giggled, used to her teasing over the years. "I know." I
sighed. "I'll head back outside with the others."

Dad strolled in then, reminding me I was missing the
action. But that's when Grams grabbed Dad and pointed
at me.

"This girl was trying to open Aria's presents," she said.

"But that is Aria." Dad's smile faltered. "You
remember Aria, don't you?"

But she didn't. At least not for the rest of the day. And

that's when the downhill cycle began. Grams had Alzheimer's disease. Birthdays were never the same.

So now, sitting here at Dad's side, smelling the sterile hospital smells, and seeing him tucked beneath crisp, white sheets, it's like I'm losing him just like I have piece by piece been losing my grams.

"I'm not as bad as I look." Dad tries to smile, but his facial muscles can't seem to pull it off.

"Why would anyone do this?" Mom wrings her hands. "The police say the intruders took nothing, but it seemed like they were looking for something."

"I could be wrong," Dad says. "But I think they were looking for the technology for the Dreamscape. The lab is too secure for them to enter so maybe they had been hoping I would keep some of the files at home."

"Oh, honey." Mom grips Dad's hand, her face shockingly pale. "First thing tomorrow, I'll call our security company and upgrade the system. And I don't want you to go back to MaxLife until we know everything is safe there, too."

Dad nods, but his eyes are distant, clouded. "I'm going to keep you safe. I will do everything in my power."

I finger the edge of the sheet, thinking how empty his words sound. People who can break into our house, destroy it, beat up my dad, what's a little security system going to do? How does he think he can keep us safe when he's lying there in a hospital bed?

WITH NO SEVERE injuries and after being watched overnight, Dad was discharged the next afternoon. But when we return home, I gasp as I stare at the disaster that greets us. Every drawer in the house is ripped open and tossed on the ground. Papers are strewn across the floor. The cushions and pillows are slashed, stuffing drifting about the house.

I press my hand over my mouth to hold back the sob.

"I can't handle this," Mom says weakly, stumbling through the mess.

Dad settles onto a kitchen chair, one of the very few that's still intact.

"You okay missing school today?" Dad asks. "Second day in a row?"

"Of course. I can't deal with school right now. How about you? I can't think of a time you missed work."

"Can't say I can either. But then there's a first for everything isn't there, sweetie?"

A sobbing sound breaks the silence. I rush to the source to find Mom by her plants, trying desperately to scoop up the dirt into piles and salvage the tattered stems and leaves. The clay pots lie shattered across the tiled floor with dirt spilled about. I sink down at her side and wrap my arms around her. The smell of dirt fills the air mixed with the sweet scent of fresh herbs.

Mom's tears spill down her cheeks as she mutters, "Why? Why would someone do this?"

"I don't know." I gather up the shards. "The important thing is we are safe and together."

"Yes." Mom presses her hands against my cheeks. "Yes, I don't think I could handle it if anything happened to you or your dad."

A knocking at the front door sends both Mom and me springing to our feet. Dad motions for us to stay where we are and creeps to peer out of the peephole. I clutch Mom's arm for support as she pulls out her phone, probably planning on calling 911. But Dad only chuckles and begins unlocking the door.

"It's the MaxLife team." Dad flings open the door. "Well, hello, there."

"How did they know?" Mom mumbles as the crew barrels inside laden with boxes of food and buckets of cleaning supplies.

"I might have texted the team to let them know what was going on," I admit to Mom.

"We're here to help." Sun holds up a box of garbage bags.

"Mission Hale is operational," Javier announces, waving a broom.

"Brought some food 'cause I knew you'd be disappointed if I hadn't." Tony hoists up a stack of pizza boxes. The smell of it actually makes my stomach grumble. I can't remember the last time I ate. Granola bars with Jake yesterday?

"He only ate most of it," Javier adds. "But he saved two of the five boxes for the rest of us."

Everyone laughs and I find myself almost joining in as I meet my team by the door. Sun hugs me while Javier gives me a kiss on the forehead saying, "¡Hermanita! We were all so worried when we heard the news."

Tony teeters the pizza tower across the room and settles the stack on the kitchen counter. He blows out a long drawn-out whistle as he studies the disaster of our home.

"They ruined you good, didn't they?" Tony says.

"Tony!" Sun clucks her tongue. "Give them space. They might not be ready to talk about it yet." Then to me, "I'm going to make us girls a cup of tea, won't that be nice? I brought some green tea from Hong Kong that I think you'll like. It's soothing on the nerves."

She starts rummaging through the mess on the floor until she finds our teapot, thankfully still intact.

"Good luck finding an unbroken cup," I mumble.

"We've got your back, Aria." Javier is already sweeping up the broken glass on the floor. "We might not be family by blood, but we are family in spirit."

I nod, not trusting my voice to speak. I've always known them to be good friends, but this takes it to a new level.

Tony marches out of the kitchen, chopping on a piece

of pizza. In his other hand, he holds a paper plate with a giant pepperoni piece on it. He passes it to me and I take it gratefully.

"I'm in charge of food, entertainment, and making sure Javier puts his share of work in." Tony winks. "Any special music requests?"

"Chopin," Sun yells from the other side of the room.

Tony screws up his face as if someone layered his pizza with anchovies. "Please," he says. "Something from this century."

The two continue to tease each other as I take a bite of the pizza, savoring the warmth and flavor. I know I should help with the cleaning, but all I can do right now is step outside. My feet lead me to Mom's greenhouse. Amazingly, it's been untouched. Inside the smells of fresh herbs and flowers hit me, dousing me with memories of summers potting plants, recording growth in Mom's journals, and clothes covered with dirt at the end of the day.

I crawl under one of the counters, not caring about the dirt-ridden floor, and munch on the corner of my pizza crust. It's good to be in a place that feels safe and untouched. I just need a few moments to pull myself together before I rejoin the others. Still, I can't help but think how ironic that in the Dreamscape, I'm the one leaping out of helicopters and jumping across pits, but here in the real world, I'm a shivering mess, huddled under the counter.

Suddenly, I'm not hungry anymore. I toss my crust in

the bin across from me and crawl back out from under the counter, squaring my shoulders and taking a long, deep breath.

"You can do this, Aria," I tell myself.

My phone beeps.

*Jake: I'm holding your car for ransom. 1.2 million for its release.*

Attached is a selfie. Jake's sitting on the hood of my car, holding a water gun and attempting a don't-mess-with-me expression.

I laugh and nibble on my pinkie. How is it that a guy I hardly know can make me laugh? My stomach flutters. It's fluttering because of the pizza, I tell myself. I've got a career to focus on and the goal to graduate at the top of my class. This whole break-in is messing with my head and drive. The last thing I need is a guy to add to the chaos. It's probably the effects of the whole rescuer/hero thing. Nothing more.

I dig through my pocket and pull out the quotes I printed off this morning. I'd been too upset to tape them to my wall so I'd jammed them into my pocket hoping they would give me the extra reassurance I needed.

*Focus only on your goal. Don't waver from forward motion.*

*Learn from your failures.*

Slowly I shuffle out of the dirt-caked corner and face my house. I take in a long, deep breath. I can do this. I'm strong. I'm the Air Girl. The one who leaps from helicopters and as I dive across fragmented memories.

I swing open the greenhouse door and ease out into the afternoon sun. But before I step inside and join the others, I pause and stare back at my phone, debating. Before I can stop myself, I shoot off a text.

*Me: You got yourself a deal.*

# NINE
## SECRETS

Once the house returned to a habitable condition, the MaxLife crew headed out, giving me one last hug and well wishes. Tony even promised to bring me Donut King doughnuts next time we do a Dream Walk together. "I'll bring the chocolate glazed kind," he added, pointing at me like this is a life or death situation. "Don't tell me that isn't your favorite. Uh, huh. Tony sees all."

I rolled my eyes, but I didn't disagree with him because he totally nailed it. Later that night, I have Mom drop me off at Jake's house. The entire ride over, we have what I call a soft argument. Neither one of us is yelling, but we're definitely not seeing things eye to eye.

"Our assignment is due tomorrow, Mom," I explain. "I have to get an A."

"I don't understand why you can't just pick your car up and come home." Mom grips the steering wheel like she's ready to pull it off. "Mr. Kores respects your father. Once he hears about what happened, he'll give you an extension."

It's true. Mr. Kores is one of those teachers who's all about understanding the student so you can better teach them. But what I don't tell Mom is I need to get out of the house. Even after we've picked up all the mess, the memory of the break-in is in every cracked object. Every stark wall. The piles of garbage lining the street. A constant reminder of the danger we're in.

But perhaps it's more than that. It's Jake. I need his carefree ways. I'm embarrassed to admit it, but I've been thinking about him, too. His eyes. How he almost touched my hair. The way he looked at me like I was the only girl on the planet.

"Please, Mom," I resort to begging. "You know how much this means to me."

She sighs but nods, lips pressed together as if she is desperate to say no. Then she flicks on the classical music station and Chopin fills the air, weaving soothing notes within the silence.

BACK IN JAKE'S sterile bedroom that could almost pass for an operating room, he pulls up the PowerPoint he started.

"I figured you've been kind of busy," he explains. "So I

took some of the topics we covered in our write-up and added it to the slides."

I look over what he's put together. It's impressive.

"How did you get those pictures to revolve like that?" I ask.

"I created my own mini-video and then made a gif out of it. Gives it the illusion that the brain is revolving."

"It's good."

"That must have been hard for the master of brain development to admit."

I shift uncomfortably on the floor where I've created note cards for my part of the speech. "How about we practice our lines? Just to make sure we've got how this works."

"I'm in." Then he pops open a prescription bottle and swallows two pills dry.

"How can you do that?"

"Do what?"

"Take medicine without water."

He shrugs as he moves to the floor next to me and examines the cards. "I've been getting severe headaches for the last two weeks. When the pain comes on, I don't bother waiting around to get a glass of water."

"You sure you're up for studying? Do you need to rest?"

"I've been going to a doctor who's been doing some tests. Maybe they'll find some answers."

I fidget with the notecards, guilt stabbing at my

stomach like a butcher. Should I tell him I've been in his brain? Maybe there's something I can do to help him.

"You okay?" His eyebrows rise and there's concern in his eyes that makes me want to reach out and touch him.

*What is wrong with me?* "No." I clear my throat. "I mean, yes, I'm okay. Let's get studying. Utilize our time."

We spend the next hour going back and forth on our sections. When it's his turn, he stands, ramrod straight, and begins reading off his card with a monotone voice.

"No!" I giggle. "You can't just read off the cards. You have to put expression in it. The cards are supposed to be a guide for you. Seriously, you sound like a robot."

"I take it robots are not your type."

I grab one of his hands to show how he can point to the screen. But the second our hands touch, I freeze. It's like I've stepped beyond the unspoken rule of no touching. I drop his hand instantly.

"Well, you know how to point." I clear my throat. "Obviously. Just put your hands out like this to show inflection."

His eyebrows rise and a smile stretches at the corners of his mouth. "You make it sound so easy."

And that's when my stomach growls. Loudly. My face burns like I've been out at the beach all day without sunscreen.

"Hungry?"

I press my hands to my stomach. "I should go. Check

on my family." I don't really want to go back home, but I should. "We're going to nail this."

He opens his mouth like he's about to argue with me, but instead nods. "It'll be my stunning pointing skills and inflection that's going to nail us the A."

I roll my eyes at him and laugh as I pack up my computer and cards. For a moment, the room had life to it, our stuff spread about. Cans of soda and a bag of Cheetos scattered on the counter. But after I gather my belongings and Jake tosses the garbage into the trash, that feeling vanishes. The room has returned to its sterile perfectness once again and I feel a wall rising up between us.

"Thanks again." I rub my hand up and down my computer strap. "I'll see you tomorrow in class."

"Wouldn't miss it."

MY ALARM GOES off at 3:30 a.m. just like it has every morning since I started working for Dad at MaxLife. Numbly I slip into a pair of jeans and a spaghetti-strapped shirt. As I stagger down the hall, my parent's voices flow up the stairs. My automatic instincts shriek to a halt. In my dazed morning routine, I forgot about Dad's injuries. Now, hearing their worried tones, the events of the past two nights ago crashes back. I sink onto the stairs, remembering how Dad didn't even want me to work today.

"You can't possibly be thinking of going back to work

this morning." Mom's voice is pinched and an octave higher than usual. "Dustin, please listen to reason."

"I'm fine." Dad grunts. "Did they destroy all the coffee cups, too?"

"The doctor said you had a concussion. You need to rest."

"I'll get coffee at the clinic." Dad sighs. "Liv, you know how much this means to me. And this latest client. He's taking us to the brink of whole new discoveries. He doesn't appear to have memory loss like his charts say, but we're going to do some more work with him again just to make sure. We've got him scheduled for this morning. The medical unit is already prepping him as we speak. I've got to go."

I stand up. Dad has to be talking about Jake! He's the only brain we've come this close to getting into the Vault. I don't even think. I dart down the stairs, plastering on a smile.

"Hey, Dad!" I say brightly. "I'm ready to go."

Both my parents frown.

"If you get to go to work, then I do, too," I reason. "Plus Mom, don't you want me to be there with Dad and keep an eye on his progress?"

"I suppose." She rubs her knuckles across her other palm like she does when nervous or unsure.

"Fine," Dad says. "Besides, we will need you. You are the best."

He smiles then and opens the door into the garage. It's

not until I slide into my car and follow Dad's SUV to the clinic that I begin to wonder about my choice. Do I really want to enter Jake's dreams? Our goal is to enter the dreamer's deepest, most precious memories. The Vault. But with Jake and I knowing each other, how would he feel if he were to find out I entered his dreams?

But there's no way he could ever find out. Right?

Lightly I touch my lips but then clamp my hand firmly on the steering wheel. Jake and I aren't even friends. Classmates. Acquaintances, really.

Today could be MaxLife's biggest breakthrough ever. This could open a whole new way for dementia patients to recall memories or even record their memories to access at a later time. The possibilities are endless. I look down at my ring glinting in the streetlights and think about Grams. This is all so much more than a guy I hardly know.

This is transformational science.

# TEN

# PATIENT 145

The whole team is already prepped by the time Dad and I enter at 4:30 a.m. sharp.

"Dr. Hale? Aria?" Sun pauses from climbing into her sleep pod. "You two are not seriously working this morning."

Nurse Debbie looks up from where she's checking the team's health scans. "Go home, Dr. Hale. Don't even think about it."

"We've got this covered," Dr. Cage, Dad's assistant reassures. "You need to get your rest."

"I'm here and ready to work," Dad says, beelining for the coffee pot. Everyone in the lab pauses and glances at each other. "I appreciate you coming in for me tonight Dr. Cage, but I think working will get my mind off things."

"I will stay and be of assistance," Dr. Cage says. "Just in case."

"I'm going in, too," I announce. "We were so close last time and today we just might break huge ground. Today we are going to make history."

I flash on my brightest smile and pretend I don't see Tony's frown or Javier's shake his head. I know what they're thinking and they're wrong. Without me, they wouldn't have made the ground we've made in the Dreamscape. The longest any team has lasted without me has been a minute. The silence in the lab hovers over me as I pop a mini-doughnut into my mouth before heading to my own pod.

"Seriously," I try to relieve the tension. "How could I sit at home and stare at the ceiling while you all are here making scientific advances?"

"Aria." Nurse Debbie fists her hands on her hips. "You're supposed to be on leave for the rest of the week."

"I'm great," I say with a mouth full, which only deepens her frown. "The joys of being young."

"She's good, Debbie," Dad says, and then to me, "But anytime you feel uncomfortable, have signs of dizziness or disorientation, you need to transition to fade. Promise?"

"Absolutely." But all I can focus on is Jake. Will he recognize me? Will he trust me more or less when he sees me? Do I really want to enter his dreams? Oh god. Maybe this is a bad idea.

"So this is the same patient we entered on Wednesday?" Javier asks.

"It certainly is. Patient 145." Dad takes a deep gulp of

his coffee and stares off at the wall as if he doesn't want to make eye contact with the team. "We nearly made it to what we believe is the Vault last time. A first attempt like that is unprecedented. Dr. Cage says the patient was willing to come back in for a second round. I think if we use the same methods as before, we can get in."

"I'm down with that." Tony fist-pumps Dad. "Let's cross our fingers he's got more hot dog stands around."

"We're not going for the food, Tony." Sun flashes him a pointed look as she snuggles her tiny frame into the folds of her pod.

"Food *unifies* people," Tony reasons. "Why do you think the dreamers are always so relaxed around us?"

"Because of the hot dogs?" I chuckle.

"You know it, baby!" Tony pumps his arms into the air before marching over to his pod.

A quick glance at my heart monitor tells me my heart rate is already elevated. If I'm not careful, Nurse Debbie is going to out-rank Dad and call me off the mission. I push aside the memories of my fall into the Void and instead, focus on the memory of Jake sitting on my car.

*Ugh*! My heart is only speeding up at the thought of seeing Jake again. In a few moments, I could be there and see his deepest, darkest secrets. Maybe this is a bad idea. Do I *really* want to know what they are?

"Your heart rate is a little high, honey," Debbie says.

"Just excited."

Debbie nods, but she purses her lips.

"Don't worry." I pat her hand. "I'll be fine. I won't do anything stupid."

"I wish I believed you," she mutters.

THE WORLD SHIFTS, fuzzy at first. Then the floor rolls beneath me like I've entered a funhouse. I hold out my hands, trying to grope onto something, and my stomach heaves like I just completed a roller coaster loop. A hard piece of metal presses against my palm and I grip hold of that, allowing the world of Jake's dream to solidify for me.

I'm standing in the foyer of a business with ceilings that stretch at least four stories high. Chandeliers dangle from above and the walls are golden, glistening with ornate mirrors and paintings. The sounds of a string quartet replace the previous tones of the sleep pod and my muscles relax. Around me, people stroll about, chatting and drinking champagne from tall flutes. The women are decked out in floor-length gowns and the men wear crisp tuxes.

Wow. I don't even know how to handle myself in this situation. A quick glance tells me I'm still wearing my jeans and spaghetti-strap shirt. *Crap.* I close my eyes, trying to visualize myself in a formal dress, but I'm coming up blank with images to help me.

"Letdown. No hot dogs." That's got to be Tony's voice.

Sure enough, Tony lounges in a settee beside me, looking completely weird wearing a formal jacket and bow tie with his flamingo shorts.

"You've got to nix the shorts," I point out.

"I know." Tony runs his hand over his dreads. "It's just they're so damn comfortable."

"Have you spotted, Ja—" I stop myself for a second and change my words. "The dreamer?"

"Not yet. But remember when I told you he looked familiar?"

Instinctively, I bite at my pinkie. *Don't say it, Tony! Don't say it's Jake from our class!*

"He looks the spitting image of that guy from our class. Can't remember the dude's name. Oh, there he is. By the piano. Woah, is he playing the piano? Not bad. Not bad."

I follow Tony's gaze and sure enough, there's Jake, working the piano like he's Mozart's second cousin. Weaving through the crowd and a group of dancers, I pick my way closer to him. My heart stutters seeing him lost in the magic of the melody. His fingers fly over the keyboards, nimble and light. His body sways to the music, hair flinging about, hanging over his eyes. I wonder if he plays in real life.

Suddenly he stops as if sensing something and looks up. At me. I freeze, not able to move in hopes he'll believe I'm here because of the dream. Not because I'm an intruder. A fake.

Slowly he stands. The music continues, even though

he's no longer playing it. The room darkens until it's just him, me, and the piano. Behind me, I feel the presence of my other teammates, waiting. Watching.

What must they think of this? Do they suspect anything?

My jeans and shirt vanish swapped with a sheer sapphire-colored dress, waving about in a sudden wind along with golden heels. My hair cascades in waves over my shoulders and as Jake steps toward me, his hand reaches out. This time he touches my hair. My skin tingles as if the air is sizzling around me.

I've never experienced these feelings in a Dreamscape before. What does that mean?

"The Vault," Javier whispers in my ear.

My eyes jerk away from Jake as I realize I'm losing myself in the dream. I must stay focused and professional.

Jake's eyes snap over to where Tony is standing on my right side.

"Uh, oh," Tony mutters. "I don't think I'm blending well in the dream."

This is one of the reasons why we try to stay unobtrusive. The moment we stand out, our Dreamers will either panic and kick us out of the dream, or they'll wake up. Both are bad.

One step, then another, Jake backs away, eyes widening, hands out at his side as if to keep his balance.

"He's panicking," Sun whispers. "Hold it together and prepare yourself. I bet we're going to enter REM."

REM is a dangerous section of a dream. It's when a dreamer is most lucid, the dreams are wildest, plus the dreamer is more susceptible to waking.

As usual, Sun is right. The room shifts and the floor warps, sending the four of us sprawling to the ground. The walls compress inward until it's only a matter of seconds before they squeeze us into pancakes.

ELEVEN

OUT OF CONTROL

The walls shudder to a stop a half-second before I fade. My vision blurs so I blink a few times allowing myself to adjust. The dream shifted, I realize as I take in my new surroundings. We're lying in a long white hallway lined with purple lockers. Jake takes off in a sprint like he's running away from us.

"Follow him," Javier says.

The four of us scramble to our feet. I kick off my heels and pump my arms, racing until I catch up with Jake.

I grab his hand to keep him from getting away, and once again, there's that shock, shivering through me as if his touch has awakened something inside me. Colors swirl around us like a kaleidoscope, and the dream switches again.

My stomach rolls and I press my eyes closed to allow myself to adjust. When I open my eyes, I realize I'm sitting in the front seat of the car. Jake grins at me from the driver's seat, saying, "Put your seatbelt on."

My hands shake. This dream is out of control. Maybe it's because usually, we enter the dreams of those who are elderly or have forgotten so much of their past. I'm not sure. But one thing I do know about Jake, he's got a wild, dangerous side to him.

I glance over my shoulder to see how the others handled the transition, but they've vanished. Our rule is to never confront the dreamer or ask questions because often it pulls them out of the dream. But I have to know where my team is.

"Where are my friends?" I ask.

"Friends?" he says.

I'm about to ask him more questions when he presses a button that says LAUNCH BOOSTERS. The car jerks forward as Jake sends it into full throttle, and my head smashes against the headrest. We fly down an open highway, whizzing by trees and houses.

"What is this?" I laugh uneasily. "A Batman car?"

He grins sheepishly. "Do you like it?"

"Uh—yeah. It's pretty awesome. Where are we going?"

"I have something special to show you."

My heart skips. Could he be taking me to the Vault?

A whoosh of air floods the car and instantaneously we are transported to the temple that I suspected was the Vault while in his last dream. The car has vanished, leaving us standing at the temple's entrance. A full moon beams pale shafts of light across the grounds. Mist floats across the stones like ghosts. I shiver and cross my arms, deciding this place is a little too creepy.

But I'm about to enter a Vault, I tell myself. This is a huge moment in dream therapy!

Like before, the green numbers move across the doors, bright like the color of Grams' ring. It's almost as if the numbers are a secret code. I squint, trying to get a better visual of it. If my mind can process what I'm seeing, the computer back in the MaxLife lab should be able to transfer these images into the mainframe at the lab.

Jake touches the door, and it creaks open. Together we step inside, my floor-length dress brushing across the crumbling tiled floor.

Eagerly, I take in my surroundings, hoping against hope it's the Vault. We're standing in a hall packed with rows of tall rectangular boxes, clear as crystal. Inside each box are all different kinds of objects. Stone pillars engraved with mathematical symbols stretch to a stalactite-riddled ceiling and vines twist over everything within sight.

I try to process what I'm seeing. This place can't possibly be somewhere he's actually been, could it? I dart a glance at Jake. A green glow illuminates his face, and his forehead is wrinkled like he's thinking.

I creep closer to one of the clear boxes and press my hand on top. This one has green symbols inside. As if responding to my touch, numbers spiral out of the box like a vortex, rising toward the ceiling.

"What do these numbers mean?" I ask.

"It's a game I created. I'll show you the others."

Intrigued, I trail after him. In the corner, I spy a box with a worn stuffed dragon inside, orange with plates running along its back. Another is packed full of super-hero action figures. Batman stands on the top, a long black cloak spilling out behind him. Everything clarifies in my mind. These are the things that mean the most to him.

A voice shocks the air, droning on about how Jake needs to choose a major for college. It's coming from a man inside one of the boxes. Computer codes float about his head and money spills out of his pockets. I recognize him as the man we saw at the table eating dinner in the dream the other night.

"Your dad?" I ask.

Jake nods, but he doesn't seem concerned about his dad. Instead, he's staring hard at the stream of code in the air.

"Is that one of your game's codes?"

"No." He rubs the side of his jaw. "This is a secret one. I found it the other day just to prove to my dad that I'm smarter than the other wannabe's at his work."

"Did he believe you?"

"I haven't shown him yet."

Suddenly, being here feels wrong. Intrusive. This place is for him and maybe someone who he trusts with his deepest, darkest secrets. Not some girl who travels weekly through a patient's dreams. Not a random classmate or an intern trying to make a breakthrough in science. An uneasy feeling sinks inside my gut. Has Jake been told all the details of what MaxLife really does? If this place is so secretive and special, would he be okay with a bunch of scientists seeing all this and studying it?

"I should leave."

"Don't." Jake turns and he cups his hands around my face, sending my heart into a fierce dive.

I stare into his eyes, and then my gaze trickles down to his mouth. I need to pull him closer. Feel those lips against mine. He leans into me.

Maybe dreams are a place where the impossible rules and thrives. A place that digs out our most secret desires.

But no. I can't.

I back away, creating enough space between the two of us so I can escape and fade.

## TWELVE
## LIVING IN A DREAM WORLD

Later that day in class, I don't dare look at Jake. Not that it matters since he isn't making any attempts either. Both of us review our presentation in the minutes before class begins and then when it is time for us to present, we manage to do so successfully. The class even gives us a round of applause.

My eyes fall on Tony, chair slightly tipped back. The only one not applauding. His eyebrows lift and he wags his finger. I can practically hear his voice in my head saying, "You've been very wicked, haven't you?"

"Fantastic and well-researched!" Mr. Kores claps eagerly. "But then I suppose we can only expect the best from the world's leading neurologic scientist's daughter."

Inwardly, I cringe as I close out our program from the school network. Why did Mr. Kores have to go say that? What if Jake puts the pieces together? I dare a glance over at Jake. His forehead is scrunched in concentration as he gathers up his notes.

"Wait," he says as we return to our seats. "Let me get this straight. Your dad is Dustin Hale as in founder and president of MaxLife?"

*Not cool.* "You've heard of it?" My voice quivers like a traitor.

"Yeah, um." He pauses which only makes my stomach twist more. "I came across it in our research last night."

I try to steer the conversation into safe territory. "I think we completely nailed the project."

"Mr. Kores seemed happy."

The next group begins their talk, and we grow silent again. He doesn't look at me now, so I trace my fingers over the edges of my tablet and bite my inner lip. The memories of what happened between us only hours ago weigh on me.

Maybe I should tell him the truth. Get it out in the open. No, that's a bad idea. It's best to pretend nothing happened. I peek over at Jake, thinking that if we hung out more he would eventually put two and two together. The guy was smart. Okay, so he's probably brilliant, which is beyond sexy.

I clench my fists. Stop that! I tell myself. What is my problem?

A message pops up on my phone.

*Tony: It was him, wasn't it?*

*Tony again: How long have you known?*

Guilt tugs at my chest. I don't respond back.

*Tony: We need to talk.*

---

TONY CHERY and I met when we got paired up for a science project and literally blew up half of the science lab. It probably was my fault since I poured the sulfuric acid into the mixture too soon, but seeing the impact of what we could do with a few liquids transformed me. He had recently emigrated with his mom and younger brother from Haiti and he didn't have many friends yet.

But that day at lunch, we made a pact. I'll never forget sitting off in the corner of the cafeteria since we not only smelled like rotten eggs, but our clothes were half-charred. The two of us were going to be the world's next revolutionary scientists. Sure, we may have nearly destroyed the science lab and were assigned detention, but we both knew we weren't like our classmates. Since then we've been inseparable, and in all of those years, we've never kept a secret from each other.

So when I meet Tony for lunch at our usual round table by the window overlooking the science club's garden, there's an awkwardness between us. I can't think of a time when I have kept something from him, much less something this major.

He stares hard at me, but I avoid eye contact and instead watch a group of eleventh graders who named themselves Goddesses on Their Knees, weeding the area and harvesting some herbs.

"I see the Hi-Hoe, Hi-Hoe club is working again," Tony breaks the strained silence before taking a bite of pizza.

I roll my eyes. "That's not their name."

"It's a way better name than Goddesses on Elbows or whatever they call themselves. Then they could sing as they worked and give themselves names that represented their personalities."

"You are out of control."

"How long have you known?" Tony says so suddenly I nearly choke on my cherry tomato. But Tony is like that. Gets right to the point, no messing around.

"Since Wednesday morning during the first dream session." I stab my fork into my salad, but I don't have the heart to take a bite. "I wasn't sure though. Still not sure, I guess. It's not like he's actually come out and said it."

"Did you report it? Tell your dad?"

"No. Not after we came so close to entering the Vault on Wednesday. But then today—"

"That's why you willingly faded." Tony points the end of his pizza at me. "Because he was going to kiss you. And you were going to kiss him back."

I open my mouth to refute his claim, but no words come out. I really wanted to kiss him, didn't I. Oh god. I hang my head. This is so bad.

"If you don't tell someone, I will. It's part of our

contract. Aria, you've got to think this through. Maybe the only reason you got so close to the Vault is that you knew him. Withholding information messes with our research."

"I never had a full conversation with him in my life until Mr. Kores put us together for the same project this week."

"My bet is he's been crushing on you for a long time. He probably digs girls with red hair or maybe nerds obsessed with their careers."

I glare at him. He laughs.

"Whatever. You've got to admit that dream was out of control. You've got to tell your dad."

"What do you know about Jake?"

"Other than he won that national programming competition last year? Not much. Rumor has it that if you need some hacking done, he's your man. But that could just be people talking. Go ahead and ask him yourself. He's headed our way."

Sure enough, the devil himself strides over to our table. Jake's holding a Coke can and hot dog. Tony looks pointedly at the hot dog. I scowl.

"Hey," I say. "Um, do you know my friend, Tony?"

"What's up, man?" Tony moves to fist-pump Jake who awkwardly returns the punch with his Coke can. "I'm in your psycho class, too. I sit in the back so I can sneak M&M's when Kores isn't looking."

"Right." Jake shifts self-consciously, tapping his can against his thigh. "So I stopped by Mr. Kores's room before lunch. He said we both got an A-plus. Thought you'd want to know."

"Great." I fidget in my chair. "Um, thanks for telling me."

"No problem." He turns to walk away, but pauses and asks me, "You busy tonight?"

"Now there's a question." Tony leans back in his chair and crosses his arms, looking way too smug for his own good.

"I can't." I don't look at Jake. "Have to work tonight."

"Of course." Jake backs away. "Some other time maybe."

I don't say anything, only watch him stride away.

"I don't like this, Ari." Tony shakes his head.

"I'll tell Dad tonight. I promise."

Tony takes a big gulp of his Power Aid and slams the empty bottle on the table. "Hmm...we'll see, won't we? Gotta jet to my last class. See you around, Air Girl."

I nod miserably. For the first time ever, I'm dreading going to work.

AFTER SCHOOL, I stop by Publix and pick out a bouquet of flowers before heading to the memory care unit of Cedar Pines. Grams' room is down the hall on the right. When I come to her door, I knock. She does better without surprises.

"Come in," Grams' voice calls out. I suck in a deep breath to prepare myself. Even her voice sounds weak and wobbly today.

"Grams!" I say brightly as I enter. "How are you doing?"

"Well, I'm just fine, thank you," she says.

She's sitting in front of the TV, remote in her hand. A stream of light spills in from the slatted blinds, creating a glow over her figure. Today she's wearing a plaid skirt and a flowered shirt. Her graying hair is curled neatly about her head. The center's hairstylist always does such a great job.

I turn off the TV and pull up a chair to join her, kissing her on the cheek and switching the remote for the flowers.

"Are you from the church?" Grams lifts up the flowers and smells them. "Oh, lilies. They're my favorite. Oh, wait. You're one of the new nurses, aren't you?"

"I'm Aria, your granddaughter," I tell her gently. "I thought you would enjoy the lilies. Studies indicate smell helps memory recall."

"Yes, well." Grams' brows knit in worry. "Thank you, my dear. But I'm afraid you must have gotten me mixed up with someone else."

I take her hand and squeeze it. "Here, let me put those flowers in water for you."

The vase is a little short for the lilies so they tilt off to the side, but it will do. I set them on the small end table by her bed, arranging them so the lily heads face Grams.

"There," I say. "Isn't that nice?"

"They are just lovely. Who did you say you were again?"

"Aria." I settle in the chair beside her.

"What a pretty ring. The color matches your eyes."

"Thanks!" I sit straighter. If she noticed the ring, it means the connection she had to it must still be there somewhere in the deep recesses of her mind. "It used to be yours and then you gave it to me. It matches your eyes, too."

She cocks her head and her fingers lightly move to her eyes. When Grams received her diagnosis it spurred Dad into the whole memory loss research. He was certain he could find a way into a person's brain—Grams' brain—to create new connections to lost memories or find a way to record current memories before they become lost.

Hence the birth of MaxLife. For the first year, I couldn't bear the thought of visiting her, seeing that glazed, distant look in her eyes. Feeling the cut of loss when she'd never remembered me.

But lately, it's been different. With every patient, we've made gains in memory recall. There's hope for Grams when before I had been watching her slip deeper into a great void. Everyone at MaxLife was determined that if we could enter the Vault, we could record the person's memories so they could access them in a different way. It would change Grams' life. It would change our family's lives.

"The last few days have been tough," I begin.

"What's the matter, dear?" Grams says. "Here, have some cookies. Chocolate chip. They always make me feel better."

I take a cookie and munch on it. "I did something I wasn't supposed to. Actually, it's more of not what I did, but what I didn't do. Is it just as wrong to withhold the truth as to tell an outright lie?"

"Well, I just don't know. Sounds a bit tricky, doesn't it?"

"It does. And then there's this guy. Jake. He's in one of my classes. We've never said more than a single word to each other before, but then he showed up in one of the dreams that my team went into. I wanted to kiss him."

Grams' eyes widen. "Kiss him? Well. Isn't that something?"

"When I saw him in class today...I don't know. He thinks everything was just a dream because he has no idea I actually entered his dream. If he found out..."

"You look troubled, dear," Grams says. "Here take a cookie. It'll make you feel better."

"Do you think it's wrong what I'm doing?" I take another cookie. "Should I tell him the truth?"

"Are you going to kiss the boy?"

"So you think I should tell him?"

"I'm ready for my medicine, Nurse Nina."

I take the cookies and set them back on her counter. Then I turn the TV back on and hand her the remote.

"It was good talking to you, Grams." I kiss her on the forehead.

She bats me away. "What are you doing, Nurse Nina? Kissing me like that. Where's the manager of this place? You should be reported."

I blow her one more kiss before stepping back into the hall. I lean against the door once it's shut and close my eyes.

The truth is it's easier to live in a dream world than face reality.

# THIRTEEN

# THE BREAK-IN

Tonight, clouds block out the moonlight as I pull into the employee's parking lot behind MaxLife. Friday nights have always been our all-nighters. Dad set it up this way since it allows Tony and me to participate since we both are still attending high school. A bunch of cars are already here including Dad's. The technicians arrive early since they usually have the sleep lab prepped for us, including the client's files and brain scans for us to review beforehand.

I climb out of my car, and Sun steps out of hers. She was waiting for me.

"Hey," she says, distractedly, checking her phone. "Ready to pull an all-nighter?"

"Not really. It's been a full week."

"I checked the schedule for next week. We only have

one client, so we'll get some downtime." Sun frowns at her phone and sighs.

"Everything okay?"

"It's Blake. He's not returning my calls."

"The blind date who ordered the most expensive thing on the menu and made you pay for it?"

She shrugs, grimacing.

"You can do better," I tell her as we head to the employee entrance.

Javier's car rumbles into the garage, Latino music blaring into the silence. He parks and Tony pops out of the passenger side, waving to us.

I pull out my key card, but just before I go to unlock the door, Sun grabs my wrist. "Don't," she whispers.

"Why?" I laugh. "Now who's the one that doesn't want to go to work?"

"Look." She points to the lock. "The green light on the lock system is on, which means the doors aren't locked."

"My dad probably forgot to set the locks again. You know how absent-minded he gets."

The four of us head into the locker room. I shoot off a text to my mom, telling her I arrived, and slip the phone into the zip pocket of my backpack. "No cell phones" in the lab is MaxLife's policy. I set my backpack into my cubby and listen to Tony talk about his latest DJ gig he's got scheduled for tomorrow night.

"The line-up of songs is killer. And I've got some new

moves, too." Tony wags his bottom and then belly. "Who's coming?"

"Not me," I say. "Too much homework."

"There's an art festival this weekend," Javier leans closer to Sun. "Interested in coming?"

"I've got a date." She tosses her boots into her cubby and slips on her silk slippers. "At least, I think I do."

"Whoo-eee!" Tony whistles. "Sun's getting some action!"

"Shut up, Tony." Sun throws her boot at him.

"Is this a guy from that dating site?" Javier scrunches his nose and rattles off something in Spanish. "How do you know if he's safe?"

I leave the three to debate weekend plans and head into the sleeping lab, expecting to find either Dad or the techs. But no one is there. Weird.

"Dad?" I call out.

I round the corner toward the offices and the lights blink out.

"Woah, what the heck?" Tony asks.

"Power's out," Javier says.

"Where's your dad?" Sun says. "His car is in the parking lot."

"Dad!" I yell again, but I'm only met with silence. "Something is wrong."

"I'll get my phone and call someone." Tony rushes to the locker room. A pounding and rattling fills the room and Tony comes back. "Or maybe not. The door is locked."

"What do you mean locked?" Javier runs down the hall only for him to return, muttering in Spanish. "Tony's right."

"I'm scared." A cold shiver scuttles down my back. "I think someone who isn't part of our team is here."

"I knew something was wrong when the outside door was unlocked," Sun mutters.

"Everyone, look for a flashlight," Javier says. "Hurry."

The darkness presses against me, but I try to let my other senses take over as I carefully work my way to the hall closet. I freeze when I hear a swish of clothing and a pad of footsteps. A grunt breaks the stillness and suddenly Javier starts yelling in Spanish. Sun screams and Tony calls out, "Who's there?"

"I got the guy." Javier's voice breaks through the chaos just as my finger clamps on a flashlight hanging on a peg inside the closet.

I flick on the light and shine it in the direction of Javier's voice.

A man wearing black pants, a black button-down collared shirt, and black shoes lies at Javier's feet. Javier whips off the black ski mask, revealing a man in his late twenties with light-colored skin, a thin face, and thinner mustache. The rest of his face is clean-shaven with fine dark brown hair slicked back with gel. He appears to be knocked out cold.

"Seems like such a normal guy for wearing a ski mask," Sun says. "He wouldn't stand out in a crowd if I were walking down the street and bumped into him, that's how completely ordinary he is."

"Except for the gun in his hand," I point out, my hand shaking so hard, the flashlight wavers about like a strobe light.

"Yeah." Tony's eyes are bugging out of his head. "Kind of hard to not miss that."

"Who do you think he is?" Sun asks.

"Don't know." Javier's eyes are calculating as he crouches at the man's side, taking away the weapon and slipping it in his jeans back pocket. "But it's like he was waiting here for us."

"But why would he come here?" My voice trembles. "And where's my dad?"

Everyone stares at me with wide eyes. I rush down the hall and check every room, searching for him. After I've scoured the entire area, I return to the group. "He's not here," I say in a frantic whisper. "Someone must have taken him. Maybe the same guys that came to our house the other night?"

"We've got to call the police, man." Tony tries the back hallway door again. "This is messed up!"

"Wait." Javier rummages through the nurse station and pulls out a set of gloves for each of us. "Put these on just in case."

"You think the police might suspect us?" Tony asks

incredulously. "Dude, our fingerprints are already all over this place."

"Javier," Sun says sharply. "I don't know what you've got planned, but we have to call the police. Every second we wait, time is ticking."

"Sun's right." I rummage through the front desk until I find the key to the locker room area and an extra flashlight. I pick up the receptionist's phone. "I'm calling my dad. I have to make sure he's okay. He'll know what we need to do."

"I'll check the breakers and try to get the power back on." Tony grabs the extra flashlight and takes off down the hall.

"How far have the police gotten on your break-in, Aria?" Javier steps to my side. "Any arrests yet? Someone hit your house and obviously didn't get what they wanted. So now they are here. What will they do next?"

I glare at him as I dial Dad's number. A ringing fills the stillness of the facility. Instinctively, I run to the sound only to find Dad's office to be a complete disaster. The chair is lying on the floor. Papers are scattered about. His computer has been shoved off to the side.

And Dad's cell phone is lying on the floor ringing.

A sick dread fills my stomach as I pick up his phone. Something has happened to him. Something awful. I just know it.

FOURTEEN
THE CHOICE

The lights flicker back on in the facility and I blink from the sudden, sharp brightness. Once my eyes adjust, that's when I see it.

At the entrance of the technician's lab, a hand lies on the floor, a trickle of dark liquid seeping out from beneath it. I hold my breath and creep down the hall. As I turn the corner, I discover the body attached to the hand. I scream again, backpedaling from horror until my back smashes against the wall. It's Craig, our lab tech. Blood has pooled up beneath him and stained his white lab coat black.

A ringing vibrates in my ears, and I start to sob.

"What is it?" Javier runs to me. When his eyes land on Craig, he gasps.

My gaze is drawn across the office to find Cheryl, slumped on the digital board, lifeless. Sun rushes to join us only to clamp her hands over her mouth.

"Oh, god." Tears stream down her cheeks. The ringing in my ears drowns out all other sounds. I stand there, immobile, as Javier checks both of the lab technician's pulses.

A flicker of light under the workstation catches my eye. With shaking fingers, I pick up the object. The Eye of God swirls before me, a universe of stars and light.

"Dad's watch," I choke.

Mom had given it to him as a gift when he won the Neuroscience Research Prize. The metal chain wristband is shattered, but the actual watch face still tells time, and the stars continue to swirl in an endless circle. Numbly, I hug it to my chest.

The room swims as if I've just entered a Dreamscape and a deep fear pools into my stomach. I pocket the watch and stalk back to where the man who is responsible for all of this lies passed out.

"Why did you do this?" I scream at him and then kick him in the side. He doesn't move. "Where's my dad? What have you done with my father?"

Javier follows me, and with a set face, he methodically works through the man's pockets and even his shoes while Tony comes to my side, wrapping his arm around me in silence.

"No phone," Javier says. "No ID. No way for us to trace him. Unless—"

He lets his voice trail off and stares up at me, eyes

granite hard. My dread has hardened into stone, lodging itself against my chest.

"This man knows what happened to my father." My words are thick and angry. "Once the police are here, we won't get our chance. So the answer is yes."

He nods grimly. "It's the fastest way. The best way."

"What are you two talking about?" Tony asks. "You're making me nervous."

"Pick him up by the shoulders, Tony," Javier commands. "I'll take his legs."

Tony doesn't budge. "Why?"

"Because we're going to find my dad," I snap. "First we investigate our way. Then we'll call the police."

"The police will know we moved the guy," Tony says. "They can figure out all kinds of stuff. And what if he wakes up and tries to kill us?"

"Pick the damn body up!" Javier says. "We'll make up some kind of lie."

When Tony doesn't move, I slip on the gloves and grab the man's legs while Javier hauls him by his shoulders. We stagger down the hall to the sleeping lab.

"The surveillance is down. I just checked," Sun announces, coming into the room. "This was a well-planned operation. What are you two doing?"

"Put him in the test sleep pod," I order.

"*What are you doing?*" Sun says, louder.

"Something bad." Tony follows us like a lost puppy.

"No," I say. "He's the one who did something bad. We're making the wrong right."

"I don't like this," Sun says.

"Prep the Dreamscape," Javier orders Sun as we drop the guy into the pod. "I'll hook him up."

"You're not serious." Sun gapes at us. "He's a criminal. An assassin. Can you imagine what's inside his mind?"

"Listen," Javier says. "When I was in high school, I got myself into a whole lot of trouble. I had no one to help me. Dr. Hale volunteered at my school as a mentor. And it's because of him I graduated high school and even college. So I owe him everything. And every second the criminals have, the further Dr. Hale gets from us. We can't waste another second."

"He's right." I rummage about until I find Temazepam, a sedative that will keep the guy sleeping for a while. We usually only rely on the Sound Oasis to put us to sleep, but today I'm not about to take any risks.

I prep the syringe, desperate to keep my hands steady. I've never actually done anything like this, but whatever. I've watched Debbie do this maybe twice. Okay, once. But as long as this creep doesn't die on us before we've finished, I'm good with the consequences.

I march over to the man. He's shifting on the table. His hand lifts to the growing knot on his head and he groans. I yank back his sleeve, but my hand freezes as I hold the syringe just above his vein. If I were in the Dreamscape,

I'd just plunge this into his veins, no hesitation. But this isn't a dream. It's real. Too real.

"Do you want me to do it?" Javier asks.

"No." I suck in a deep breath and plunge the contents of the syringe into his vein, hoping my aim was good. His eyes start to crack open, but Tony throws a towel over his face.

"Can't have him seeing you," Tony explains. "Just in case."

The man's body falls limp again.

"Guess I better add injections to my resume." Then I stare at Tony. "If our friendship ever meant anything to you before, you'll help me. Please tell me you're in."

The Adam's apple in his throat bobs. He lifts his chin slightly and his dark eyes stare into mine. "I've got your back."

Meanwhile, Javier straps the sleep mask over the creepy man's eyes. Sun comes over with a laptop with the Dreamscape program opened on the screen.

"What's this?" I ask.

"Your dad put a new portable prototype on this laptop. It doesn't have all the bells and whistles and can't record the session like the main system, but it's exactly what we need. If we do it on the main system, everyone will know what we did."

"They're going to find out either way," Tony says as Sun clips a wire from the passed-out man's sleep mask to the laptop.

"Then let's hope we find out where my dad is and why this guy was here."

Sun's fingers fly over the keyboard as she types in the program's sequence. "Okay. He's in."

"You stay behind," Javier tells Sun. "Monitor the Dreamscape, okay?"

She nods, but her face twists like she tasted something bitter. "This is completely illegal, you know. We don't have a signed release. We could totally lose our licenses for this."

This makes me hesitate. What am I doing? I fiddle with my sleep mask. This is my dad and I'm totally okay with doing whatever I can to find him. But my friends don't have to do this. "Sun is right. This is not your problem. It's mine and my family's. I can't have you risking your careers to help me. You should leave. Just give me an hour before you call the cops."

"Too late for that, Air Girl." Tony huffs as he climbs into his pod. "This whole thing is stupid. But you are right. If this was my mom, you'd do this for me. You are family. If you go down, I go down."

My throat is dry. "Thanks, Tony."

"It goes the other way around though, too." He points a finger at me as the top lowers over him. "I go down, you go down."

"I'm good with that," I say.

"Trust me, hermanita. I'm not sitting by and letting

this criminal get away with this." Javier hops into his pod and pushes the button to bring the top down.

My mind whirls as the sleep pod lowers over me. What will we find once we enter this assassin's mind?

# FIFTEEN
# BREAKING THE RULES

I hunker to the ground in the darkness. It's the odd smells I first notice. Diesel and tar. I grope through the inky blackness and touch firm rubber. A tire? The room grows in lightness, just enough that I can make out my surroundings. We're in a warehouse. A metal cross-beamed ceiling stretches above me and to my right are tall shelves filled with boxes. Forklifts are stationed in a line like soldiers on the left. Soon I discover I'm hunched beside a black Cadillac.

Somehow I need to convince our assassin to show me where my dad is. This is new territory for me. Usually, our team just follows or gently guides the dreamer. Never have we made demands or coerced someone to do what we wanted.

Voices spill into the darkness on my right. Three men.

One is thin and tall with brown skin, sunglasses, and a crew cut. The other has white skin, about as fair as mine, and he's got light hair, white along the edges. His face is wrinkled and he's heavier set. The third is our dreamer, the assassin.

"Don't take my codes," the light-haired one begs. "I'll be ruined."

"Too late," the dreamer says. "You got what you deserve."

"Are you ready?" Sunglasses asks the dreamer.

Before I have a chance to step out and confront our dreamer, the room shifts, and the dreamer and Sunglasses are in the Cadillac. The car's engine roars to life. Startling, I realize they're about to leave. Without me. I can't let them leave me behind, so I whip open the backseat door and barely slide into the backseat when the car takes off.

"I wondered where you were," Javier says from where he's already sitting in the backseat. He shuts the door just as the car peels out of the warehouse.

"Where's Tony?" I whisper.

"No clue." Javier's eyes are dilated, and I know he's freaking out.

Back in the lab, he had acted so brave and confident, but here in the dream, he knows what I know. Without the trained technicians monitoring the Dreamscape and Debbie keeping an eye on our vitals, anything could go wrong.

Like what happened to Carol two weeks ago. She's a team member I don't usually work with since she usually comes in while Tony and I are at school. But when Tony called in, she covered for him. Our team was following a dreamer through a department store. The place was massive with floor after floor of perfumes and shoes and purses. Carol and I split up, one of us taking down the shoe aisle while the other trailed behind the lady in the purse aisle. I never saw Carol again in the dream.

Then as the rest of our team woke up, Carol continued to sleep. I skipped school to stay by her side. Five hours later, the technicians finally pulled her out of the dream. We had to keep the dreamer asleep all those extra hours to make sure her brain waves weren't interrupted. It can happen if you lose yourself in the dream rather than staying aware that you are in someone else's dream.

The car stops abruptly, pulling me back to the moment. Right away, I notice our surroundings are starting to dissipate.

"We're about to fade," Javier says. "Our dreamer must have left the car."

Panicked, we dive into the front seat, but instead of landing in the front of the car, our bodies drop onto a wooden floor. Totally confused, I take in my new surroundings to discover we're in a room with eight men sitting at a table, knitting with long silver knives. Our assassin is there too in the center of the group. Desperately, I try to make myself look different to not throw him out of the dream. I imagine myself with short, white hair.

I blink. "Okay, so I think this is the weirdest dream I've ever been in."

"I'm telling you," Javier says. "The weird factor never ceases to disappoint."

A tall woman wearing a black business suit with black hair swept up in a fancy bun marches to the table like a sergeant. Every so often, she pulls out a baton and smashes it on the table demanding them to knit faster. The men nearly jump out of their chairs each time, their knives clicking as they obey her command.

Suddenly, she whips around and stares pointedly at Javier and me on the floor.

"What do you think you are doing?" She leers at us, red lips pulled deep into a frown. "Sleeping on the job?"

I shake my head frantically, surprised the dreamer used someone else in the dream to communicate with us. I try to get to my feet, but I can't seem to move.

"Where is Dr. Hale?" I ask the dreamer. He pauses from his knitting, knives jutting up at the ceiling, and frowns at me. "Tell us what you did with him."

"GET UP!" the woman screams. "Whoever produces the best afghan first wins the million dollars. Everyone else dies."

"Afghan?" Javier whispers, clearly as confused as I am.

"Let's just go along with this," I say. "Maybe there are clues here that can help us."

Finally, my legs obey me and move. Even still, my legs are sluggish like a knife slicing through butter. Javier and I drop into two empty chairs, joining the other knitters at the table. I pick up the two knives lying before me, trying to figure out what to do with them.

"I'm finished!" the dreamer calls out.

He leaps over the table and produces a few rows of plaited yarn. I'm waiting for her to tell him it isn't an afghan, but she doesn't.

"We have a winner!" she proclaims and lifts the limp patch into the air. "Bring the prisoners to me."

The dreamer hurries to the far wall where long black boxes are stacked up. He lifts the handle of one of the boxes and drags the box to the lady.

"The package is prepped and ready for transportation." The dreamer lifts the lid of the box.

I drop my knives and yarn. A sick feeling slides through me because I think I know what's inside the box. I don't want to look, but I know I have to. Once again, my legs drag as if I'm slogging through a marsh until I make it to the side of the box. I'm terrified to look inside, and yet terrified to not. Swallowing hard, I lean over and take a peek.

My heart stops for the briefest of seconds. Dad is there! He's lying inside, chapped lips closed, face pale, and wearing his lab coat with the MaxLife insignia patch on the upper right-hand corner of his chest. His gray-blond hair is tousled, and there's a streak of fresh blood that trickles down the side of his face. Dark blood stains are smeared over his white lab coat.

I back away from the box. No, not a box. Casket.

"No!" I choke.

My knees buckle, and I desperately claw at the box as if that can somehow fix everything.

"Stay calm, Aria," Javier says, and then he touches my dad's neck. "I feel a pulse. He's alive. They must have him in a deep sleep."

The room shifts again and everything around us vanishes. As my body acclimates, the roar of airplanes rage into my ears, and a warm breeze teases at my hair and tickles my skin.

Planes, a control tower, runways fill up my line of sight. We must be at the airport. The woman and dreamer stand in front of Javier and me, the black box sitting on the ground between them. A plane taxis and stops not far from us, its bright lights blinking through the harsh darkness. Men run up and roll the casket across the runway toward the plane. I try to move to stop them, but it's like my whole body is paralyzed as I watch the ramp lower from the back of the plane and two men haul the box with Dad inside up the ramp and into the belly of the plane.

"This money is yours," the woman is telling our dreamer. I swallow, trying to focus my mind, remembering this is only a dream. The lady flips open the lid to a wicker picnic basket, stacked full of bills. The dreamer goes to take it, but she clamps the lid shut. "It's yours as soon as you terminate the rest of the team."

"I will not fail," the dreamer says.

Enraged, Javier balls up his fists as if it's taking every ounce of his willpower to not throttle her. My head whips back to the plane as the engines roar to life. My knees buckle and it's suddenly hard to breathe. I wheeze in as much air as I can and start crawling to the plane.

"Dad!" I scream out his name, gravel digging into my knees and palms. "Stop the plane."

The Dreamscape shifts and it's as if someone has grabbed my chest, looped a chain around it, and yanked on it full force. I'm pulled backward, arms stretched for the plane. Swirls of gray spiral around me and darkness drags me backward.

My chest squeezes so tightly that I can't breathe. And then bright lights are blaring down on me. I'm in my sleeping pod, curled up in a ball. My mask is gone. It's hard to focus because the Dreamscape still has a hold of some part of my brain. My heart thuds against my chest like I'm sprinting.

I roll onto my back, trying to pull my scattered thoughts and emotions into check when a face looms over mine.

Blue eyes. Blond hair hanging loose. Sharp jaw, clutched grimly.

The face with lips I had dreamed of kissing stares

down at me. Anger, rage, and fury has replaced the soft-
ness it once held.

"Jake?" I choke out the word.

*Not enough air.*

*Need air.*

"You screwed my family and me over." He spits out
those words. "You're going to pay for what you've done."

# SIXTEEN
## $81 MILLION

Jake. Here at MaxLife.

Why is he saying I screwed his family? Nothing makes sense. I must still be dreaming. Maybe Dad isn't captured after all, and I'm in bed sleeping.

"What are you doing?" Tony yells. "You're going to kill her!"

Sleeping mask askew on his face and ropes dangling from his wrists, Tony wobbles over and slams a hard punch to Jake's jaw. Jake stumbles backward and drops to the ground.

"Guess I didn't tie you up well enough," he mutters, spitting out a drop of blood.

Then, still swaying, Tony staggers to my sleep pod where I'm gasping for air. He presses an oxygen mask over my face. The cool air rushes down my throat and I suck it in hungrily.

"She's hyperventilating," Tony lectures. "What kind of moron are you? You can't just rip people out of the Dreamscape!"

"I didn't know!" Blood streams out of Jake's nose, and worry has replaced the rage in his eyes. "Is she going to be okay?"

The room swims into focus. Sun is sitting by the laptop, but her arms are strapped to the back of the chair. To my right, Javier is slowly rising up in his pod. He runs his hands through his hair. His eyes are bloodshot as he lumbers to his feet, looking strung out.

"Who are you?" Javier eyes Jake who is wiping the blood from his nose with the back of his hand.

"His name is Jake Sutherland," Tony says grimly. "He's our dreamer from Wednesday."

I take the oxygen mask off and manage to sit up. The room shifts slightly. "Tony, I'm glad you're okay," I manage to say. My throat is dry. "I didn't see you in the dream."

"I got kicked out right away," Tony explains as he grabs a pair of scissors and cuts through Sun's bindings. "Good thing I did because Jake could've killed us all."

"I didn't know—I had no idea—" Jake shudders, rubbing his hands over his face.

"What are you doing here?" Javier asks. And then to my shock, he pulls out our attacker's gun from his pocket and points it at Jake.

"Woah, man." Jake holds his hands in the air. "I honestly didn't know that waking her would be dangerous.

Haven't you already done enough damage to my family? Do you really need to kill me, too?"

"I ask the questions," Javier growls. "You answer them. What are you doing here?"

Jake licks his lips and takes us all in, lowering his hands. I press the oxygen mask back to my mouth, trying to push out the memories from the dream. The memory of the casket and plane. And Dad leaving. Oh, god. My eyes water. If I even think about that, I'll fall apart.

"I found out the truth of what you guys are doing here," Jake says. "I left a thumb drive with all the data I discovered with my mom. So if I go missing, you'll be the first the police come to."

"What kind of coo-coo are you talking about?" Tony asks. "We're not going to kill you. Right, Javier?"

Javier shrugs as if killing Jake doesn't sound like such a bad idea.

"Dude, we're memory and dream specialists," Tony says. "You've got us mixed up with someone else. You should leave."

"No, he can't," Sun says. "He's seen too much."

"Oh, I've seen way more than whatever you're doing to that guy there." Jake points to our attacker still sleeping. "After some digging, I put the pieces together what happened. My dad manages confidential accounts for the Federal Reserve Bank in Atlanta, and they were hacked with codes only he and I knew. Millions of dollars stolen."

"Listen," Javier says. "We have our own troubles, but we're not stealing money."

"How could we steal millions of dollars?" Sun asks. "That's absurd."

"81 million to be exact, and everyone is pointing fingers at my dad for it. He was fired from his job. And get this. It happened the very day after my second visit to your company for headaches. Coincidental? I don't think so. I think you guys are behind it."

"Are you *serious*?" I drop the mask, shooting him an incredulous look. "Your dad's been fired and you're blaming us? You nearly gave me a heart attack. Like seriously, you are messing with technology you can't possibly understand. This facility isn't a place to play around with like your tech toys back home. We don't play games. Besides, right now my dad has gone missing, and people are dead. So excuse us if we don't care a damn about your dad's job."

Jake's eyes widen and his face pales. "Dead? Your dad is missing? Have you called the police? Why are you lying around sleeping then?"

Sun eyes him warily. "We were just about to before you nearly added to the death count."

"Something isn't adding up." Jake's focus shifts to our captive who has started to stir. Sun jumps up and quickly injects him with another dose of Temazepam. "Wait a sec. You were stealing information from him, just like you did from me, weren't you? Don't tell me you don't do that because I already hacked into your system. I read the files and saw the video footage."

"Steal information?" Tony asks. "Dude, you really don't know anything. We are scientists who help dementia patients retrieve their memories."

"You've got us confused with something else." I shift on my pod because technically we were stealing information from our attacker's mind. Not that he didn't deserve it. "You need to leave. We have to find my dad and sitting around talking to you isn't helping."

"You pretend to help people, but what you really do is steal their data. Who knows! Maybe you steal people's memories, too. Did you ever consider that your father might be in on all of this? Maybe he's not kidnapped. Maybe he took the 81 million and ran."

He didn't just say that!

"Get out!" I scream, rising up out of my pod. "How dare you insinuate my father would do any of that."

I literally launch myself at Jake, but Tony holds me back.

"You know what the crazy thing is?" Jake's face is red, and his hair is sticking up on its ends. "I actually liked you. I thought you were smart and—I don't even know. But now I'm going to make sure my father sues your company's ass off until every last penny is gone."

"You weren't the only person who was wrong about someone," I spit the words back at him. "I always knew you were hiding something. But now I see you for who you truly are."

"You've got it all wrong, Jake," Tony says. "You heard her. Get out or *we* sue you. How many times do we have to tell you we're scientists, not criminals?"

"Now that's a lie," Jake scoffs. "I was referred to MaxLife for a CT scan to diagnose a headache. Except you know what happened? I fell asleep and dreamt about you four while showing you the codes. Don't you find that a little suspicious? It wasn't until a few hours ago when my mom got a call from the feds saying my dad was under criminal investigation that I started retracing my steps.

"That's when I hacked into your system to discover— low and behold! —you not only go into people's dreams, but you video them. Trust me, I found the video where I showed you the room with boxes. Those were codes to get into the SWIFT system at the Federal Reserve."

I press my fingers to my temples, trying to process what he's saying. I can't deal with all of this.

"Are you even supposed to know those codes?" Javier asks. "That sounds suspicious in itself."

"Why don't you worry about your own business," Jake shoots back. "And I'll worry about mine."

Except what if Jake's telling the truth? After everything I experienced in the last fifteen minutes, I don't know what to believe anymore.

"It doesn't matter," I tell him darkly. "I was just in that man's dream and saw them take my dad away in a casket.

So that's all I can think about right now. Besides, we don't read code. Those numbers are totally meaningless to us. For all we know, they were jellybeans. Or flying aliens."

"Jake might be onto something," Sun interjects. She sinks into a chair and clasps her hands over her knees. Her face is a greenish color as if she's come to some horrible conclusion. "What we see is reimaged into the mainframe. Anyone who works the tech or your dad could have seen those numbers and passed or sold them on to someone."

"Exactly!" Jake points at me. If I wasn't so weak, I'd slap him. "That's exactly what happened. Yesterday after-noon, someone transferred 81 million dollars from the Federal Reserve Bank to an unknown account. A crew is trying to follow the money trail as we speak."

"You can say whatever you want." I fist my hips. "But my father would *never* do anything like that."

"Not your father." Sun nods to our sleeping attacker. "What if *he* used us to steal the codes so he could steal the millions?"

"But that doesn't explain why they came back here and killed people," Tony said.

"And took my dad," I add.

The room falls silent, and we all turn to the man still sleeping.

# SEVENTEEN

# WE SWORE WE'D NEVER DO IT

"We need to look into Jake's files and see if what he's saying is true," I say. "The biggest red flag is that all our clients have dementia. Not headaches."

Sun begins typing on the computer. "I found his file," she says. "Apparently, Dr. Langer's office referred Jake to us for a diagnosis so that part of his story is true. And right here is your signature, Jake. You signed off on the intrusive exploratory therapy, among other things."

"I didn't know that intrusive exploratory therapy was letting my classmates into my brain," Jake says. "This is some sick prank."

"I don't have time to worry about Jake and his stories," I cut off their conversation and begin turning off the equipment. "If that assassin's dream we just entered is accurate, this murderer is thinking about shipping my dad off on a plane to who knows where. I have to go to the airport and see if I can find whoever took my dad before they leave."

Sun rewinds the data from our visuals of the dream. "The airport you saw in the dream is Orlando Executive Airport."

"We don't know if that dream is what he was planning on doing or already did," Tony points out. "Or it could be just wishful thinking."

"I know, I know," I huff. "Dreams are just expressions and ways our minds deal with things. But it's our only lead. We've got to try it." Then I head for the door, saying, "I'm not sticking around for a second longer. I'm finding my dad."

"Wow." Jake sucks in a deep breath. "You people sure take dreams to the next level."

"I'm coming with you," Tony says. "You're not going there alone."

"No." I pause. "We nearly lost you in the Dreamscape because we didn't have backup technicians or a nurse at our sides. This is all too dangerous, and I don't know who or what I'm going to run up against. I'm not risking your life for this."

"Dr. Hale is like a second dad to me." Tony backs up to the hallway, arms out. "I'm coming."

"Are you all insane?" Jake says. "We need to call the police. This is way out of our league."

"Absolutely," Javier says. "As soon as we think this

through. First off, we need to move the killer's body out of the sleep pod."

I nod. "Erase evidence of what we've done."

"We also need to remember that when the cops get here, everything will be taken into their custody," Javier adds. "We should take Dr. Hale's laptop with us."

"On it." Sun closes Dad's laptop and slips it into the carry-on bag. "And all of the gear," she adds. "Just in case."

The realization of what they're saying hits me. We gained information from the sleeping intruder about my dad. If we don't find my dad at the airport, we may need to go back through the data to find another lead. Or we may need to enter more people's dreams to learn more answers.

Slowly, I nod. "Good idea. Whatever it takes to get my dad back."

Instantly, Javier begins collecting the Temazepam, which we could use if we don't have our pods or access to the Sound Oasis, and emergency meds. Sun grabs the sound wave frequency earplugs and the Sound Oasis microchip, which when activated into the system, sends out sound wave frequencies that tricks the brain into sleeping.

"I'm taking the NightFlash, too." I slip the long bar that projects pulsing blue light into the air. We rarely use it, because people don't connect to the Dreamscape as well with it, but if someone still can't fall asleep with the Sound Oasis and we don't want to use Temazepam, it's our emergency backup. "Just in case."

"Whoa, whoa, whoa." Tony holds out his hands. "You're talking about more than just a run to the airport. This is a crime scene. We can't just take the stuff and jet. How will that look to the cops?"

"They won't know." Next, I grab everyone's sleep masks and put them in the case with the sound devices Sun collected. "Not if we don't tell them."

"Trust me," Jake says. "They'll figure it out."

I glare at him. "Then we'll find my dad before they put the pieces together."

Meanwhile, Tony and Jake move the assassin out of the sleep pod, tie him up and dump him back in the hallway.

Sun scans the room. "I think we're ready."

"Don't you dare call the cops until we've been gone for five minutes," I tell Jake. "This guy here is responsible for killing two of our techs in the next room and kidnapping my dad. Once we're gone, you can believe whatever you want. Just don't contact me."

"I'm coming with you," Jake says. His face is serious and focused as if he, too, has come to a new realization.

"Like hell, you are," I shoot back. "You nearly killed me."

"Take me or I'll tell the cops everything." He crosses his arms. "You know that if your patients found out that their dreams could be stolen, you'd be sued and shut down in seconds."

"You're blackmailing us now?" I snap. "Way to build team confidence."

"Listen, if you didn't scam the Federal Reserve Bank, then someone else did. And this 'therapy' you guys have got going on is the closest link to the crime I've got to proving that my dad is innocent. You have a dad that needs you and so do I. Maybe if we can work together, we can help both our dads."

I huff, hating that he's right. "Fine. Whatever. Just don't cause trouble." I flash him a warning look. I don't have time to deal with his needs because I need to focus on saving my dad. I turn to the group. "We got everything?"

"He's coming with us?" Javier frowns. "I don't like it."

"Oh yeah, I'm coming." Jake holds up his phone and pushes play. Our voices come over the speaker. "Otherwise, I'm going to play them this recording where you talk all about how you are stealing evidence from a crime scene."

"See." Javier glowers, his face darkening. "This is exactly why we can't trust this guy."

"We need to hurry," I say. "Every second we wait, the farther the kidnappers get from us."

"Fine," Javier concedes and points to Jake. "But I'm watching you."

There's a moment of hesitation where we stare at each other, wide-eyed, hearts pounding as we hold packed bags full of resources to do something we swore we would never do—enter people's dreams without their permission. To use the Dreamscape for our own gain.

I push those thoughts away and instead focus on the task at hand. Rescuing my dad.

"Good. Then let's go." I stride out the door.

EIGHTEEN
INVESTIGATING


We all cram into Javier's car. With every second we spend wasting time, debating on who sits where and what to do, my nerves tighten until I'm sitting in the backseat, a complete mess.

Once we are on our way to the airport, I call my mom while Sun calls the police, alerting them of the break-in and murders.

"Mom," I say once she answers.

"Aria? Is everything okay?" Her words slurred like she's half asleep. I've woken her up.

"Is Dad home?"

"No," she says. "He's at work with you. Right?"

"He's not there," I say. "You should probably sit down for this. There was a break-in at MaxLife, and well, things aren't good. Two of our lab techs were killed, and um... I don't know where Dad is. I'm trying to find him."

"WHAT?" She screams and I hear a thump. Did she fall out of bed? I almost wish I hadn't called her, but it's better she hears this from me than the cops. "You need to get out of there and come home. It's not safe."

"I'll be home in an hour," I say. This doesn't help, instead, she starts to yell for me to come home so I have to resort to yelling back to get her attention. "Mom! I'm safe and with the team. We're going to check one more place where we think Dad could be." Then I soften my tone. "One hour. I promise."

When I hang up, Javier is pulling into the Orlando Executive Airport. "This looks familiar," he says. "Just like the dream."

"Yeah." I lean over the front seat squinting into the darkness. "But the place is dead. There aren't any planes taking off."

Once we've parked and climbed out of the car, we rush inside the main terminal, a small building compared to Orlando's International Airport. We search the area until we find a security guard.

"Are there any outgoing flights right now?" Javier asks.

"At 1 a.m.?" The guy laughs. "Not in this airport. Where are you planning on flying?"

"Have there been any that have left in the last hour?" I venture.

"Sure. But they were all private planes." The man scrutinizes me warily now. "We don't give out private flight information."

Defeated, we settle into the rows of hard seats.

"It was a long shot." Javier shrugs. "Maybe the assassin's dream was a memory from a different situation. There's a strong chance that dream led us in the wrong direction."

"What do we do now?" I say. All my hype and bravado has seeped out of me, leaving me with an awful headache. "We can't just give up."

"It's late," Sun says. "And the trail is cold. Aria, you know I want to be there for your dad. If it weren't for him, my father wouldn't have gotten the treatment for his mind that he needed. I owe Dr. Hale so much. But as much as I hate saying this, it seems like we've got to rely on the police."

"I've been thinking this all through," Jake says. It's the first time he's even spoken since we left MaxLife. "And I think I've figured out how this all played out."

"Okay, Obi-Wan," I drone. "Enlighten us."

"Someone must have seen me trying to hack into the Federal Reserve Bank and guessed I saw the codes. Someone who was also trying to get the codes themselves. Remember how I got those headaches? What if they weren't coincidental but concocted by that very someone to get me to go to MaxLife. I mean, they could have very easily bribed my doctor to set me up with MaxLife for further tests. Then while I was dreaming, you all went into my brain and recorded me showing you the codes. Afterward, all the thieves had to do was retrieve those video files either by hacking into your system or from one of your staff. Boom. They got the codes."

"That's pretty out there, dude," Tony says.

"But for 81 million?" Jake shrugs. "It was a cheap and easy con."

I pull my knees against my chest and nibble on the corner of my pinkie. Now that I've calmed down, I see Jake's point and why he blamed me. The thought of someone taking what we do and using it for their own gain never crossed my mind. We've always been about helping people and making their lives better. But what makes me sick inside is to even consider the fact that someone in MaxLife could've sold the information we gathered.

"So that's why you thought it was my dad or even me who was a part of this," I say.

"Except none of us were explicitly looking for those," Javier says. "It was pure chance. Aria, you were the one who actually discovered the codes in Jake's Vault. Did you know to look for those codes or was it just a coincidence?"

I dare a glance at Jake. He's looking at me with pain-filled eyes. I was the one who lied and betrayed him. But could my involvement have been more than we had realized? Was this all my fault?

"I never knew anything about codes," I whisper. "But after I saw Jake in class, I put two and two together that the dreamer was Jake. I should've said something to the team, but I didn't. I guess, I felt like we were so close to making a breakthrough that I couldn't, or didn't want, to stop and think through the consequences of it all."

Everyone is silent as the enormity of the situation slides over us. Finally, it's Sun that breaks the silence.

"My vote is we each go home and think through this," she says. "Maybe the police will come up with a solution. We've risked a lot to be here and to have done what we did."

I scuff the end of my shoe across the linoleum floor, hating to admit defeat. "Fine, but I'm not giving up on my dad. He's in trouble and I'm going to find him no matter what."

"There's something else," Jake adds. "This whole dream thing you guys do, it's more valuable than you're giving yourself credit for. You are essentially looking into people's thoughts, searching for memories, finding their deepest secrets, and potentially discovering things even your patients can't remember. Put that into the wrong hands, it could be dangerous. And worth way more than $81 million."

# NINETEEN

## HACKING FOR THE GREATER GOOD

I sit alone in the parking lot in my car after giving the police my statement. The car's frame barely holds my panic in check. Dad's watch is clutched in my palm, and I stare at the stars swirling over its surface. A weird part of me believes that as long as the stars still move, Dad is still alive. It's silly and stupid, but I want it to be true.

Everyone else has headed back home after giving the police their report. Except I can't seem to get my act together and turn on the car. Not with all the horrors of tonight raging through my mind. The technician's blood pooling out of him, staring at Dad in the casket and then watching them roll Dad up the plane's ramp.

I lean onto the steering wheel and let the sobs escape.

Someone knocks on the window, and I literally jump in my seat and scream. It's Jake, standing outside of my car door. I bristle and frantically search the car for a tissue.

Here I thought everyone had left. How long has he been standing out there?

Once I blow my nose, I lower my window. He's got his arms crossed, back to me as if he's uncomfortable.

Fabulous. He probably heard me crying.

"What?" I ask. I know I sound curt and annoyed, but this hasn't been a stellar day.

"Listen." He scuffs at the ground with his shoe and then turns to look at me. There's pain in his eyes and all my defenses fall away. Okay, so maybe this hasn't been a good day for either of us. "I wanted to wait until the others were gone because I know this sounds stupid after you totally entered my brain and spied on my inner secrets, especially since I nearly killed you, but I trust you more than the others."

I run my finger along the edge of the windowsill unsure how to respond. What he says is probably true. I was the one he let into his Vault. Dad's theory is that only when a dreamer really trusts someone do they let them in there.

"Okay," I say hesitantly.

"I think with a little work, I can figure out where the money went."

"How does that have anything to do with me?"

"Ever heard of War of the Realms?" When I don't respond he sighs. "I actually do more than just *play* video games. I also design them. War of the Realms is one of my best sellers. I'm not trying to brag here, but I'm on my way to being one of the best game designers in the world. And not such a bad hacker either. I might be kind of awkward around cute girls, but computers and I are tight." He crosses his fingers, and if I weren't so upset, I might have actually smiled. "Wherever this money went, I'm willing to bet I can find it, and that it will also lead us to your dad."

"Now you've got my attention."

"You want your dad," he says. "I want to extricate my father from ties to this mess and clear my family's name. My dad is a jerk for leaving my mom and me, but sometimes he's a pretty cool guy. We have this love-hate relationship. It's... complicated. The reality is if I hadn't stuck my nose in where it didn't belong and gotten the codes from my dad, none of this would've happened. I don't know what you saw in that dude's dream back at MaxLife, but maybe with a little digging, I might find something. Then you can tell me if it rings any bells. What do you say?"

I don't have to think this through. I'm desperate with no leads whatsoever. "I'm in."

"Cool." His face shows surprise like he hadn't been expecting me to so quickly agree. "But all my hacking has to be done on my computers and server."

"You want me to go to your house?" I eye him suspiciously. "Are you going to try to kill me at your place?"

"Listen," he says. "Back there at MaxLife, I didn't know what was going on or exactly what you were doing. I shouldn't have overreacted. I get it if you can't trust me. I'm just trying to help my dad. Somehow someone used me to get this data. I need to make this right."

It's the earnestness and believability in his expression that wins me over. Or maybe it's the fact that I've been in his dreams and know him better than I should. "Let me just tell my mom and then I'll follow you to your place."

Mom wasn't too happy about me not going straight home, but since she's on her way to the police station, she was a distracted mess. Not that I blame her.

At Jake's house, I expect to head to his room where we studied, but instead, he goes to the back of the house and steps outside to the pool deck. The water glows a Caribbean blue and the bushes around it are lit in soft yellow spotlights. The warm air settles heavily on us as I hurry after him.

"Where are we going?" I ask. "Isn't your room back there?"

He stops suddenly, his shoulders tense. "What I'm about to show you, I've never shown to anyone else. Well, except for my mom, but she doesn't count since she's always too busy checking her phone to really notice anything. And my dad hasn't stepped foot in this place since he walked out on us five years ago."

"You're freaking me out," I say.

He shakes his head and presses his lips together. "It's not a big deal. Well, what I mean, it is for me. For you to be there. And I'm an idiot." He chuckles lightly to brush off the honesty of what he just said, but even in the semi-darkness, I can make out a blush burning his cheeks.

"No." I reach out and lightly touch his arm. He jerks slightly and I wonder how long ago it has been that someone touched him. I mean, like *really* touched him. "You're brilliant. I know that from when we worked on the project together, and of course, everyone at school thinks you're some kind of hacker legend. I don't know about this place of yours, but if it means it can get my dad back, you can one hundred percent trust me."

He stares deeply into my eyes, and then, as if he sees something that confirms my words, he turns and strides down the stone path to another building that looks like the pool house. This one is designed just like the main house, but it's smaller. He pulls up a plate revealing a keypad and presses his thumbprint against it. A scanner blinks green.

"Paranoid much?" I say overwhelmed at the amount of security he's got.

"Very," he says and opens the door. "The tech in here costs a fortune, but it would take years for me to recover what I've done to the systems."

AC hits me as we step inside, instantly cooling the layer of sweat on my skin. The air smells clean and free of any one particular smell. Automatic can lights flicker on, filling the hall with a cozy glow. Framed and hung on the walls are posters of superheroes. I study them as I follow Jake down the hall.

"What are these?" I ask. "They look old."

"They're classics. Part of my collection."

He motions me down the hall and we step into a wide-open room. The walls hold shelves filled with all kinds of paraphernalia of superheroes. A figurine of Batman leaping off a building. A Superman cereal box. Action figures of every Marvel comic I could possibly imagine and then more.

"Wow," I mutter. "This place is like a sanctuary to Marvel and DC Comics."

"You could say it's a passion. My dad might never see me, but he sends enough cash to keep me busy."

Screens black out the windows and a glance at the ceiling reveals more windows above except these aren't covered. Stars blink through from the skylights.

Jake moves to another section of the room. Three giant TV screens hang on the wall, images of a world that looks fantasy-like are on them for screen savers. He heads to a long desk where three large computer monitors are positioned to form a half-hexagon. A large plush chair on rollers sits in front of the entire system and he plops down into one and starts typing, his fingers flying over the keyboard. Code pops up on the screen, numbers and letters all in rows.

He's a king in a kingdom I don't even understand.

As he works, I wander to the far side of the room. Sketches of people, hand-drawn maps, printouts of geological charts, and photographs of people are tacked to the wall.

"What is all of this?" I ask.

"It's the brainstorming wall for my newest computer game. What do you think?"

One of the drawings catches my eye. Jagged snow-capped mountains, a verdant green valley, and thatched huts. The hut looks like the spitting image of the one where Tony ate hot dogs. I've been here before. In his dream.

I step away, a little freaked out.

"It's pretty impressive," I say. "I like the creatures you've created."

"Yeah," he says vaguely. "They all have different powers. Still trying to figure out what the one beast with the horns can do."

"What if a person who harvests them can grind the horn up for strength, but the negative is once it's ingested in a player's system, they become wild and untamed like the beast."

"Nice!" He turns away from the screen to look at me. My face burns under his admiration. "So it's like a punishment for tampering with nature."

"Exactly." I edge to his side, trying to figure out what he's doing. "Is that the hacker's code?"

"This is the SWIFT code the hackers used to trick the National Reserve Bank's system," he explains.

"What exactly is swift?"

"SWIFT stands for the Society for Worldwide Interbank Financial Telecommunication. It's a communication network for banks worldwide to transfer money. I've been trying to piece it all together so I could be wrong. But my best guess is that on Thursday, February 7th, someone from MaxLife took the images from my dream showing them my dad's access codes later that morning.

"Then using those codes, someone on the inside at the Federal Reserve was able to plant custom malware. When I last talked to my dad, he said that the malware contained sophisticated functionality to interact with local SWIFT Alliance Access software to transfer money without anyone knowing."

"So this was not just a small operation," I say. "It was all well-planned and thought out."

"Well, what do you expect when we are talking about stealing millions without leaving a fingerprint?"

"Good point."

"Whoever developed the malware-enabled software had excellent coding skills and clear knowledge of how SWIFT codes work. No red flags were raised. My dad said the only reason we know about this is that the Bangladesh printer wasn't working properly. When they restarted it, all these red flags showed up saying a critical system file was missing."

"I just can't process how they couldn't have left a trail to a person's account or to someone who withdrew the money."

"They definitely covered their trail, but no one is that good. With a little poking about, I'm determined to find their digital fingerprint. What I'm doing now on these two computers is trying to hack into the National Reserve Bank again and try to see where the money went."

"You can do that?" I ease onto one of the rolling chairs. "Is that safe?"

"They've got the whole system on a heavy lock-down. I've had my servers on search since before I went over to MaxLife. See this here?"

"That line?" Everything I'm seeing doesn't really make sense. My expertise has always been studying brain waves and reflecting on how the mind operates and its inner workings.

"Yeah." He taps the screen where a bar is moving up and down on the right side. "It's been searching for a breach in the security walls. So far, no luck. I've also reached out to a friend of mine on the Dark Web. He owes me a favor."

"You trust people on the Dark Web?"

"You have a better idea?"

"Point taken."

He gets up and opens the refrigerator. It's packed with Coke bottles and water on the top two shelves. The bottom is full of chocolate pudding.

"Thirsty?" He holds out a Coke.

"Sure."

He pops open the bottle's screw top and passes it to me. Then he takes one for himself and downs a swig.

"It appears as if you're a Coke connoisseur." I take a sip.

"It's the only true soda if you ask me. And it has to be in a bottle, not a can."

"Picky. Next thing you're going to tell me is that it has to be at a particular temperature."

"Coca-Cola recommends that it be kept at 38 degrees F for ideal drinking satisfaction."

"Wow. You are serious." I suppose it's a little strange, but there's something quirky and compelling watching him lean against the frig so sure of who he is and what he wants.

"To hackers and heists." I clink my bottle against his.

"And being smarter than the best."

But then his expression grows serious. He grabs another chair and sits with his body facing the back of the chair. "This is the thing." He stares at his bottle. "I don't want to get your hopes up. We might not be able to get inside their server, and even if we do, it could take hours, weeks even, and then the money trail will grow cold."

"I get it. No guarantees. So we just sit here and wait?"

"Pretty much."

"Or we could play with Batman and Superman." I cock my head to the side, smiling.

"When I was a kid, I wanted to be a superhero more than anything. Every time we had a career day in my elementary school, I said I wanted to be a superhero. Until $5^{th}$ grade when my father said that wasn't a real occupation. I had to be more practical like a teacher or a fireman, but ideally a businessman."

"Growing up sucks," I say.

"You seem to be in an awful hurry. Taking advanced classes. Working a full-time job while going to high school."

"Maybe it's being an only child to two brilliant scientists and trying to live up to their expectations. Everyone's expectations. When Dad got the Neuroscience Research Prize for his Memory Recall Therapy, one of the neurosurgeons came up to me and said there was no way I'd ever live up to my dad's reputation. I don't know why, maybe just being stubborn or wanting to prove him wrong, but that's when I decided I would be a neuroscientist."

Both of us sit there as if unsure of what to do with all of our new understanding of the other. I fidget in my chair, wondering if I've shared too much, but it's out there now and I can't take it back.

Suddenly a beeping fills the large room. Jake rolls his chair over to the computer, pushing aside the large leather one as he stares intently at the screen.

"We're in," he says, reverently. "My underground hacking buddy came through."

I rush to his side and watch as a 3D rendition of a door opening fills the monitor. Jake's fingers fly over the keyboard and the screen takes us down a hallway and then stops at another door.

Access code requested, the screen reads.

"What does that mean?" I ask.

Jake doesn't respond, instead, he types. LX11822OP5991.

Then he lifts his hands and holds them midair as if frozen. We wait as the computer reads, Requesting access.

And then: Access granted.

"Yes!" Jake high-fives me. "We're in!"

I literally do a little jump like I'm a kid who got a secret pass into the candy shop.

*I'm going to find you, Dad.*

"Okay," he says. "We've got to move fast. In and out before I leave too long of a trail."

"How do you keep your trail hidden?"

"I'm bouncing off servers like every 14 milliseconds," he says as he types furiously. "Even if someone tried, it would take them months. But I'm not taking any chances."

I drop into my chair, crisscrossing my legs while hugging my Coke bottle. Mom always told me that observation and patience are supposed to be a scientist's best friend. But it's not a natural skill of mine. I'm more of the girl who leaps into the throes of something and thinks about the consequences later on.

"I just need to go through the system and see which accounts the money was deposited and if it's been transferred or withdrawn." After a few minutes of him scanning the three screens and typing some more, he finally logs off and exits the system. "We're out."

He leans back in his chair and despite the cool of the room, a trail of sweat trickles down the sides of his face.

"So? Where did the money go?"

"Bangladesh."

"Bangladesh?" I ask. "But why? And who? Who took it out?"

"Don't know." He rubs the side of his face in thought. "It was withdrawn Friday morning from Bangladesh Bank before they had any clue of what was happening. Or at least it looks that way. I guess it makes sense. It was Bangladesh Bank who alerted us to the red flags when they noticed their printer failure. Maybe someone there purposely turned off their printer so the money could be transferred through."

"So they must know who withdrew the money."

"Maybe." He tilts his head to the side and his fingers fly over the keyboard, his forehead scrunched in concentration. I lean closer to see he's on the Bangladesh Bank's website. "Well, this isn't good. They've got an internal security system and I have no way of accessing it remotely. It would have to be done there. My guess is the feds will be getting involved once they discover what I have. Then they will begin working with the bank to discover who took the money."

"But what about my dad? We could be waiting weeks for them to apprehend this person and the trail might go cold by then."

"It's Saturday afternoon there and the bank is closed.

Everyone is probably freaking out. $81 million is a whole lot of cash to lose."

"Bangladesh," I mutter again. "Maybe that's where the plane went to. Can you access the airport's computer systems to see if any planes went there?"

He purses his lips and leans his head back as if surprised I asked. "I'm afraid that's out of my expertise. The only reason I was able to get into the National Reserve is that I learned all the access codes. I've been in and out of their system for years thanks to my dad."

"So I have to fly out to Bangladesh and find out for myself?"

"Wait a sec. You're not actually thinking of going to Bangladesh, are you?" When I don't answer he says, "Sounds dangerous. I don't like it."

"If that's where Dad is, that's where I need to go."

"You need to leave this up to the feds. They're the pros. What if I'm wrong and the money and your dad aren't linked? What if I'm completely off base on this?"

My mind feels like it's whirling a million miles faster than the 268 miles per hour in which the brain can actually move information. While he begins his mad hacking skills, I pull out my phone and call the team on video chat because I think Jake is right.

My dad and the money are connected.

# TWENTY
# TAKING MATTERS INTO OUR OWN HANDS

Amazingly everyone is awake, probably because like me, they're still freaked out about what happened only hours ago.

"Let me get this straight." Javier's lying on his couch with his phone propped up on one of the cushions. "Jake really believes that the $81 million was wired to Bangladesh?"

"Yep," Jake says, not looking up from his computer screen.

"Aria, why do you think your dad is where the money is?" Suns asks. "How do we not know Jake isn't just using us to get things worked out for his dad?"

"Because I'm not the jerk you believe I am," Jake says.

"Jake says the money was transferred to an account at the Bangladesh Bank in Dhaka," I say. "I'm just throwing out the idea that maybe Dad was taken there since that's where the money is."

"How did Jake figure this out?" Tony asks, skeptically.

"He has a friend on the Dark Web helping him out."

"And we trust this Dark Web guy?" Tony lifts his eyebrows.

"There's no reason he'd give me wrong information," Jake reassures. "Besides, he owes me."

"It could be a she," Sun points out with a smirk.

"What if we just went to Bangladesh and checked it out for ourselves?" I propose. "I know, it's a wild idea, but it's the best one I can think of right now. Jake said the system isn't available remotely, so if we could get in there and check it out ourselves, we could find out what really happened."

"Definitely a bad idea," Tony says.

"I'm stuck on the idea that Bangladesh is on the other side of the world," Javier says. "And why we are involving Jake."

"We need him," I say. "We can't follow the money trail without his skills."

Javier doesn't respond, but his grim look on my phone's screen says everything. He's not happy.

"You sure did a 180," Tony mutters. "Not two hours ago I had to hold you back from scratching his eyes out."

"Well, that's still an option." I look pointedly at Jake who rolls his eyes. "But until he proves himself not valuable, I think we should keep him around."

"Feels great to be needed," Jake says sarcastically.

I decide to steer the conversation back to the task on hand. "So what are our options? Wait for the police to investigate? How long will that take?"

"Too long," Jake mutters.

"I've got some money saved up," I barrel on. "We could get the first flight out to Bangladesh. Get a jump on this."

"Or I could call my brother," Sun suggests. "He might be open to letting us borrow his plane."

My eyes bug out. "Now we're talking."

"Get out! Your brother has a plane?" Tony says. "Slick. You've been holding out on me."

"Because when I mentioned my boat." Her eyes narrow. "You bugged me to take you out to the lake every day until I did."

Tony whistles. "This girl has had a ride of a lifetime all this time and I never knew."

Sun's family is mega-rich from her father's business in Hong Kong. She doesn't need to work, but after my dad helped her father with treatment on his brain and memories, she applied for a job at MaxLife. She said, "Dr. Hale changed my perspective on what I do with myself in this world. It's time I start changing the world rather than just shopping the world. Well, both actually if I can."

"Bonus is everyone's passports are up-to-date," I remind them. Suddenly our Belize trip last month is proving to be more useful than we first thought. I turn to Jake. "Except for you. Do you have a passport?"

"Thankfully, yes."

"It's too risky," Javier says. "And what will it look like to the police? They could easily be coming to our doors for further questioning."

"Which is why we should leave now," I say.

"We're putting a lot of our faith in a guy we hardly know," Javier warns. "I don't think this is a good idea. It feels too rash."

"He can hear everything you're saying," Jake says loudly.

"And what about your moms?" Sun adds. "You three may be eighteen, but will they actually let you leave the country?"

Tony is silent while Jake says, "I'll convince her. Not a problem."

I bite my inner lip, not wanting to answer Sun's question. The hopeful feeling of finding Dad is crumbling and I can't let that happen. "Let's just say hypothetically, Sun's brother came through and I convinced my mom that this is a good idea, I don't see why we can't leave tomorrow."

The whole team is silent.

"We would need visas," Jake says, already typing. "I'll check to see the requirements for the Asiana Visa. Okay, here it is. Looks like they can be applied for online as long as your background check clears. The biggest issue is once a visa application is submitted, if the applicant qualifies, the process takes a minimum of 24 hours to complete. It's cutting it close."

"Can you have your Dark Web friend help us out with that, too?" I ask. "Or we can pay for it to be expedited."

"See if there is a way we can sign up under Scientific Research," Javier recommends, which makes me hopeful he's seeing Jake as an ally.

"That's a lot of favors to be asking." Jake groans. "I'll see what I can do."

"I don't know, Aria," Sun says. "It's not impossible, but definitely a challenge. I'll call my brother and see what mood he's in and if he's got plans." She winces. "And if he's still mad at me for not calling him on his birthday. He was pissed over that."

"I've got MaxLife's credit card," I add. "At least for now until the board of trustees realizes we're spending the company's money without their permission. Tell him the business will cover all costs."

"Is no one else realizing what a bad idea this is?" Tony's face is practically pressed against his computer's camera. "We're dealing with professional hackers, thieves, kidnappers. Murderers. This is way out of our area of expertise."

"Which is why you should stay home," Javier tells him. "I'm sure your mom won't allow you anyway."

"Oh, I'm coming, bruh." Tony pops open a bag of chips and begins eating. "I'm just saying we need to be aware. Besides, how can I say no to a private jet?"

"Danny hasn't agreed to it yet," Sun warns. "And don't make me regret asking him."

"Text us first thing you hear something, okay Sun?" I ask. "In the meantime, I'll have Jake send you all the link for the Asiana Visa application. Tony, Javier's right. No one has to come because this could get dangerous. We don't know what we're up against and your mom and brother need you."

Once I hang up, I lean back in my chair and stare at Jake as the reality of what's happening begins to sink in deeper. "Do you think he's okay? My dad?"

"I don't know. But I do know mine isn't. Mom just texted and said he's been taken someplace else for further questioning. She doesn't know where they took him, but she's one hundred percent sure he's going to jail."

I press my hands over my face, wishing for yesterday morning when my biggest worry was whether I'd ace the assignment or not. How can my whole world just change within a few hours?

I manage to get a few hours of sleep before Mom wakes me. Saturday became a day of long talks with the police, which actually felt more like an interrogation. It was grueling and depressing when the police told us they didn't have any leads on Dad's whereabouts. It got worse when they told us he's one of their suspects in the murder of our technicians along with the intruder we tied up.

Their only lead seems to be in the intruder, but I get the feeling they aren't getting much from him.

The day improved dramatically when Sun sent me a text saying Danny okayed the trip as long as I get my mom's signed permission on a form she attached. Another bonus was a text from Jake saying applying for our visas under Scientific Research got us an expedited Asiana Visa.

Nothing is holding us back. Knowing we are going to

do something rather than just fill out paperwork and answer the same questions over and over again to the police, calms me.

But I don't even get a chance to talk to Mom about the trip until we trudge back into the house after being at the police station all day.

"I'm going to Bangladesh to find Dad," I blurt. Then I hold my breath, waiting for her to explode.

I'm not disappointed.

"Bangladesh?" Mom sputters, her eyes popping out of their sockets. "What do you mean you're going to Bangladesh? Is this some kind of joke?"

"Nope. I'm dead serious."

"Whatever for? Why would anyone take him there? Also, no. Absolutely not. I don't even—I can't do this."

It's too complicated to explain how we think that Jake's dreams, the $81 million bank heist, and the intruder's dream are all linked. Just thinking about it from her point of view makes our theory sound insane. Which, it probably is, but desperation does that to a person. I decide to keep things simple.

"Sun's brother has a plane and he's offered to fly us there tomorrow. We think there's a chance the kidnappers took Dad there. It will be a quick trip. We won't even be there more than two days."

She gapes at me like I told her I'd signed up for a one-way trip to Jupiter.

"Did you not hear me? You cannot, under any circumstances leave the country. And you definitely should not go where you think the kidnappers are! What are you thinking?" She starts pacing the room and launches into a ten-minute lecture on how irresponsible and unreasonable my idea is. Finally, she crosses her arms and plops into a chair at the kitchen table with a tired sigh. "Leave this for the police to figure out. They'll find your father. I know it."

Statistics say that with every hour passing, the slimmer the chance of that person found is." I rub my arms and grit my teeth. "We're running out of time and after talking to the police today, I don't have much confidence in them. They're making Dad sound like he's the murderer and thief!"

"They are the experts in this, not you." With shaking hands, she rubs her eyes and blows out a long breath. "Right now, we just need to be here and ready for when your father returns."

I'm so tired, I could fall asleep standing up. Maybe I am sleeping, and this is a horrible dream I can't control or escape. Discouraged, I turn to the kitchen counter and go about the task of making tea for both of us. I set our mugs on the counter, souvenirs from when we went to the Association of Dreams conference last year. Mine is a thick square celadon mug from Seoul that I bought at a local market while Mom's is her favorite teacup from Japan with a blue rim, dainty and delicate like her. This year, the conference is supposed to be in Warsaw and Dad was hoping to present the overview of the next stage of his studies on the Dreamscape.

My stomach churns. Now I don't even know what the next few hours will look like for us.

I place the tea bags into our mugs, trying to think about how I can convince her.

"I'm eighteen, Mom," I said. "If anyone understands this situation, it's our MaxLife team. We're going together and we can help each other out with the leads we have. I know the police will be on this, but I bet we're already one step ahead of them."

Mom remains silent. I'm not sure if she's thinking through what I'm saying or if her mind is locked away in her horror of Dad's disappearance. I pour hot water over the teabags and then add a teaspoon of sugar to mine, tapping the spoon against the rim twice. Just like I've done for the last seven years. I've always heard that when people's lives spin out of control, they revert to what they can control or what they know best.

"Honey, you're too young to understand the full complications of all of this situation." She closes her eyes and sighs in exasperation. "You need to leave this up to the experts. They've been trained for this kind of stuff."

I go to hand Mom her teacup, but her hands hang on her knees limp. So I set the cup beside her, then grab my own mug, soaking its warmth between my palms.

"I'm going to call Aunt Stacey," I finally say. "She'll want to be here to help out around the house."

Mom runs her hands through her hair, which is wild and sticks out like carrots. Dark circles ring her eyes, and her skin looks pale, too pale. She doesn't even bother with the tea, instead, she stands and shuffles to the counter. She pops two sleeping pills into her palm and swallows them without any water. Then she pads out of the kitchen toward her room.

"We'll talk about this in the morning," she says over her shoulder.

When her door shuts, I abandon my tea and storm into my room. I clench my fists in frustration and then pound them into my pillow until I've no energy left, and I sag onto my bed.

I get what she's saying, but she doesn't realize how much we already know about this crime and how deep it is. There's no way I'm going to tell her that I broke the rules of MaxLife to enter an assassin's dream or had Jake hack into the Federal Reserve or work with someone on the dark web.

I just need to focus. I shuffle to my mirror where all of my motivational quotes are written on sticky notes. One in particular catches my attention.

*The moment you give up is the moment you let someone else win.*

I peel that note off my mirror, staring at those words, letting them wrap around my mind and soul. Then I pocket it along with a few others. Taking a long, deep breath, I pick up a pen and print out the form Sun sent me. Before I can stop myself, I scrawl Mom's signature on the form. Technically I don't need her permission since I'm eighteen, but Sun's brother is covering his bases. I stare at the paper, hoping I'm making the right decision.

By the time she wakes up, I'll be gone.

## TWENTY-TWO
## FLIGHT TO BANGLADESH

Even though the sun has barely cut over the horizon, it burns bright against my eyes. It's too happy for all of the emotions rolling through me as I slip on my sunglasses and toss my suitcase into the backseat of my car. The palms wave over my head and the air smells like the fresh blooms that Mom has planted in our front yard. When I crank the engine, I cringe that Mom will hear it, but she doesn't come out. I thank the sleeping pills she took last night.

After I park at the airport, I stare out into the predawn light, the silhouette of the airport cutting against the dawn. Am I making the right choice by doing this? My nerves grate like knives, sharp against my skin. But sitting around and waiting for the police and the feds to come up with theories and answers isn't going to solve this. Sometimes you have to stand up and take action. Sometimes you have to take matters into your own hands.

Somehow I manage to pull myself together and get out of the car, striding down the long parking lot to the airport terminal.

At the ATM, I withdraw money from MaxLife's credit card, feeling no guilt for what I'm about to do. This is for Dad. He would do anything and spend any amount of money for me.

I find the others in the lobby sitting on the hard plastic chairs. Tony has his headphones in and is mouthing words to himself, patting the armrests of the chair. Javier is reading the newspaper while Sun is talking to a tall, thin man with dark hair and an angular face. He's Asian and looks a lot like Sun so I'm guessing this is her brother, Danny.

I scan the area for Jake and finally spy him standing by the window, staring out at the planes. His shoulders are hunched as if he's bearing the weight of the world on them.

"Hey," I announce myself to the group once I'm close enough.

They all look up at me and the Sun's brother comes over to introduce himself.

"I'm Danny." He shakes my hand. "I'm sorry about your dad. I'll do whatever I can to help. Dr. Hale was a good man. He's been a big help to our father restoring some of his memories."

"Thank you," I say. There are no words for how grateful I am. "For everything."

"You sure your mom is okay with this?" Danny asks. I dig through my purse until I find the form with her fake signature on it. He takes it from me, and after glancing at it, shrugs. "I haven't been to Bangladesh in some time, but my pilots are the best. We'll get you there in no time."

The others stand to join us, and we all roll our suitcases and equipment over to security. Once through, we head down a series of corridors and take the elevator out to the tarmac.

"Your moms are okay with this?" I ask Tony and Jake as we head outside.

"She's a little preoccupied visiting my dad in jail," Jake says darkly.

"I might have made it seem like a work trip." Tony grimaces. "I'm surprised your mom didn't flip out about you coming."

"She wasn't thrilled." I shrug and force one foot in front of the other. That keeps me from freaking out and turning on my heels and leaving. "Besides, it will be a quick trip. Two days max."

My head swims with the image of Mom curled up at the kitchen corner and her disheveled appearance. I force myself not to think how she'll go ballistic once she discovers I've left. I manage to console myself with the thought of the note I left her and the email I sent this morning on her behalf to Aunt Stacy. Knowing my aunt, she'll jump in her car first thing and drive over from Tampa. Mom will be okay with her there.

As we all enter the plane, Tony whistles. "Man!" he says. "This is one sweet ride!"

"Sit wherever you are most comfortable," Danny says. "It might feel slightly cramped since usually it's just me and my executive team that flies. But it will be easier than flying commercial. Drinks and snacks are in the back galley and feel free to pop any of the freezer food into the microwave."

Sun kisses him on the cheek and says something to him in Chinese. I take in the cream-colored soft, cushiony chairs and how each has plenty of legroom and a window. "Wow," I say. "This is like flying first class but better."

Everyone thanks Danny and the mood of the group has definitely improved. Well, maybe everyone except Jake. He keeps quiet as he settles into a chair and checks his phone.

"He's a good brother," I tell Sun as I push up my suitcase into the section that Danny indicates for us. "You're lucky."

"He is." She smiles. "But he works too hard. We would all be happier if he found himself a wife and had a few kids. Might settle him down some."

"Like you're one to talk," Danny says, laughing and poking her in the back. "Miss Neuro-scientist."

When I settle into a seat, it's so soft and large that I know I'll be fast asleep once we're in the air. I snap on my seatbelt and glance behind me to see Jake sitting there, a computer on his lap while talking to Danny about internet connections. Javier has seated himself directly across from Jake, crossing his arms, and I bet, he's sending mental daggers at Jake.

Once Danny strides away, Jake's eyes catch mine. I whip back around to face forward, my heart skittering.

What is wrong with me? How can I be mooning over a boy when my father has been kidnapped? Guilt charges through me and I force myself to not look at Jake as the plane begins to taxi down the runway. I need to stay focused on finding Dad. That is what's important. As the engines revs up, Sun reaches her hand out from across the aisle. I grab her fingers and she squeezes mine.

"We're going to find him," she says. "I know it."

Whenever we're working in the Dreamscape, I always rely on her instincts. She understands emotions, the inner feelings of a person's mind like no one else. I would trust her with my life.

"If you think so," I say. "It must be true."

I pretend I don't see that flash of doubt cross her features or how she moves her head to look forward instead of looking me in the eye.

The plane lifts into the air and I tell myself this is the solution. We're going to find Dad and get the $81 million back so Jake's dad can be cleared and not go to jail. Then we all won't live the rest of our lives torn up by guilt at what we've done.

The engines roar. The cabin shudders. And I don't care if I'm placing all my trust in a lie.

Bangladesh. I step out of the airport and it's like entering another world. People bustle past to jump into taxis or rush to meet up with family or friends. Cars are honking uproariously while drivers call out for our group's attention for us to ride with them instead of the taxi Danny ordered us. Even the air smells different. More like a big city instead of the salty air of Florida.

I drag my suitcase across the bumpy pavement to the back of the taxi van Danny ordered us. We traveled eighteen hours, arriving here in Dhaka, Bangladesh on their Monday morning, and even with a private plane, we look a little haggard in our wrinkled clothes.

"Tell me the hotel is close by." Sun tosses her carry-on into the back. "I'm desperate for a shower."

"By the way," Tony whispers to me. "If my mom calls looking for me, tell her I'm staying at a friend's house."

"Wait, what? She doesn't know you're in Bangladesh? I thought you told her it was a work trip."

"Shhh…" Tony glances around to make sure no one heard before slipping his luggage next to Sun's. "Dude, chill. There's no way she'd let me skip school. I'm surprised your mom said yes."

"Me too." I try to push away the thoughts of Mom's text that greeted me when we landed.

Basically, since I'm not acting like a responsible adult, I'm grounded for eternity. I remind myself this will be worth it once I find Dad.

"You lied, didn't you?" Jake whispers in my ear as I'm about to get in the van with the others. "Your mom didn't want you going on this trip."

"Shut up and get into the van," I snap. "And don't you dare tell anyone that or I'll tell the group about your Batman obsession."

"And there's the red-haired fire I've been waiting for." He grins and jumps into the van.

"Head for the Purbani International Hotel," Danny tells the driver once we all settle inside. Then he peeks his head around the front seat to talk to us. "It's the closest hotel to the bank and only eighteen kilos from here. The hotel is in the older section of the city so not the newest of places, but it should work for what you need. I also checked on the bank's hours. It opens at 10 a.m. so that gives you two hours to get settled into your rooms before heading over there."

Except as we leave the airport, traffic keeps our taxi van moving at a snail's pace. The van is stifling hot and the scent of petrol from the highway penetrates the air despite the AC's best efforts to cool us down. Horns blast through our silence while pedestrians weave in and out around our van, some even tap on the doors and windows, waving.

An elephant charm dangles from the driver's mirror and music blasts from his speakers. I peek out my window and soak in the eclectic mix of shops and hundreds of people going about their daily business. This is a city of chaos and constant motion. We pass by a mosque and then just a few minutes later, we turn the corner where a Hindu temple stands, the golden peaks gleaming against the cloudy sky.

A woman holding a tiny baby races to our taxi, pounding on the glass windows while holding out a palm for money. Her eyes stare vacantly at me as if they've already lost hope. I want to help, and against our driver's warning, I roll down the window and slip her a five-dollar bill.

Instantly, our van is swarmed by what feels like a hundred beggars. Our driver spews off what sounds like a lecture in Bengali at me while the others try to keep the grabbing hands from tearing at my clothes. Thanks to our driver, we manage to get away without hurting anyone, but I can't stop myself from looking back out the rearview mirror, wishing I could do something to help them.

Finally, after what feels like an eternity, our driver

pulls into the large parking lot of our hotel, which is a tall V-shaped white building that looks like it could've had a new paint job a decade ago.

"It doesn't look like much," Danny says with a grin, "but they serve excellent curry."

"Man, somebody give me a bed," Tony mutters. "I could really go for a long dreamless sleep."

My stomach is twisted and queasy from the start and stopping of the car so I'm relieved to step out of the taxi. The air burns hot against the back of my throat, reminding me of the scorching days in Florida when the forest fires are out of control. The bellhop smiles at me, asking in a lilted English accent if he can take my bag, but I thank him and continue into the main lobby.

The white tiled floor gleams, reflecting the ceiling lights. Two large stone elephants stand like sentinels on either side of a grand stairway. The walls display murals of countryside landscapes and tall, ornate golden pillars spike up, climbing to the ceiling.

"After everyone has dropped off their bags in their rooms," Javier says. "Let's meet back here in the lobby to make our plan. If all goes well, we could be flying back to home early tomorrow."

My room isn't anything fancy, but for just over a hundred U.S. dollars a night, I'll take it. The white tiled floor continues into my room, keeping the area cool.

I set my suitcase on the chair by the window and draw back the curtains to take in the view from eight stories up. I suck in a breath. Dhaka is one huge, sprawling city, with a rolling landscape of buildings, some spiking up like jagged peaks. Some sections look appear more like shanties or small crumbling square concrete structures. There are so many buses, cars, motorcycles, and those cute cycle rickshaws I spotted on the way here.

Even though I've only been here a few hours, I can already feel the tempo of the city. It's alive and wild and full of the unknown.

The need to freshen up drags me away from the window. I pull out a pair of khaki pants and a long-sleeved shirt to not draw any attention to myself. I debate on what to do with my hair, but end up just brushing it out, too tired to deal with it. Once I change and splash water over my face, I tuck my purse strap over my shoulder and head back downstairs.

In the back of the lobby is an area set with tables and chairs surrounded by tall fake palms strung with colorful lights. The hum of soothing Bangla music fills the lobby. Jake and Javier are already there, laptops opened and talking.

In a way, it's weird seeing Jake with my team, acting like he's a part of us. My emotions roll over me and I can't make sense of it all. One moment, my heart flutters at seeing him. The next, there's that anger that if it weren't for him and his nosing around in his dad's bank, none of this would've happened.

"Hey." I stroll up to their table where he's sipping a Coke. "What trouble are you two getting us into?"

"I think I can do nearly all the searching remotely," Jake says, eyes intent on the screen. He clicks on his keyboard and then swivels his screen so I can see it. Why does it seem like he's avoiding eye contact with me? "But to get into the system, I'll need to have one of you place some Botware into their computer system."

"We're scientists," Javier says. "Not criminals. We've no idea how to do that."

Jake shifts in his chair. "What are you implying? That I'm a criminal?"

"He's not," I say quickly. "Except why would we need to get anywhere near one of the bank's computers? It will look suspicious, won't it? And after this whole heist disaster, they'll have security at its all-time high."

"Good point." Jake shrugs. "I guess that's where your ingenuity comes in."

"Ingenuity?" Sun asks as she sails into the lobby, her black hair fluttering around her chin. She's applied fresh red lipstick and classic black pants and a flowered blouse. As she settles beside me, I feel like a rumpled mess compared to her classic chic look. "If you're looking for brilliant ideas, I'm here."

Jake holds up a thumb drive. "We need an excuse for you to insert this into one of the computers at the bank."

"That's it?" Sun scrunches her nose. She waves her hand at a server who rushes over to our table. "Green tea for two and scones all around. Can't have our brain cells cannibalize themselves to gain energy to ward off starvation now can we?"

"That's true?" Jake asks.

"Yep." I nudge him. "So if you want to stay smart, don't starve yourself."

Javier leans back in his chair and takes a gulp of his coffee. "But it's more than that, isn't it? We have to insert the thumb drive and then take it out."

"I need about five minutes to connect to the server through the thumb drive," Jake acknowledges. "And then ideally you'll need to take the drive out, otherwise we'll leave behind a digital footprint and evidence. Well, the reality is we're going to be leaving a digital footprint regardless. There's just no way around it, but if we can avoid drawing attention to it and making it easy to be traced back to us, that's better."

"What exactly are you doing with the drive?" Sun asks. "You think you can access the files to see who withdrew the money?"

"I doubt I'll be able to do that." Jake rolls his neck. "Hacking into the bank's server would take more time than we have today. But from what I've been able to figure out is that the surveillance cameras are on a different system, which I should be able to access easily."

"And if we're caught?" I cringe at the thought.

The others suddenly look highly interested in the plate of scones the server delivered to the table.

"Listen." I fold my hands. "This mess is Jake's and my problem. You both don't have to go. Just coming all this way is moral support and that in itself is huge."

Jake looks up at me, his gaze intense and on fire. He means business, but I can't quite read what's going on behind his eyes. One thing I do know is through all of this, I need to stay focused on Dad. Those flutters in the pit of my stomach can't become anything more than that.

"Oh, I'm in," Javier says. "There's no way I'm not helping out with this."

"This discussion is a waste of time." Sun sips her tea. "We've already said we're willing to take the risks. If it weren't for your father, Aria, my father wouldn't be alive right now. So let's just focus on how we can get this surveillance data and go from there."

I share an idea to execute our plan and the others add in their thoughts. By the time we finish, I'm feeling like we might actually be able to pull this off.

"I like it." Jake closes his laptop. "Let's do this."

"What about Tony?" Sun's eyes wander to the elevator. "He hasn't come down yet."

"He probably fell asleep." Javier chuckles. "Let him be. No need for him to get into any more trouble than he already is in."

We head outside and call a taxi at the bellhop station. I clutch my to-go cup of tea that I requested, needing the hot drink to relax me. Javier and Jake take the first taxi while Sun and I take the next one. We decided it was best to keep as separated from each other as possible just in case.

Our driver ends up dropping Sun and me on the wrong side of the road. A group of sellers hawking their wares, calls out to us. The interesting part is they're all well-dressed like businessmen, wearing black dress pants and button-down collared shirts. A woman selling woven baskets stands to our right. She's wearing the traditional wrap dress and her head is covered.

Sun and I cross the street, darting past a tiny red bus and avoiding a group of rickshaws careening down the road. Once Sun and I step onto the sidewalk in front of the bank, we both let out a sigh of relief.

"Whew!" Sun swipes a stream of sweat from her forehead. "Next time, we need to make sure our driver lets us off on the right side of the street."

"That really didn't help calm my nerves."

The Central Bank of Bangladesh is a seven-story white building lined with palms and gardens. On its sides rise up tall glass-paned towers along with a sprinkling of small dirt-streaked structures. The contrast of new and old, rich and poor, sitting side by side is startling. But even the scenery can't distract me enough from thinking about what we're about to do.

Tall trees rise up around us with twisted vines blocking off some of the blazing sun's rays. We stroll up to the metal gates of the bank and check in with security at a white stone building. They pat us down before we enter through the security scanner.

"Are you sure this is going to work out?" I whisper, my heart thumping in my chest.

"Don't talk." Sun walks briskly, smiling as if nothing could possibly be bothering her. "You're making me nervous."

"Fabulous. Now I'm completely freaking out." I clench the cup holding my green tea, wishing I hadn't brought it along.

"Think of this like a Dream Walk. Except *please* don't go jumping out of helicopters."

I snort and roll my eyes. Still, she's right. In the Dreamscape, I'm always the bravest on the team. I don't hesitate, instead, I follow my instincts. Why can't I do that in the real world? Why shouldn't I? But then, the real world and the Dreamscape have totally consequences.

The moment we step inside the foyer of the bank, I pull the thumb drive out of the pouch in my purse and slide it into my palm. Mentally, I force Dad's face into my mind, praying that we are one step closer to finding him.

"How about that man at the desk back there," I suggest. "His desk is out of the way of traffic and his computer looks easy to access, not boxed into a cubicle like the others."

The two of us beeline across the lobby. As we walk up, the man looks at us in surprise. He's wearing a sharp black suit and his shirt is buttoned and crisply ironed. His dark black hair has been smoothed back and his mustache twitches as he takes in the two of us.

He rises from his seat, eyebrows lifting. "Can I help you, ladies?"

"Why yes!" I say eagerly. I plop down in one of the two chairs in front of his desk while Sun, following my lead, sits in the chair beside me. My phone beeps and I glance at it.

*Ready*, it reads.

I eye the computer on the man's desk. It's turned on and opened to an Excel spreadsheet. Except he's got a computer model where the hard drive is separate from the monitor. It will be really awkward if I were to stretch across his desk and plug in the drive.

"Err…" I pause to read the name on the desk. Mr. Bosu. I switch my accent to sound Australian. "Mr. Bosu. Good day, mate. My friend, Tara Karin, and I are here to tour your bank. We're from Australia and thought how fun it would be to visit your bank. We are both in school and considering a career in banking."

I cringe over my Australian accent, which sounds more like an American wannabe. I can only hope he's never met any real Australians.

"Well then, how nice to meet you." Mr. Bosu smiles tightly and picks up a pile of papers, straightening them. "You must excuse me, but we are not doing tours today or offering career lessons. It is a rather bad day for such matters."

"Of course. So sorry to be of inconvenience." Sun clears her throat and clenches the sides of her chair. She's going to back out! We can't just leave without at least trying. Quickly, I stand and cry out.

"Oh!" I set down my tea on Mr. Bosu's desk and gaze at the marble globe resting beside his nameplate, pretending to be completely infatuated with it. "That *is* the loveliest object! You must tell me where you found it. I simply cannot go home to Sydney without its replica."

"Why, thank you," he says, surprise in his voice. "It was a gift."

I pick up the globe and while doing so, pretend to accidentally spill my tea. Dark liquid spills across his desk, racing over his papers like a flood escaping a dam. Eyes wide and yelling words I don't understand, Mr. Bosu waves his hands about, spinning around in search of something to mop up the mess.

"Oh, bloody cuppa," I cry out, trying to maintain a semblance of an accent. Sun covers her mouth. She's laughing at me! I glare at her. It's not my fault I've never been to Australia.

"Here!" Sun leaps up and grabs his arm, leading him to the next desk over where a tissue box sits. "This will do the trick."

When their backs are turned to me, I slide between the desk and the wall. I lean over and snap the thumb drive into the hard drive on his computer. Then I start my stopwatch, hoping Jake will get his data downloaded sooner than later. Meanwhile, Sun holds the tissue box just long enough so that when he turns back around I'm by his desk, pretending to save his desk things from my tea.

Mr. Bosu mops up the mess, rattling off a tirade of words in Bengali, which I'm guessing aren't so complimentary of us.

"You must leave now," Mr. Bosu says, jaw tight. "As I explicitly said before, today is a *very* busy day."

I check my phone. No word from Jake or Javier. My stopwatch warns me that only two minutes and ten seconds have passed. Jake thought he would need at least five minutes. This isn't good since we can't leave the thumb drive otherwise the authorities could trace the data source.

"I simply can't leave your desk in such a muddle." I run about the desk, taking the tissues from his hand and mopping up the liquid. "You must let us help you tidy up your workspace. There's a good man."

"I suppose," Mr. Bosu grudgingly allows.

"And you can't have that desk all sticky with tea," Sun adds. "Let me go to the loo to gather up some wet paper towels. Those should do nicely."

She returns to finish up the cleaning while I attempt to set everything back into place as slowly as possible. I check my stopwatch and we've now surpassed five minutes without any word from Jake.

"There now," Sun says. "Everything is spit-spot."

Now it's my turn to raise my eyebrows at her word choice. Somehow we've veered from Aussie to British. She winks at me, smirking.

"Yes," Mr. Bosu says. "Thank you and a good day to you both."

"Wait!" My mind frantically scours for another thing to do or say to keep us for a few more minutes. "A photo-graph! Yes, that's what we need. To remember our *lovely* time with you, Mr. Bosu, from this *lovely* bank."

"I do not take photos and certainly do not have the time." His mouth has literally turned downward in complete annoyance.

"But you've been so kind." Sun lightly touches his arm. "It will only be a quick photo."

He clears his throat, his face smoothing out. Then he mutters an okay under his breath. That's Sun for you. She can convince anyone to do what she wants them to do.

Sun and I crowd in on either side of Mr. Bosu behind his desk. I hold up the marble globe and then we take a selfie. By this time, a lady has come up to the table, holding a stack of papers and frowning at the three of us. Other people around the bank are also staring at us, which is bad. How am I supposed to get that thumb drive out with everyone looking?

"Fantastic!" Sun says once I snap the photo.

"Let me just check it." I'm stalling for time. *What is taking Jake so long?* "Make sure it's not blurry."

My phone beeps and I read the text that pops up.

*Done.*

Finally!

"I suppose we must be off then," I tell Sun. She nods, understanding my message. I move to take a step toward the desk to return the globe but pretend to trip.

The globe falls out of my hands.

"The globe!" I scream. I drop to the ground right beside the computer console, pretending to catch it.

Everyone's eyes turn to watch the globe roll across the floor. Meanwhile, I yank the thumb drive out, pocketing it in one quick motion. Sun races after the globe and snatches it up, handing it over to Mr. Bosu. The two of us then rush out of the bank, looking incredibly guilty. Adrenaline is still pumping through my veins as we step out into the blazing heat.

The tension in my shoulders loosens and that surge of victory floods me like those times in the Dreamscape when I made it through a dream transition and didn't get knocked out.

I slip on my sunglasses and purse my lips.

"Not bad for the real world," I say.

"Good on ya, mate," she agrees, giggling. "We aced that mission."

We exit the bank's gates into a world of honking horns, the push of crowds, and jammed-packed streets.

"You do know your Australian accent is god-awful," Sun says as the two of us clip down the dusty street side street toward the café we are supposed to meet the guys at.

"I used all my TV experience to replicate my accent to perfection."

"It was evident," she says sarcastically, but her cheeks are flushed and eyes bright. Despite her tone, I know she's pleased with our outcome.

Rickshaws pass by us, their drivers asking if we'd like a ride while street vendors continue to entice us to try their food. Electric wires cut across the sky above and dust kicks up in the air from the traffic. The shops' doorways and windows are wide open, allowing me to peek at what they're selling. I'm guessing they keep their doors open to not only tempt shoppers inside but also to allow some type of breeze to pass through because it sure is hot here.

Soon we find our rendezvous location. Café Burger. A tin-roofed awning juts out, providing shade over plastic tables. Javier, Jake, and Tony are sitting at one of them, staring intently at a laptop.

"There they are," Tony says, spotting us. "Little stinkers. Leaving me behind like that."

"Hey," I greet them. "Where were you this morning Tony?"

"Why didn't you wake me up?" He crosses his arm and glares at me like he's completely offended we left him behind.

I pass Jake the thumb drive, ignoring Tony. Jake slips the thumb drive into his computer. "Now for the truth. Let's hope it works."

"We made a bit of a scene," Sun says. "Actually, Aria made a scene. I picked up the pieces. Or, more accurately, mopped it up."

"Any trouble?" Javier asks.

"Just a super annoyed banker." I drag a chair over and join them at the table.

Jake's fingers fly across the keyboard and after a few clicks, video clips pop up organized by dates. Jake chooses this past Friday at 11 a.m. Bangladesh time, which would've been after we entered Jake's dream Eastern Standard Time.

"The person we're looking for should've come into the

bank around this time," he says. "It's just before the Bangladesh Bank discovered the money was transferred and lost. Actually, it wasn't until after the Bangladesh Bank's printer was fixed that they saw all the reports coming in."

"Sounds like someone rigged the printer as well," Javier mutters.

"There are so many people." Sun studies the footage. "How will you know who it was?"

"Eeny meeny miny moe," Tony jokes.

"Here." Jake points to one of the tellers where a man with dark hair and a suit stands, his back to us. A teller hands the man a stack of cash.

"That looks pretty suspicious, doesn't it?" I ask.

"Maybe." Jake sighs. "Keep watching that clip while I continue working on the coding to see if I can get into their system."

"In the U.S.," Javier says. "If you withdraw large portions of cash, it alerts the feds for suspicious activity."

The man on the screen talks to the teller, nods a few times, and then signs a paper. He taps his pen on the paper three times. I can't help but wonder if that was just a nervous habit or if it was a signal. In the Dreamscape, it would mean something: impatience, excitement, or the beginning of a transition to a new dream segment. But in this real-life scenario, there doesn't seem to be anyone else suspicious there. The teller passes the man a slip of paper.

"What is that?" I ask.

"A check for a million dollars?" Tony guesses.

"No." Javier squints at the screen. "Doesn't look like it."

It's when the man turns to leave, we get our first good look at him. He's a native of Bangladesh. Brown skin, fairly young looking with glasses and short, black hair. But it's when he glances up at the camera, my heart stutters. It is as if he's staring right at me. As if he were concerned about surveillance.

"Whoa," Tony says. "Tell me you didn't see that."

"He knew someone might be watching him," Javier mutters. "Amateur."

"Or he wanted us to think he was an amateur," Sun points out.

Moments before the man exits the building, our Mr. Bosu strides up to him and shakes his hand.

"Look!" I say. "It's Mr. Bosu and he's talking to the guy who supposedly withdrew the millions."

Jake pauses from his search. "That's odd."

The two chat for a brief minute before stepping off to the side, out of the camera's view.

"Something's going down," Tony says.

"Let me check the other cameras." Jake begins going through the different pieces of footage. "This is too coin-cidental."

Sun and I order sodas while Jake keeps searching, but after nearly an hour, he leans back in his chair, tossing his hands up.

"I've got nothing," he says. "It's like they both disappeared for ten minutes. And look here. Your Mr. Bosu pops up again back on the screen by his desk. And then at that same time, in camera sixteen, the other guy leaves the bank, empty-handed."

"Okay," Javier admits to Jake. "You're not so bad. Maybe Aria was right to let you come along on this mission."

"Do you think he gave Mr. Bosu the money?" I wonder.

Jake rubs his chin. "Don't know. It will take some digging, but I have a feeling the money never left the bank with that man. We don't even know if the money was picked up here. It could've been transferred elsewhere after this bank. And I don't have the means to find out. I'm sure the feds back home are working on this right now."

"So basically our trail has ended and it's getting colder by the second," I say. Unable to deal with that thought, I push back my chair and stride to the other side of the café underneath a TV where a newscaster relates news of flooding in the south.

"What if we got answers our way," Javier says.

"Dude, no." Tony shakes his head.

My body goes rigid. I know exactly what he means and I know exactly how wrong that would be on so many levels. I pull up our family photo from my phone. My finger traces the outline of Dad's face, and it takes everything inside of me to push down the sobs that threaten to release from deep within my chest.

I turn back to face the group. "Yes," I say.

They all stare at me, a mix of horror and understanding. No one says anything at first. And then Tony sighs, sinking his head into his palm. Sun presses her lips together and Javier doesn't look up from the napkin he's folding.

I'm surprised it's Jake who speaks first. "I can get Mr. Bosu's address," he says. "We can pick him up and bring him back to the hotel."

"We brought the supplies, right?" My voice is tight.

"Yes," Sun says and then clears her throat, looking away.

Because the moment we didn't call the cops at MaxLife and entered our intruder's dream without his permission, deep down we knew it was our means to an end. After all, it was the only way.

Wasn't it?

TWENTY-SIX

# A MEANS TO AN END

I wait in Javier's hotel room, pacing the floor, my nerves are at an all-time high. Sun sits in the lone chair by the window staring down into the city of Dhaka below. We told Sun's brother we were going to sleep early due to jet lag. No need to get him involved with more than he already is. Javier, Jake, and Tony left two hours ago to intercept Mr. Bosu from work. The plan was for them to find a way to bring him to the hotel while Sun and I prepped the room for a Dream Walk.

Then once we're finished, we'll put him back in a taxi and send him home, none the wiser.

"It will work," I tell Sun.

She won't look at me. I clench my fists, hating myself for putting her through this and yet, desperate for her to stay because ultimately we need her to run the Dreamscape from the outside to make sure everyone remains safe through the whole procedure.

I hate the waiting, so I decide now is a good time as any to call Mom. It'll be early morning for her. It only rings once when she picks up.

"Aria?" Mom asks. "Tell me you're almost home."

I lick my lips, sagging against the wall. "Not yet. We're hoping to be back tomorrow morning for you if all goes well." I shut my eyes, hating how I'm holding information from her. What kind of person was I becoming? "Any news on Dad?"

"Nothing." Mom chokes up then and there's a muffled sob on the other end. "They are now saying he was kidnapped just like you thought. The man they found in his office still hasn't talked, but the cops think they wanted him for the dream technology. Can you believe that? This is all about his work! I warned him he was tampering with things he shouldn't touch. But he never would listen to me. Now look what happened!"

My legs are jelly, and I sink down on the bed. "He meant it for good, Mom." I stare at our equipment, all ready to be used. "You have to believe that. We just had a big breakthrough with the Dreamscape. It's going to help Grams. I know it."

"When you get back we need to talk about your research and your career plans," Mom says. "This dream stuff is too dangerous. You're a smart girl. You can work with me. You could be an amazing botanist. Maybe it will be through plants that we can find a way to heal Grams."

"I've got to go. I love you."

"I love you, too, but come home, okay?"

I hang up, thinking through our conversation. Suddenly, my perfectly planned-out life is spinning out of control. Not only am I missing tons of school, but I've no idea where Dad is or what my future will be. I straighten my back and press my fingers against my temples. I can't think about all of that. I need to focus on getting Dad back. Once he's safe, I'll figure out the next steps.

Noise in the hallway jerks me back to the door. I rush to the peephole to spy the group lugging Mr. Bosu in their arms. Quickly, I unlock the door and throw it open, allowing the guys to come stumbling inside. Then I shut the door behind them and click the locks into place.

"Had to give him some sleeping juice," Tony says, huffing. "The dude started asking too many questions."

"Put him on the far bed." Sun picks up the syringe of Temazepam, and after swabbing his forearm with antiseptic, plunges more of the liquid into his system. "I'm not taking any chances. And he'll be fine. It's fine."

I stare at her. It's as if she's saying that just to convince herself we're making the right choice.

"He's actually helping save people's lives," I add. "And who is to know if he isn't guilty himself? If that doesn't work we can always try the NightFlash."

Sun dismisses the idea. "It never connects the sleepers to the Dreamscape properly."

"One thing I do know." Jake grunts as he tries to put both of Mr. Bosu's legs on the bed. "He's not as light as he looks."

"No joke." Tony has grabbed bath towels and starts mopping his face with them, tossing a towel to Jake and Javier. "Let's get this over with. I don't like any of it."

"Agreed," Javier says. "Sun you work the Dreamscape's control panel while we three go in. You all know the drill."

He's right. We've worked together more times than I can count. This is like eating popsicles on a summer day for us. But the thing is, being in this room, outside of MaxLife, everything feels different. Off.

"I'm going to hook my computer up to the Dreamscape," Jake says. "I'd like to run a diagnostic on it to make sure no one can hack into your system."

"They could do that?" I ask.

"Definitely." Jake touches a few buttons. "Especially because this Dreamscape is wireless. Later, after we're done, I want to load up an anti-hacker software as well, and a failsafe, too. Hey, Aria. Do you know who your father used as the prototype for the Dreamscape? Like whose brain is the alpha?"

"He actually used my grandmothers and mine to help set up his research. Why?"

He lifts his eyebrows at this, but then just shrugs and

says, "Just curious. It's got a very complex system that mimics a human's brain really well. It's actually an incredible invention of your dad's."

"He is brilliant," I whisper, suddenly feeling the need to get into this dream and find the answers we've been seeking.

Sun slips a Neuro-Read Sleep Mask over Mr. Bosu's eyes and a set of headphones that will project the Sound Oasis to him. Before we had the fancy chairs, we used these headphones, but it's been a while.

I shove aside the knot in my stomach and lie on the floor on one of the three mats that we created from towels and pillows. I click the transmitter button on the strap of my sleep mask so my brain waves connect to the Dreamscape.

Sun doesn't waste a second. The Sound Oasis emits the cry of gulls and the crashing of waves, filling my consciousness. I'm taken far away from this old hotel room where I'm lying on the floor.

I push aside all doubts and fears and allow myself to sink far and deep into the Dreamscape.

I'm standing in a posh hotel lobby. Chandeliers gleam from above, scattering shimmering light across the floor, and just to my left lies a restaurant with white tablecloths and twinkling candles. Silverware clinks and a band plays traditional Bangla music. My hand gropes the air until I find a wall where I'm able to steady myself. A rush of bile fills my mouth and a piercing jab stabs against my temple.

I whimper.

Slowly I take even breaths. This transition is far more difficult than any other I've encountered, and if it was any other situation, I'd have faded right away. Without our chairs back at MaxLife's lab, this transition into the Dreamscape is hell.

"Dad," I whisper, reminding myself why I'm doing this. "Find him."

These thoughts pull the room into focus and I'm able

to take one, two, three steps. I scan the crowds of indistinct faces in search of Mr. Bosu, our dreamer. I find him sitting at a table beside a massive buffet table piled high with mounds of food. He's talking to someone.

I weave through the restaurant full of faceless people until I come to a table where Tony sits. He's eating a giant plate of rice with vegetables with a stack of naan bread piled up on the side of the plate. A chagrined smile crosses his face.

"You can't be serious," I tell him, hands on my hips.

"It relaxes me." He shrugs. "Habit, you know? Besides, this naan. To die for."

Javier strolls past us, a frown on his face. "Focus, you two!"

Nodding, Tony sets down his fork and joins me as we ease into the chairs at a table beside Mr. Bosu. I pick up a fork, side glancing over at our dreamer who is with a woman at the table. The two aren't talking. The woman is passing spoons across the table, piling them high in front of Mr. Bosu.

"Spoons?" I ask questioningly to Tony who only shrugs and piles rice onto his naan.

I tip my chair back to get a better look at the woman, trying to look as nonchalant as possible. My guess is she's a foreigner to Bangladesh, maybe Chinese. Her black hair is tied back at the nape of her neck. She has large, luminous eyes and a full mouth lined with red lipstick. She's wearing a strapless, black sequined gown with a choker of diamonds ringing her neck. Basically, she is drop-dead gorgeous, and from the glazed look in Mr. Bosu's eyes, he agrees. There's something familiar about her that niggles at the corner of my mind, but I can't place it.

"Are we going to sit here all day while this lady passes him spoons?" Tony asks. "Because this is going nowhere fast."

"You're right," I say. "We need to shake things up."

I rise to my feet when I spy Sun and myself sitting at the table on the other side of him. I freeze, shocked because I've never actually seen myself in a dream. At one of Dad's conferences, I remember him saying hypothetically it could happen if the dreamer knew the Dream Walker, but that has never been the case since we didn't know our clients.

Except for Jake, that is.

I ease back into my seat. "Tony, look! Sun and I are sitting at that table. We must be a part of the dream."

"Ooo." Tony scrunches his face and shakes his head. "Not cool. You've got to keep it on the low. If he sees you, it could freak him out and wake him up. Which we *definitely* don't want to happen."

I consider my options. In the past, I've always been the one who was able to think outside of the box and break through the boundaries that were in our path to help us stay in the dream. But now that I'm actually in the dream, it changes everything.

Javier hunkers down at my side. "You have to fade. If he sees you, it could ruin our opportunity."

His tone is insistent, unwavering. Back at MaxLife, I would have to listen to him. It's part of our protocol since I'm technically still an intern. Javier's been our team leader ever since I started working for the company. In our handbook, it's listed that to disobey the team leader, we are subjected to a reprimand. I've never questioned his authority before, but then my dad's never been kidnapped, forcing me to break nearly every rule in our code of ethics.

"I can't leave," I say. "You know I'm the best here at thinking outside of the box. I'll just stay in the background and watch. As long as he doesn't see me, we should be fine."

"It's your hair." Javier rubs his temples and throws his free hand up in frustration. "Sometimes it works in your favor to get the dreamer's attention, but in this case, it's not."

Unconsciously my fingers twirl around a strand of my hair. Deep down, I know he's right, but I can't. I just can't leave. If we don't get information from this guy, it means our trail has gone cold and I can't think beyond that because the ramifications are too huge.

So I shake my head ever so slightly, pressing my lips together. I imagine myself with different colored hair.

"White?" Javier asks. "No offense, but I don't think you could pass for a grandma."

"It's the best I can do," I mutter. It's not a great

disguise, but it will work if I stay focused on it. "Now get off my case."

"Fine." He shoots me a scathing look. "But if this goes down, it's all your fault."

*Ouch.* But yeah, I deserve that.

Javier moves to a table near Mr. Bosu who is now sitting completely surrounded by golden spoons. Meanwhile, Sun and my dream self are inching closer to Mr. Bosu's table. My dream self holds a large bowl full of dark liquid and I have a twisted grin on my face. Seriously, I resemble the witch from Snow White holding out a shiny apple. Except I'm wearing jeans and my nose doesn't have warts bubbling over it.

"Girl," Tony says. "Look at that evil gleam in your eyes. What is that?"

"I don't think he likes me." I grab the edge of the table as my dream self looms over Mr. Bosu and his piles of spoons.

"What are you doing with that bowl?" Tony asks.

"I've no idea."

Dark liquid pours out from the bowl, pooling over his head, shoulders, and body, and then it cascades over the spoons. But the liquid doesn't stop there. It rushes through the whole restaurant, washing over the pristine whiteness into a dark inkiness. The liquid rises higher and higher, forcing Tony and me to stand.

My dream self still holds the bowl, and the black liquid continues to pour out like a waterfall. Everyone in the restaurant begins screaming and the beautiful woman at Mr. Bosu's table vanishes. Mr. Bosu waves his arms around, screaming.

"We have to calm him down," I say. "He's entering the REM cycle, which means he's about to wake up!"

Suddenly calm music washes across the room. Mr. Bosu's screaming ceases and his eyes blink rapidly. The people in the restaurant stop yelling and splashing.

It's Bach's cello Suite No. 1 in G Minor—one of Mom's favorites. Instantly, I'm reminded of her, and a flash of guilt streaks through me, churning in my stomach until I feel like I'm going to throw up. Yes, my dad is important, but I also have a mom who is sitting at home worried I might never return. I swallow the lump in my throat. Would she ever recover if she lost both Dad and me?

No, she wouldn't.

The room shifts until everything vanishes except a spotlight beaming down on Sun, sitting in a chair, eyes closed as if drinking in the music, and Mr. Bosu. The music plays on while the rest of us hover at the edge of the Void. A door opens and a wedge of light slices through the darkness. Mr. Bosu turns his attention to the door and begins walking, and then running, toward it.

"He's transitioning!" Tony says.

Javier and Tony burst into a sprint to follow him.

But I don't move. All I can think about is Mom all

alone, that distant look in her eyes the night I left. Maybe I should never have left.

My legs remain rigid as I watch them rush through the door. Bach continues to play, Sun's bow flying over the strings, her eyes closed as if she's engulfed in the melody.

The door slams shut, and darkness swoops around me.

I peel the mask away from my face and toss off the headphones. I take in my surroundings and remember I'm in a hotel room. In Bangladesh. My stomach rolls. Ugh. I'm going to get sick. I haven't thrown up after visiting the Dreamscape in a long time. I stumble into the bathroom and barely make it to the toilet before I throw up. My hands won't stop shaking, even after I wash them and splash water over my face.

"Are you okay?" Sun races to my side. "Why did you fade? What happened?"

"It's fine. I'm fine. Just didn't acclimate well."

"Okay, you had me worried there." She squeezes my arm. "Take your time and get some water. I've got to get back to monitoring the Dreamscape."

Before I've taken two steps out of the bathroom, Jake is

standing before me and wraps his arm around my waist to steady me.

"You okay?" he asks.

I look into his eyes to find real concern. Maybe it's the whole queasiness of not being in my sleep pod or it's having everything flying out of my control, but suddenly I want to leave the whole dream thing behind and just sink into his arms and pretend we're back at his house prepping for another psychology presentation.

"I am now." My voice is a whisper, meant only for him.

His eyes lower to focus on my lips. "You did the right thing. Getting out of there. But I've got to say the dream version of you was pretty kick-ass."

I roll my eyes at that, and he helps me to the dresser where Sun has Dad's laptop set up and the lone chair pulled to it. Behind us lies Mr. Bosu on the bed, still sleeping. Tony and Javier are also still sound asleep on the other floor mats. I dig my fingers into my jeans pocket until I'm touching Dad's watch. Somehow it makes everything better.

"Next time," I say. "Let's get the hotel suite."

"Next time?" Jake grins as he hands me a water and a package of some type of cookies we bought at the hotel gift shop. "Are you like asking me out on an extended date?"

I hit him on the arm, but Sun shushes us, glancing furtively at the sleeping figures.

"They're at some type of resort at the beach," she explains. "I just can't pinpoint where it is at."

I squint at the screen as I take a sip of water. The top window has three streaming codes running across it, one from each dreamer. Then below that is the dream sequence music that Sun is inputting into the dreamer's ears. Finally, in another box is the visual display. There's a slight delay as the computer tries to transfer the three dreamer's visuals into one, but it gives a fairly good representation.

Thatched-roofed cabanas overlook an ocean with crystal blue water. Palms wave across a purple sunset. The place is like paradise. But instead of relaxing by the beach, Mr. Bosu, still wearing his suit, is running along the shore, panting heavily.

"What's he doing?" I whisper.

"It looks like he's trying to run away," Jake murmurs.

Suddenly my dream self appears and begins gliding across the beach, holding that globe from his desk. I'm now wearing a bikini top and a sarong wrapped around my waist. My hair flies about me and my green eyes glow, staring intently at Mr. Bosu like I'm some type of enchantress.

"Wow," Jake says. "You look sexy."

"You're kidding, right?" I mutter.

"What are you holding?" Jake asks.

"That stupid globe from his desk," I say. My stomach rolls again and a trail of sweat beads along my forehead. "I was trying to use it to distract him as I took out the thumb drive."

"Wait, look," Sun says. "You're doing something with it. Wow, it's like he's really terrified of you."

"Or maybe he thinks you're bad luck," Jake adds. "Red hair and all. Didn't you spill tea all over this desk?"

Mr. Bosu backs away from me. On the bed behind us, the real Mr. Bosu begins muttering words I can't understand.

"He's talking in his sleep," Jake whispers. "Is that bad?"

"Not unless he wakes up." Sun moves the mouse over the screen and clicks on a calming sound sequence.

But obviously, that doesn't work because Mr. Bosu turns away from my dream self and takes off running down a cobblestone path with bamboo fences lining the way.

"He's going into REM again," I say.

"Let's try this sound then." Sun clicks on a 'waves crashing' button.

Instantly the rush of crashing waves fills the Dreamscape. Everything else is silent. Mr. Bosu's feet slow to a brisk walk. He rounds the corner and stands in front of a bamboo door. It rattles as he tries to rip it open, but it remains locked in place.

Sweat drips down his face as he glances over his shoulder.

"The dude looks freaked out," Jake says. "For some reason, he's really scared of you, Aria."

"I don't like it," Sun says. "It's like he knows who Aria really is."

"Look there." Jake points to the top of the screen where a sign reads: Surfside Resort and Spa.

I shrug. "It could be a clue, or it could mean nothing."

"Often dreams are representations of actual things," Sun explains to Jake. "Like if you see a mode of transportation it could be a reflection of the direction you are taking in your life or how much control you have over it. Or if you encounter paralysis it could mean you feel a lack of control, or it just could be that between REM and waking. Most of what we do is guesswork. Having a patient's psychoanalysis is what really helps us."

Mr. Bosu continues to rattle the door for a while until soon he sinks to the ground and in a rush, all fades to complete darkness.

"What happened?" Jake says, alarmed.

We all turn to those sleeping. Javier and Tony both stir.

"He's waking!" Sun scrambles to the counter and puts more Temazepam into the syringe. "Can't have him wake up."

She plunges the liquid into his system and then unhooks him from the Dreamscape. Meanwhile, Tony and Javier are sitting up. Tony staggers into the bathroom and throws up. Javier remains on his mat, looking paler than usual. Dark circles ring his eyes and his cheeks seem hollower.

"You're not getting enough to eat," Sun scolds him, but she gently places her hands on his shoulders.

Javier takes the water Sun offers him. "The transition is rough without the equipment we have at MaxLife."

When Tony returns to the room, I pass him a water bottle as well.

"Tell me we've got food here." Tony picks up a package on the counter and holds it up, frowning. "What's this?"

"A local snack," I say, and then grab one and toss it to Javier. "They're like sweet crackers. Not bad."

"But a burger would be *good*," Tony points out.

"You guys should get him into the taxi sooner than later." Sun is nervously massaging her fingers.

"Yeah," Javier says. "Just give me a minute to recover."

"Any leads?" I ask.

"Nothing," Tony says. "After you left, we entered a beach resort. Didn't seem like anything nearby either."

"Yeah, it definitely didn't look like something from Bangladesh," Javier says. "There was an ocean, so maybe it was the Bay of Bengal. But the dream was too restless."

"There was a name that popped up on the screen," Jake says. "Once we get this guy on his way, I'll do a little research on it."

"What are you going to do with him?" Sun asks.

"Don't worry," Javier says. "We'll leave him in a nearby bar passed out in a chair smelling like liquor."

While the guys pick up the still sleeping Mr. Bosu and lug him out of the room, Sun and I pack up the equipment.

"We'll be back in a few minutes once we get this guy at his next location," Javier says.

After they leave, my whole body feels even weaker than before. It's like the moment they took Mr. Bosu away, any hope of leads went with him.

"You have to come to grips with the fact that we might not be able to track down your dad," Sun says. "We've broken so many laws and your mom must be wanting you back home rather than overseas."

"So do you think this is the end?" I ask.

"I think we should go back home in the morning."

The truth is, I can't accept that. I won't accept it. To go back home empty-handed kills me. I pull out the note I stuffed in my pocket before I left home.

*The moment you give up is the moment you let someone else win.*

I abandon the packing to sag into the chair and begin reviewing the footage from the dream. It's not long. Maybe five minutes or so. I always find that strange, how dreaming feels like it's so long, but in reality, it can be but moments. The brain is an amazing thing in that way. Finally, I come to the end where the sign Surfside Resort and Spa pops up on the screen.

Sun moves to stand over my shoulder, resting her hand on my arm. "That's a resort. The kidnappers wouldn't take your dad there. You know what my guess is? That man who withdrew the $81 million gave a portion of it to Mr. Bosu who managed to hide the transaction trail."

"The golden spoons represented money," I say numbly.

"Exactly. Maybe Mr. Bosu was planning a vacation or a getaway at a resort except after you left the bank, he internalized your actions. Maybe he felt that your hair symbolized danger. That's the only explanation. That's the one that makes the most sense."

"I'm going to my room." I don't even look at her or ask if she's okay if she packs up the mats and towels. I can't deal with any of that right now. All I want to do is go back to my room and cry for the rest of the night.

# TWENTY-NINE

# IF GIVEN A PENNY, WHAT WILL YOU DO WITH IT?

I had planned to cry my eyes out once I got back to my room. But I can't. Instead, I lie on the top of my sheets, staring at the ceiling, running through every scenario, every event that happened so far in my head. There has to be something I'm missing. Some clue.

A knock on the door pulls me back to reality. A glance at the clock tells me it's three in the morning. I must be jet-lagged because right now I feel wired.

The last thing I want to do is answer the door, but I trudge over and stare through the peephole. It's Jake. I lean against the door, debating whether to open it or not. Another knock.

"Aria? It's Jake. I thought maybe—um, I think I figured out what resort that was in the dream."

I bite my lip, remembering a quote I stuck to my mirror last month.

*If given a penny, what will you do with it?*

I open the door. Jake stands there, one hand in his pocket as if he doesn't know what to do with it while the other holds his laptop to his chest. He's changed into khaki shorts and a simple white T-shirt that says Geeks Rule the World.

"I like your shirt." I open the door wider. "Come in."

He pushes back the hair hanging over his face and steps inside. "Sun said you needed space and I get it if you don't want to talk long, but I found something I think you'll find interesting."

"I'm glad you came." I sit on the corner of my bed while he strides over to the single table and chair. He pops open his laptop and once it turns on, he spins the screen around so I can see.

"I did a quick search for resorts with the name Surfside Resort and Spa. There are two significant ones. One is in Destin, Florida so that's close to home for us. And the other is in Boracay, Philippines, which is not so close."

"Sun had a theory." I pick at a thread on my shorts. "That he was probably a player in this heist and this resort might be where he wanted to go with the money he was paid off to keep quiet."

"Yeah, she told me that, too. But I'm not convinced. Look at these pictures. They look just like the ones from the dream. I bet he's been there."

"He could've seen the photos online and then

dreamed about it. That's not uncommon. I mean, who wouldn't? It's a gorgeous place."

"Then there's this." Jake then pulls up another set of pictures of a woman. "I scanned the face in the dream and ran a facial recognition on her."

"You have that technology?"

"Well, I may have hacked into someone's system." He shows me a screenshot of her.

"Wait." I suck in a breath. "I remember now. She's the same woman that I saw in the intruder's dream at MaxLife."

"So that gives us a definite connection to her. Her name is Zhang Lau."

I stand, my heart racing. "Did you know that a person only dreams of people that they've seen before in real life or like in a picture or TV? Which means there's a real chance that this lady is a factor in all of this."

"Sun knows all about this lady. Apparently, she's her father's arch-enemy. Lau has stolen data from Mr. Li's business and has tried to scam him more than once."

"So she's got a history of criminal activity. She fits the profile."

"And listen to this," he continues. "She's a casino owner of like more than a dozen casinos as well as a few resorts. Including—"

"Surfside Resort and Spa," I finish for him, my heart hammering.

"Bingo."

I could kiss him right now. I jump up and down instead in excitement.

"This is it! You've found the connection we've been looking for! We need to go to the Philippines. Like tomorrow."

"Maybe." Jake's expression holds that wary look, and his eyes won't meet mine. "One thing I do know is now I have something to report to my dad about theories of where the money went to. But I can't promise that your dad will be at this resort. In fact, I highly doubt he will be."

"You may be right." I inch myself closer to Jake. "But this is the best lead we've gotten yet. It proves there's a connection between the Federal Reserve Bank heist and my dad's kidnapping. We can't ignore it."

From where he sits, he looks at me, standing over him. Suddenly all I can focus on is his lips and the intense need to kiss him.

I reach down and trail my finger along the edge of his T-shirt collar, pulling him closer. His hands fall to my hips, and I know I should resist these feelings. Keep this relationship purely business and stay focused on our mission. There's a slogan on my mirror back home about staying focused, but somehow I can't remember what it was right now.

All I think about is how good it feels to have him so close. He rises to stand up, his hands trailing up along my back as he does. I shiver from his touch, my skin electrified. His lips are so close to mine. We hesitate for a moment. Inches, maybe less, stand between our lips meeting. His breath smells like mint, and as his palm cups my chin, his skin burns hot against mine.

I tell myself to back away, but instead, I break the distance between us. My lips press against his, which are warm and hungry for me. His arms engulf me as my hands wrap around the back of his neck, drawing him closer so our bodies are pressed against each other. His fingers tangle through my hair, and I lose myself in the passion of the kiss.

A ringing cuts through the fog of passion. My body snaps rigid and I jerk backward, away from Jake's arms. It's my phone.

Still breathless, I flip it over. Mom's number is listed as a missed call.

"It's my mom." I straighten my hair, not able to make eye contact with Jake. "I should call her."

"Right." He clears his throat as if he wants to say something but then picks up his computer and marches to the door.

"Jake," I call after him. He stops and swivels around, his eyes hopeful. "Don't tell the others on the team. About us. We should stay focused on our task. You know—"

What is wrong with me? I can't seem to formulate a single sentence.

His jaw tightens, but he says nothing. Instead, he nods and then exits the room.

What had I been thinking to kiss him? Was that wrong

or had it been the most right thing I've ever done? I've no clue.

My fingers trail along my lips. I've only been kissed one other time by Kores Borden in ninth grade. It was one of those slobbery, wet kisses. A great way to turn a girl off forever to kissing.

But Jake's kiss...

I sag onto the bed, closing my eyes. My skin still tingles everywhere he touched me. My body sings from passion that I never knew could possibly exist.

THIRTY
HUNTED

The next morning as I pack up my bags, there's another knock on the door. I open it to find a tray sitting on the floor with a plate of muffins, tea, a rose, and a note that reads: I'm rooting for you. A quick glance down the hallway and I spy a man wearing the hotel staff uniform briskly exiting the hall into the elevator.

I bend down and pick up the tray.

"How sweet," I mumble as I head back into my room. The card isn't signed but I'm guessing it's from Jake. A smile plays over my lips, and I wonder if I made the wrong choice last night to send him away.

The hotel phone rings. I pick it up to hear Sun on the other line. "Where are you?" she asks sharply. "We need to get out of here now."

"Sure," I say. *Wow, she's in a bad mood.* "I was just on my way."

There isn't time to drink my tea, but I take the rose and a muffin and tuck them into my travel purse, which I slip under my shirt for safekeeping. Then I grab my suitcase and I step out into the hall, patting my pants pocket to make sure Dad's watch is still there. When I enter the lobby to meet the others on our team, Danny's and Sun's heated voices catch my attention.

"You said it would be just one location," Danny says.

*Uh, oh.* Danny doesn't want to take us to the Philippines. Last night after talking to Jake, I called up Sun and told her our theory. She agreed to try to convince Danny to take us there next. But it's not looking good. I look over to Tony and Javier sitting on one of the padded benches along the wall. Tony shakes his head and crunches up his face as if to say not to get involved.

Sun stares down at her nails and then looks back up at Danny, flipping her hair back. "The Philippines is our last stop. I promise."

"What were you all doing last night?" Danny sideglances to look at me and then at Tony and Javier sitting in the lobby, pretending they aren't hearing a word of the fight.

"We had to review some footage," Sun says vaguely.

"You promised no more lies." Danny crosses his arms, eyebrows lifting. "But I saw them with that man."

"Hush, will you!" Sun whispers harshly, glancing about the lobby.

There's something about her look that sends a spark of

fear up my spine. Now it's my turn to search the area, but nothing out of the ordinary catches my attention. There's a couple eating breakfast in the dining room, a man reading the newspaper in one of the chairs, and then the hotel staff.

"Let's go," Sun blurts out harshly to the guys and me, interrupting my fears.

"Good idea." I hurry after her, rolling my suitcase along. I'm not sure what it is, but there's something about this place that's getting to me. Or perhaps I'm just letting Sun fluster me. The thing is, she's usually the calm, relaxed one so to see her out of sorts is unnerving.

"Have you guys seen Jake?" I search the area for him.

"Haven't seen him since last night," Javier says.

The taxi van pulls up and the others start loading their suitcases inside. Still no Jake. I rush back into the lobby and finally spot him, leaning on the counter of the concierge's desk.

"Jake!" I yell. "Are you coming?"

His hair is completely disheveled, and he's still wearing the same clothes as last night. As I hurry over to him, he rubs his forehead, a wild look in his eyes.

"What's wrong?" I say. When he won't look at me. I grab his sleeve. "What happened?"

"My room," he says distractedly. "This morning I got a call from the concierge saying I had a message from my dad, but when I came down, they told me no one from their desk had called."

"We can assure you no calls were made from our desk," the concierge interrupts sharply, clearly offended over Jake's accusation. "But I am calling the police for you. We will get to the bottom of this, sir. You can rest assured this is unacceptable for our hotel."

"What's unacceptable?" My voice is now a high pitch.

"When I returned to my room." Jakes takes in a long, shuddery breath and shakes his head as if saying it will finally make what he's about to say come true. "It was all gone. Everything except the clothes on my back and phone. Even my computer."

"That's terrible." I release his arm in shock.

"Here's your passport and wallet, sir," the receptionist says. "We will be reimbursing you for your room due to the incident."

Jake takes his possessions and pockets his wallet. "Guess it pays to put valuables in the hotel safe. We should go."

"But your computer. Don't you want to file a police report?"

"It's a huge loss, but not worth the time to stick around." Then he leans in closer to me, whispering into my ear, "Someone knows what we're doing. We're probably being watched right this minute. We need to get out of here."

Numbly, I nod. Is that why Sun is so upset? I clutch the rose tighter as we head for the exit. From the corner of my eye, I eye the man reading the newspaper. Is there something odd about his position or am I just paranoid? Suddenly, I feel like I'm in the Dreamscape and I need to pay attention to anomalies. They're clues for us to change directions or to interject in the dream to get a different outcome.

And though this isn't the Dreamscape, there's that nagging feeling in the back corner of my mind. I glance over my shoulder. The man has lowered his paper and is rising to his feet, eyes intent on me. My heart catches in my throat and I whip my head to face forward. I try to be nonchalant as I step outside, but I know it's too late. The newspaperman knows I'm aware of him.

"That man back there," I whisper.

Jake glances over his shoulder and nods. "Yep, he's got to be one of them watching us." He's about to enter the taxi van but pauses.

"What's the matter?" Danny asks, obviously eager to get moving. "Where's your suitcase?"

"Where were you, man?" Tony asks. "We were worried about you."

"Will you two hurry and get in the car?" Sun twists her sunglasses in her hands. "I've got a bad feeling about this place."

"I'm with you on that," Jake says as the two of us climb in, joining the others.

Our van's backseat is lined with a beaded interior with charms hanging from every place that something could be hung from—the handholds, the bars holding up the headrests, the mirror, and sun visors. The driver greets us and then starts the engine, rolling out to the traffic of the busy street.

"Did you order this taxi?" Jake asks Danny.

"Sure did," Danny says. "We can't get one this size last minute."

"Then we need to get out of this taxi ASAP." Jake taps the driver on the shoulder. "Let us out. Now!"

"You okay, man?" Tony asks.

"Everyone out!" The moment the driver slows down, Jake flings open the door and jumps into the busy road even before the van comes to a complete stop.

"What is wrong with you?" I yell at him.

I scramble out of the van, marching over to where he's unloading the other's luggage from the back and tossing it onto the sidewalk. The rest of us stand off to the side, gaping at him in shock.

"Call me paranoid," Jake says, huffing. "But I would feel better in another taxi. We passed a taxi stand a little ways back."

Our driver throws his hands in frustration at us and begs us to reconsider. Meanwhile, we each grab our luggage and trail after Jake down the street to where a line of taxis wait.

"I can't believe you made me jump out of a perfectly good taxi," Sun mutters while Danny complains the whole way about why he even took us here and how we're ruining his new shoes.

After sweating in the intense heat and breathing in the fumes from the highway, we arrive at the taxi station. Since the cars are too small for us all to fit inside, we realize we're going to need to split up into two cars.

"Everyone loads up in pairs into one of these," Jake says. "Meet up at the airport."

Javier and Tony hesitate and begin questioning Jake, but Sun cuts them off.

"Everyone just shut up and listen to Jake," she says. "The truth is he might be onto something. Back at the hotel one of the men was taking my picture. I have a feeling it's not because he thinks I'm a movie star."

Danny and Sun slip into the first taxi and Javier and Tony join them. They pull away and I'm about to get into the second taxi with Jake when a driver calls out of his window. I realize it's the driver from the taxi van we just left. He has parked at the end of the line of taxis.

"Hello, miss!" The driver waves to me. "Please, you cannot leave. I was told I must drive you to the airport."

Guilt tugs at me. This man's life can't be easy. The least I can do is pay the guy for a missed job. I open my purse, pay him, and hurry back to the van.

"Aria!" Jake yells. "It's too dangerous."

And that's when the bomb explodes.

# THIRTY-ONE
# BOMB ATTACK

The boom vibrates through the air, ricocheting a tremor through my core. The van lifts off the ground and instantly bursts into flames, exploding before my very eyes. Jake grabs me and throws me to the ground and then lands on top of me as burning heat consumes the air around us. My cheek smashes against the gravel pavement. Heat scorches my lungs and skin, singing my hair. Vaguely, I realize Jake's using his body to protect me. Wreckage clatters around us and he cries out as his arm cradles around my head.

Complete terror races through me, incapacitating my ability to move. My mouth opens and I feel the scream exit my throat, but all I hear is a thrumming ring vibrating around me, consuming all other sounds. Dust fills the air so I'm unable to see anything other than the pebbles on the ground.

"We have to get out of here," Jake says through the ringing in my ears and helps me stand back on my feet.

Somehow I'm able to move, one step after the next. Smoke and dust and unbearable heat swirls around Jake and me. My vision is teary and blurred, and all I can focus on is that Jake is alive. His face is blackened, and his shirt is shredded, but he's here. The fumes constrict my lungs and I cough, needing air. Jake presses me to him, his whole body shaking.

Screaming suddenly shocks the silence and though it feels as if my ears are full of cotton, I don't miss the wails and shouts. I move my legs faster until we reach the taxi we were supposed to get in earlier. Jake throws open the door and the driver starts talking frantically.

"Take us to the airport." Jake yanks out all his cash and tosses it into the front seat. "Hurry!"

Tears stream down my face, and I can't stop shaking. "Please."

The driver appears as frantic as we must look. But he turns around and somehow pulls into traffic, weaving through the people waving for him to stop.

"We're moving," Jake whispers.

I clutch Jake's shirt and bury my head against his chest. And start sobbing. It's ridiculous, but I don't care. I can't look up even though our driver is talking a million miles a second to us. Sirens break through the screams, but soon it all fades as we speed away, far from it all.

As the minutes tick away, the screams and sirens are

replaced with honking cars and the drone of engines. I'm not sure how long I cling to Jake, but soon I'm able to pull myself upright.

A quick glance at Jake's shirt tells me it's completely soaked from my tears. And then my eyes trail up to stare at his face. Dust cakes his cheeks and a streak of blood runs from his ear down to his neck. His eyes are wild and blood-shot, shifting from the driver to glance at the traffic on either side of us.

We must be closer to the airport and on the highway because the taxi has increased its speed.

"Did you see the others?" My words come out choked and gritty.

With the pad of his thumb, Jake lightly touches my face. "You're bleeding."

"It doesn't hurt. I'm fine."

"Sorry."

"No." I shake my head vigorously, trying to force the panic at bay. "You saved my life. What's a little cut anyway? But your neck. It's bleeding pretty badly."

"We'll get cleaned up and changed at the airport. I feel bad about leaving, but it wasn't safe there. We had to get away. Whoever did that must have been close by."

"Someone wants us dead. I can't believe this actually happened."

He doesn't say anything, instead, he gives me a sad smile. My head pounds and my entire body feels numb.

"Wait," I say. "My suitcase. It's still at the curb."

"What about your passport?"

I touch the travel purse I tucked under my shirt. "No, my passport and money are still here, but everything else I brought with me is lost."

"We can replace clothes," Jake says. "That's not a big deal."

"Yeah, you're right."

I lean back against the seat, listening to the music from the taxi's stereo boom around me. Normally, I might be annoyed by such loud music, but in this moment, it's drowning out the horror I've just experienced. I pull out Dad's watch. The face has a jagged crack down the center where I must have fallen on it, but the stars are still swirling.

*He's okay*, I tell myself. *You're okay. You can do this.*

"How did you know?" I ask as we turn into the airport area. "To get out of that van."

Jake presses his lips together and runs his hands over his face. "Just had a bad feeling. Sun was right. We were being watched. And after they took all of my stuff, I knew they meant business."

"They're trying to stop us. We must be close to finding out something that they don't want us to discover."

"Too close."

The taxi pulls up to the curb and we crawl out. My legs nearly buckle beneath me, and I reach Jake to keep my balance. He pulls me close.

"Aria! Jake!" It's Sun, waving to us from just ahead. She's with the rest of the crew and they all rush to us.

"What happened to you two?" Javier asks.

Once we tell them the details, they stare at us in shock. Sun drags me into her arms.

"This is out of control." Tony joins in with a group hug. "Not cool. I'm so glad you're okay."

"Let's talk about all of this in a safer place," Javier says, smart-thinking as usual.

"What we need is to get out of this country," Danny mutters in a low voice, "before the authorities realize that bomb was meant for you. I don't know what you're all involved with but it's too dangerous for my liking and somebody—" He looks pointedly at Sun "—isn't telling me everything. Regardless, let's focus on getting through security before any of our names get red-flagged."

No one disagrees. We head directly to the bathrooms, and I open my purse to see what little belongings I have left. The rose Jake delivered to my hotel room is crushed and the petals have been ripped off the stem. For some reason, that's the last straw for me and I sag onto the first bench I can find. I hold the petals in my palm, and stare at them, wondering how we got to this moment.

"Are you okay?" Sun hunches down in front of me.

"I'm fine." Total lie. "I didn't get to eat breakfast. Maybe if I eat something, I'll feel better." I pull out the smooshed muffin from my purse as if to prove my point.

"Why do you have a rose?" Sun asks. When I shrug, she narrows her eyes. "Where did you get it?"

"I think Jake got me it. It was outside of my room this morning along with this muffin and tea."

I'm about to take a bite of the muffin when Sun rips it out of my hand.

"What is your problem?" I snap.

"Jake?" Sun calls him over. "Did you give Aria this flower and muffin?"

I gape at her. Why is she embarrassing me? Doesn't she see how upset I am?

His forehead crinkles. "No."

The others have gathered around now, staring down at me and my rose.

"Did anyone here give this to Aria?" Sun presses. When they all shake their heads, my heart sinks into the deepest pit of my stomach. She takes the rose and holds it up in the other hand, saying, "You were specifically targeted. I bet the muffin is poisoned and they knew exactly which room you were in."

She marches to the trash can and throws them both away, brushing her hands off once finished.

"Wow," Jake says. "These people are covering all of their bases."

"I can't deal with this," Tony adds. "Man, oh, man."

I grit my teeth, feeling numb. I had just been about to take a bite of that muffin. If Sun hadn't taken it from me, it is a very good chance I'd be dead.

"Too many close calls," Javier says while Danny starts swearing over and over, pacing back and forth as the realization of the kind of trouble we are in hits him.

"You should freshen up." Sun is back to acting like my big sister. "Here, you can borrow my clothes and apply this antiseptic to your wounds. They don't look so good."

I stand on wooden legs and take the clothes, pushing past the others to the bathroom. Once in the stall, I sag to the ground, choking back sobs. I don't care that the floor is grungy. It's probably cleaner than I am. My chest constricts and I'm finding it hard to breathe.

*Stay strong,* I tell myself and dig out Dad's watch from my pocket to stare at the swirling Eye of God. *One step at a time.*

I'm pulled back to June 11th, a day I'll never forget. It was our big breakthrough with the Dreamscape. I wasn't a part of the crew at that time, instead, I'd just hung out at the lab to help Dad out over the summer months when I wasn't in school. I loved being there, in the heat of groundbreaking science and watching my dad work. Many people thought of my dad as eccentric, odd even. He has a way of mumbling to himself when thinking through hard problems.

More often than not, he'd even mumble at the grocery store as new ideas hit him. People would side-glance at us, but I didn't care. Because I knew what they didn't. Those mumblings were the workings of a genius.

The Dream Walker crew had just finished another

entry into the Dreamscape, but the dreamer kept rejecting the crew's presence in the dream and would wake up. This had been their twentieth attempt and tenth dreamer.

"We are so close," Dad told me as the crew began waking up once again. "If only I could figure out how to convince the dreamer that the crew is a part of their dream. Or become so obscure that they become one with the wallpaper."

I'd been sitting cross-legged on the counter, nibbling on a bagel, studying the footage of the Dreamscape they had just exited.

"I think it's the way the crew enters the dream." I paused the footage. "See where Javier is standing and how he is staring at the dreamer. It's not natural. Javier needs to act like he's a part of the dream, not entering the dream."

Dad straightened from where he was sagged over in his chair. "You might be right."

"Let me try it," I begged Dad. "I think I can do it."

This was like the hundredth time I'd begged Dad to let me into the Dreamscape so the last thing I expected him to say was yes. But on June 11th, he did. And when I entered that dream with the team, I was hooked. It was the longest a crew ever had lasted in a dream. When I woke up from the Dreamscape, it was as if MaxLife had finally come to life. The room was full of shouting and high-fiving. We celebrated by going out for fresh doughnuts. My favorite.

"You're our good luck charm," Dad had told me.

I licked off the chocolate glaze from the corner of my

mouth, not able to hold back a wide grin. I was hooked. I was their lucky charm! Ever since that day, I've been a part of the MaxLife team and I've never looked back.

Now, as I sit here on the floor, I feel anything but lucky.

My hands shake so hard that it's tricky to slip on Sun's clothes. Once I've changed, I splash water on my face.

The girl I see in the mirror is one I can hardly recognize. Slowly, I apply the antiseptic cream to the scrapes and cuts on my face and arms. My cheeks look a lot like Javier's with that hollow quality from not eating enough. Dark circles ring my eyes and my hair is tangled, red curls out of control. I clutch my brush firmly so as to get a grip on my treacherous nerves and begin to comb out the knots.

What am I even doing here? The bomb had been more than a warning. It had meant to kill us.

If I'm going through all of this, what must my dad be dealing with? Much worse, I'm guessing. The chances of him being alive—No, I won't go there. I won't entertain the possibility. Tears well up again, but I shove them back and swallow the lump in my throat.

"I can't stay away," I whisper to my reflection in the mirror. "I will hunt them down until I get my dad back. Nothing is going to stop me."

I straighten my shoulders, pull out a tube of lipstick, and slather it on. These people want to mess with my life, fine. But that means I'm coming for them.

When I step out of the bathroom, Danny, Sun, and Jake are arguing. Tony leans against one of the walls, shoulders hunched, while Javier stands by the group, rubbing his chin and listening to the argument.

"What's wrong?" I ask as I step into their circle.

Jake's face is flushed as if he's really upset. "Danny won't take us to the Philippines."

"It's too risky," Danny says. "You just saw what happened back there. Has it not occurred to you that we almost died? No amount of money is worth losing your life over. I know you want to find the money for your dad and clear his name, but this is where I draw the line. These people obviously want you to stay out of their business and we are no match for them."

"Maybe you're right," I say. "But look what we've done. We have gotten further than the feds back home."

"That's because they're doing it *legally*." Danny holds his hands up in surrender. "Listen. I was all with you. Trust me. But it's been more than forty-eight hours since your dad and the money went missing. And the trail is ice cold. I don't know what you want to do in the Philippines, but I'm guessing more trouble."

"I can't give up," I say. "I won't."

"You are free to do whatever you want," Danny says. "But Sun, if you don't come back with me, I'm telling Mother. You know how she is."

We all look over at Tony. He shrugs and then plugs in one earbud, looking at the crowds of people lining up to come through security.

"And your parents?" Danny looks at Jake and me. "Are you sure they would be cool with this trip to the Philippines knowing our taxi was just bombed?"

He's got a point. Mom would one hundred percent have a heart attack. Not that I'm going to tell him that. So I say, "What you've done for me, Danny, bringing us to Bangladesh, it's more than I can ever thank you for. I'm indebted to you."

I suck in a deep breath, hating the idea that I'm going to have to leave my friends because the reality is I'm not sure I can continue on my own, but I can't give up. "Actually, I'm indebted to all of you. Thank you for being here with me through this, but Danny is right. It's too dangerous. I can't ask you to continue."

"This was always our choice," Javier says. "You never forced us."

"I think we all know this is where our paths split." I try to smile at them, to show them I'm okay with the separation. "I'm going to continue on to the Philippines. I've got MaxLife's credit card."

"It's only a matter of time before the feds freeze all of MaxLife's accounts," Danny points out.

Sun crosses her arm. "Aria, you don't even know for sure if that resort is the right lead."

"You're right, Sun. But I have to try. I could never live with myself otherwise."

"I don't like it," Sun says.

"I'm going with you," Jake jumps in. "I don't have anything to my name other than my travel documents and wallet, but that doesn't matter."

"I'm going, too," Javier says and picks up the Dreamscape equipment bag as if it's decided. "I'm seeing this to the end. Dr. Hale gave me back my life. I'm going to make sure I do the same for him."

Tony shuffles over to me and wraps me in a hug. "I wish I were better cut out for this kind of thing. But this stuff is way out of my league. Besides, I got to get home. Pronto."

"I'm glad." I hug him back. "It's better this way. Safer."

And then our team parts ways. One group returning to the United States, the other to the Philippines. As I stand at ticketing, I watch Sun, Tony, and Danny head through security.

I hope I made the right choice.

Relief floods me when we all manage to get through security without any trouble. I stop at the ATM and withdraw a large amount of cash while Jake and Javier head to the convenience store to stock up on drinks and snacks. We have two hours before our plane departs for a ten-hour flight with layovers in Kuala Lumpur and Manila before we land in Caticlan, Philippines so Jake and I purchase some clothes and a duffle bag each before getting lunch. We even have time to use the computer station area to do some research on the area and I send an email to Mom telling her I'm doing fantastic and plan on being away for a few more days since we are hot on Dad's trail.

I wonder if she can read through my over-exuberance.

As we board the airplane, it feels weird to not be with the others, and I keep checking my luggage and pockets, feeling as if I'm forgetting something.

"You can take the window seat," Jake offers as we come up to the aisle where our seats are located.

Worn out, I lift my newly purchased carry-on into the compartment above, which holds all the Dreamscape supplies in it and a bunch of Sun's clothes that she gave me. Then I slip into the seat. Jake settles in beside me while Javier sits in the seat across the aisle from us.

"Feels weird to not be carrying anything," Jake says, slapping his legs and giving me a wane smile.

"I'm sorry about your computer. That was like your baby, wasn't it?"

"It's fine. Well, it's not fine, but there's nothing I can do about it. Last night as soon as I realized it was taken, I launched my self-destruct code to have it do a remote wipe."

"What's that?"

"Basically it's a sleeping virus I always load on my laptops. I can wake it up using a code and it will wipe out everything on that computer's hard drive."

"Seriously?"

"Originally I had put it there in case anyone tried to steal my computer to get access to my video games." He snaps on his seatbelt and then begins to review the movie selections available for the flight. "I never thought I'd be protecting your Dreamscape or my research from bank robbers or hiding the research locations that I visited online. I don't want them to know we know about Surfside Resort and Spa."

"I'm sorry you lost everything."

He shrugs. "I've got it all on the Cloud, but I was attached to that laptop. I'm planning on putting one in the Dreamscape laptop so no one can steal your dad's work. It's safer that way."

I rest my hand on his before I realize what I'm doing. When our hands touch it is almost like sparks skitter over my palm. Quickly, I pull back my hand, tucking it into my lap. I had reached out to him out of a natural instinct, but is that what I want?

"Thanks." I peek over at him. "I'm glad you're here."

His eyes drop to my hand. "So you thought I'd given you that rose."

"Either you or Sun," I mumble. Embarrassment over the whole thing forces me to focus my gaze away from him and out the window to the runway where small trucks are making the last-minute preparations for us to depart.

"I wish I had given it to you."

This pulls my attention back to him. "Really? That's um... sweet. Our kiss last night. I don't know what that was. Or what I'm even feeling. Like maybe I have all these feelings inside because you're here helping me out. I don't want you to think..."

*Ugh. I am completely ruining everything!*

But he laughs. "Are you saying you have sick patient syndrome? You know, when a patient falls in love with the person that's caring for them."

"Maybe." I giggle at the thought. A flight attendant

strolls by, reminding us to keep our seats upright during take-off. When she leaves, I say, "It's just that I want to stay focused on doing what we came to do. Get my dad and make sure your dad isn't being blamed for the crime."

"Right." He nods, pursing his lips. "Me, too."

The plane begins taxiing down the runway. I can't help but feel tension from Jake. I did say the wrong thing. I am an idiot.

The plane shudders around us and then slowly rises into the sky. Outside, the ground falls away. Wisps of clouds swirl around the plane as if dragging us away from the chaos that we experienced. Sitting beside Jake and pretending there's nothing between the two of us becomes harder than I expected. I'm reminded of how I clung to him, my head resting against his chest after the bomb. His strong arms wrapped around me. The warm kiss that sent shivers racing through my body.

More than anything, I want to sink back into those arms and just forget everything that happened in the last few days.

"Glad we got out of there safely," Javier says from the other side of the aisle. "Better get some rest you two while you can. Once we arrive in the Philippines, we'll be hitting the ground running to make our connection flight to Caticlan. We'll also need to make up an alibi of why we're there."

I nod, but a sinking dread in my stomach worries me that trouble will somehow find us.

## THIRTY-FOUR
## AN ISLAND RETREAT
### BORACAY ISLAND, PHILIPPINES

Once we land in Manilla, we take a hopper flight to Caticlan, and then a short bus ride to the jetty port. Out the window, I watch locals harvest rice in the endless rice patties or pedal their bikes alongside our bus.

Finally, we arrive at the port. I step outside and I'm greeted by a gentle, sweet-smelling sea breeze. The air is moist and warm, and despite the last few days, my muscles relax. I lift my head back, gazing into the sky, a cerulean blue. Palms wave beside bamboo-thatched huts lining the edges of the sand road.

Just ahead, the ocean slices off the horizon from the harbor where we will take the fifteen-minute boat ride to Boracay Island.

"I feel like I'm a world away from home." I eye the crystal-clear water.

"Seriously. This place is incredible." Jake shoulder's

the new duffle bag he bought at the airport. "Better than on TV."

"I hope you're right about this resort, hermanita," Javier says, leading the way onto the ferry. "We just spent a huge amount of MaxLife's money."

"My dad is worth any amount of money," I say.

But the reality is what if we arrive at Surfside Resort and Spa and find no leads? What if it's a dead end and here we are heading toward an island at the far reaches of Earth, hanging out at a gorgeous resort, wasting time and money?

I push those thoughts away as we settle at a table on the ferry and begin making our game plan.

"I'm thinking we should separate once we exit this boat," Javier says. When I begin to resist, he holds up his hand. "Hear me out. Whoever was following us knew which rooms we were in because they trashed Jake's room and left possibly poisonous food outside of your door. They also knew which van we would be leaving and when we were departing."

"But won't they be looking for six of us, rather than three?" I note. "And how could they possibly know we are here?"

"Maybe," Jake says. "Unless they saw us part ways at the airport."

"That's unlikely," I say. "Besides, they wouldn't let us get this far."

"Regardless," Javier says. "If Jake is correct about

Zhang Lau being the owner of this place, we're entering our enemy's own territory. We need to go to the extreme to stay low-key. My suggestion is to take on alibi names and only use only cash while at the resort."

The engines for the boat roar to life and soon we're zipping across the Indian Ocean, heading for the nearby island. Though we are under a covering and sitting at a table, the wind blows across the deck, forcing us to pull in closer so our voices don't spill onto other tables.

"Here's what I was thinking," Javier says. "The two of you should be a newlywed couple and I'll be there on vacation from a business trip."

"Married?" I laugh.

"Woah, man, aren't we a little young to be married?" Jake's eyebrows lift at the suggestion.

"You are both eighteen, right?" Javier says. "So for this trip, let's say you're twenty. That's believable. You can say you were so madly in love that you couldn't wait another day to be apart."

"Why do we have to be married?" I ask. "That's ridiculous. Why not just be a dating couple?"

"Because whoever bombed us in Dhaka won't be expecting it if they follow us here," Javier says. "They'll be looking for three singles traveling together but staying in separate rooms. And they definitely won't be looking for a married couple. Plus, I'd feel better about you not being alone at night. Just keep your hands to yourself, Jake. No messing around." Javier's expression turns dark, and he glares at Jake.

I glower at him. "I'm not rooming with him." Jake has one elbow propped on the table and is grinning wickedly at me. "Look at him. He's smirking like the devil himself. Besides, I can take care of myself. I don't need to be babysat."

"I promise to keep my hands to myself." As if to prove his point, he lifts both hands in the air. "But Javier is onto something. It's safer this way. Besides, we won't be there long. A night...two at the most."

I cross my arms, eyeing the two of them.

"We'll make sure the room has a couch," Jake adds.

"Which you'll sleep on," I say.

"Which I'll sleep on," Jake repeats.

"Fine. I guess."

"Good," Javier says. "I'll try to get a room as close to you as I can. When we arrive, we need to make no eye contact. Only text messaging."

"Sounds doable," Jake says. "My main goal is to get into the main office and do some research on their system."

"I like that," I say. "Maybe we can get an idea of why Mr. Bosu came here and where this Zhang Lau might be holding my dad."

"Good," Javier says. "Once we get settled in our rooms, we'll do some surveillance and figure out when would be the best time to access the resort's files. Also, keep an eye out for a place we can meet should we have to talk in person."

---

THE SURFSIDE RESORT and Spa is even more quaint and romantic than I imagined after seeing it in Mr. Bosu's dream. The taxi drops Jake and me off at a rounded white building tucked into a thicket of bamboo and palms. Plumeria and hibiscus grow along the stone path leading up to the front doors. I lightly touch one of the plumeria's petals, thinking how Mom would love the flowers here. Then guilt stabs me. I can't think about her right now.

"Well, darling," Jake says, a twinkle in his eyes. "Looks like we've arrived."

I roll my eyes. "You're not going to call me darling during our entire stay here, are you?"

"You mean during our entire *honeymoon*." He wraps his arm around my shoulder and grins down at me. "Would *sugar* be better?"

"Ugh." I shrug out of his arm and grab my carry-on, but I can't help but smile a little. As difficult and awful these last few days have been, having Jake here has kept me sane.

Besides, without him, I wouldn't have gotten this far in finding clues to Dad.

We traipse into the lobby of the resort where calm, lilting music is playing. A woman with long, braided black hair, wearing a traditional dress sashays over to where we are standing. She holds out a tray with glasses of juice, a wedge of orange pinned onto the edge of the rim. We both take a glass.

"Maligayang pagdating sa Pilipinas," she greets us, dipping her head in a bow before leaving.

"Thank you," we both say.

The juice is sweet and fresh. I could guzzle it in one gulp.

Jake moves up to the counter and smiling at the clerk, says, "Good afternoon, my wife and I are here for our honeymoon. We would like to get a room."

"Excellent," the clerk says. "If you will give me your credit card and passport, I will get you processed."

"We'd like to pay in cash in advance," Jake says, and I pull out a stack of US dollars. "And Laura, my wife, is rather famous and would like our names to remain anonymous. This would be our gift to you for keeping it quiet."

"Oh!" His mouth widens into a big O shape when Jake passes him a couple of hundreds. "A movie star. Of course. I can absolutely accommodate you."

"Great." Jake beams and then pulls me in close and wraps his arm around me possessively. This time I smile and play my part.

"You'll be wanting one of our special rooms for newly-weds," he says with a wink.

"Well, we are newlyweds." I bat my eyes up at Jake. "Aren't we, *sugar cakes?*"

"Err..." Jake says, clearly flustered. "Yes. Definitely."

"Excellent." The clerk prints out a receipt once Jake pays for the room. Then he passes over an old-fashioned metal key, the layout of the hotel, and a printout of the daily activities for the week. "Your bungalow is just out these doors and down the path on the right. It is number five. Congratulations!"

"Bungalow?" Jake questions.

"Thanks!" I take the handouts and key. "You get the bags, *sweet cakes.*"

"No problem, *darling*," Jake says and trails after me.

I refer to the map as I meander my way out of the lobby, taking in the natural wood floors and walls, and cream-cushioned furniture. When I step outside, the area is oddly familiar. A bamboo-roof pool bar sits on a huge deck area with white umbrella tables. A pool glistens a bright sapphire with guests swimming in it while others sunbathe on lounge chairs. Palms and pockets of flowers are tucked along the perimeter to provide the feeling that we've been transported to paradise.

"This was one of the areas that Mr. Bosu ran through in his dream," I say excitedly.

"Except there aren't tangled vines and fences," Jake points out.

He's right. There are only beautiful gardens here and a band is playing fun, carefree music by the bar. Beyond the pool area, lies the beach and ocean. The sky is already hugging the water in a swirl of pinks, oranges, and purples.

"This place," I say, breathlessly. "It's so romantic."

"Too bad we can't enjoy it."

My face blushes bright red at his inference. I quickly refer to the map again. "Looks like the bungalows are in that tree area by the beach."

We discover the line of huts propped up on small piers over pearl-white sand. I clamber up the steps of Bungalow 5, insert the key in the lock, and step inside. A giant king-sized bed fills nearly the entire room. To the right is a chaise and a dresser where I set down the papers the clerk gave me. The bathroom is nearly as big as the main room with a Jacuzzi tub, glass-walled shower, and a vanity with silver, fluted edging. Vases filled with fresh-cut plumeria are scattered about the room, their smell intoxicating, and a bowl of assorted exotic fruits that I have no idea what they are rests on the bedside table.

Jake whistles as he ventures inside, dropping the bags by the door. "This place is *sweet*." His eyes make a quick scan of the room, but when his gaze lands on the giant bed, his face flushes. My face burns over the situation we have gotten ourselves into.

"So this is your room." I tease and point to the bathroom, trying to lighten the tension.

"Hilarious." He leans against the doorframe, his hair falling into his eyes. More than anything I want to go and wrap my arms around him. "How about you take the tub and I'll take the bed?"

We stare at each other for a moment. The memory of

our brief kiss in Bangladesh is at the forefront of my mind. What would it be like to kiss Jake without holding back? To let go of all my inhibitions and tuck my body into the folds of his arms. Since our last kiss, I've dreamt of kissing him more times than I'd like to admit. Dreams are always wild, but they're fleeting, a tease of what reality holds.

An expression crosses his face. Is that yearning? Desire?

"Maybe we can decide later," Jake finally says, looking away.

"Yeah." I clear my throat. "Good idea."

What is *wrong* with me? I need to stay focused on our plan and finding my dad. Not mooning over a classmate I hardly know.

"We should've gotten two rooms." I cross my arms, hating how uncomfortable this all is, and yet even more so how the idea of being here with Jake sends shivers of excitement through me.

Jake picks up a piece of fruit from the fruit bowl and takes a bite of it. "Not bad."

"I'm starving. How about we freshen up? I could really use a shower after that explosion. I feel so grungy, and the airport bathroom just doesn't cut it. Then we could go have some dinner."

"Sounds great to me." Jake throws himself on the bed, leaning against the pile of fluffy pillows with a sigh.

"That's my bed you're getting dirty."

He takes another bite of the fruit. "A little dirt won't hurt these sheets."

I huff and march over to grab my bag before locking myself in the bathroom. Having a hot shower transforms me into a new person. When I change clothes and finally exit the bathroom, I feel as if I've escaped the horrors of the bomb.

Almost.

When I step into the cool air-conditioned room, the lights hadn't been turned on and the glow of sunbeams cascades through the slatted blinds. Outside, waves crash against the beach, and the fan above whirls. It's so peaceful.

Jake is fast asleep, his chest rising and falling, fruit still in his hand and resting on his chest. My heart pangs for him. Seeing him this way, he looks different. Less guarded. Vulnerable. I pad to the bed and slide next to him, wondering if I should wake him or let him sleep.

I trace the lines of his face with my finger, noticing each freckle, the scruff growing on his chin from not shaving, the indent of his earlobe. The smooth curve of his lips.

*No. Do not look at his lips!*

I shake his shoulder. We need to get some food and do some surveillance. This isn't a vacation, after all.

"Took you like an eternity." Jake groans and blinks before climbing out of bed. "Man, this international traveling is rough on the system. I don't even know what time or day it is."

Once he showers and changes into a new set of clothes that he bought at the airport, we hide our bags under the bed and make sure we take anything we don't want stolen.

"After the last time I was robbed, I'm not taking any chances," Jake says. "There's no place to really hide anything here, but it will slow them down at least."

Outside, we take the path that winds back toward the hotel, but before we enter the pool area, I pause to take a good look at the ocean. It's light enough for me to make out the whitecaps and the lift of the waves.

"Wait a sec. I want to take a moment to enjoy it," I whisper to Jake. "It's soothing."

He slips his hand in mine. It's casual as if he had been reaching out as a friend. But I know better. I should pull away, but instead, I look up into his eyes. They glisten in the growing darkness and light a fire within me.

"You can take a moment," he says. "You can take as long as you need. What has happened over the last few days—"

His words fall away in the thick night. I step closer to him. I know I shouldn't, but being with him makes me feel safe. It makes me believe that everything will be okay in the end. This place is ours and ours alone. It's as if we've stepped into our own Dreamscape where anything can happen and everything should.

I press my hands on his chest, feeling his firmness.

"Aria." He says my name like I'm a star in the sky.

He leans in and I don't push away. Before I can even think, his lips are on mine. Soft and eager. I clutch his shirt, pulling him even closer. His breath is minty and I'm lost in the passion of his kiss. His hands cup either side of my face and I slip my hands around the back of his neck, letting myself drown in his embrace.

Time flashes away and I literally forget where I am until a burst of laughter from a group strolling down the path rips me back to reality.

Heists. Murders. Kidnapping. Bombs.

It all rushes back against me like a raging storm. I push myself out of Jake's embrace. The world feels colder, distant without his arms wrapped around me.

The laughing couple passes by us, not even giving us a sideways glance.

"Well." Jake's voice is husky and deep.

Every ounce of my body aches to just step back into his arms and forget the madness around me. I reach for his hand and our fingers intertwine. He lifts up my palm and kisses it.

"Sometimes I feel like I've lived most of my life in a virtual world," he says. "But being here with you, it's like I'm breathing for the first time."

My words jam in my throat, my emotions running wild. I don't know how long our paths have crossed, probably a hundred times since we've had a number of classes together. The truth is, I never gave him a second thought before all this happened. I was only focused on my career and my goals. What else did I miss?

We stroll to the pool bar area and find a table near the edge which gives us a clear view of the pool and the resort's main building. Torches flicker around the pool's perimeter, casting golden beans across the water. The server comes over and hands us menus.

"I'm so hungry." I glance over the menu. "I could eat everything in the kitchen."

"Same." Jake laughs.

We order lumpia to share and then Jake ends up ordering pancit palabok while I choose sinigang. I lean back in my chair, nibbling on my pinkie, studying the people eating, chatting at the bar, and the few swimmers splashing in the illuminated water.

"What's going on in your head right now?" Jake asks, leaning forward.

"I was just thinking how much this moment feels like a dream. I know that sounds cliché and all, but when you enter a dream, there's that sense of otherworldliness to it. Like you don't belong there, and yet you are. If you let that feeling continue, the dreamer senses it, and sometimes that wakes them up or they dismiss you from the dream."

"How do you keep that from happening?"

"For me, it's about believing in the reality of the dream." I fiddle with my napkin. "So far, it's worked well."

"Sun mentioned to me while you guys were in the banker's dream that you were the turning point for MaxLife. What did she mean by that?"

"I don't actually know, but before I joined the Dream Walker team, they always got kicked out of the dream after a minute or so. But when I went in, that all changed. We could stay in for long periods of time. Now, everyone's a lot better at sticking with the dream longer. But I have the record of staying within the dreams the longest. I think it's about the mindset, you know? Believing in the dreamer's dream."

The server delivers our food, and we eat in silence for a while, savoring the food.

"The only good thing that has happened to me in the last few days is I'm not getting those headaches anymore.

After everything that has happened to us, I'm beginning to wonder if my headaches were orchestrated because they spurred me to go to MaxLife for treatment. I was totally played. I guess it feels good to be doing something about it rather than just being used."

"Are you still upset at me?" I finally dare to ask the question that's been haunting me. "For entering your dreams."

"Upset?" His eyebrows rise as if surprised and then he shrugs. "I guess I'm more upset that this all happened. But as crazy as this sounds, I'm kind of glad. I mean, did you ever in a million years think we'd be hanging out together like this?"

I laugh. "No, I guess not. Everything for me has always been about college and my future goals."

"If we get back to our real lives—"

"You mean when."

"When." He nods, running his finger along the condensation of the glass. "I don't want things to be awkward or weird between us."

I stiffen, unsure how to take that. Did he mean things would be over for us once we got back? Or did it mean that he wants to continue as we are now? Before I can process that, a text pops up on my screen.

"It's from Javier," I say.

*Meet me by the door of the back office in five.*

# THIRTY-SIX
## SLEUTHING 101

I scan the area until I spot Javier sitting at a table on the other side of the pool. He stands, and turns to face us, but pretends he doesn't see us. I pick up my phone and type: *Copy that.*

He glances at his phone, tucks his hands into his pockets, and turns to stroll leisurely back into the resort lobby.

"Copy that?" Jake lifts his eyebrows.

"This is a secret mission, and you should take it seriously."

"So I take that to mean no kissing." Jake rises, a mischievous grin playing on his lips.

I roll my eyes at him but smile self-consciously. "I just hope we don't come all this way to find nothing." I leave some cash on the table.

I'm about to take off, but Jake pulls back on my arm. "No offense, but you need to chill out. You don't look like you're on vacation, but rather like you're engaging in some secret mission. Perhaps you should treat this more like one of those dreams in your Dreamscape."

"Right." I roll my shoulders. "That's a good point. Sounds like something Sun would tell me."

Thinking about her sends a pang through me. I know it's best Tony and Sun aren't here, but that doesn't make me stop missing them. Jake grabs my hand and squeezes it. I freeze for a moment, still unsure where things lie between us.

"Don't worry," he says, sensing my hesitation. "I won't bite. Besides, we're supposed to be a married couple on our honeymoon. Remember? We've got to play the part."

I shuffle alongside him, my mind whirling, trying to process everything. Beside me, Jake saunters along, but once we enter the cool lobby and head down the corridor, his body stiffens. The lilting Filipino music fills the hallway, but instead of soothing me, it only makes me tense.

At the office door, we find Javier. He's inserting a key into the lock. The entire wall of the office is glass. So much for hiding.

"Took you two long enough," he mutters, never once looking up. That's Javier. Focused and yet able to perceive everything around him.

"We didn't want to look too obvious." I slide in beside him, glancing around.

"Where did you get the key from?" Jake asks.

"I may have stolen it," Javier says. "You two stay out

here while I go in and make sure we are at the right place. Knock on the glass twice if someone comes down the hall."

"Got it," I say as he slips inside and darts over to the desk. I lean against the wall, rubbing my arms, hating how exposed I feel. "I never saw myself creeping around hallways and snooping in offices."

"Maybe we'll figure this all out tonight and get a lead." Jake shifts before me and I can read the lack of confidence in his expression. My heart sinks.

Footsteps pound the wooden floor around the corner. "Someone is coming," Jake whispers.

Instantly he leans into me and holding my shoulders against the wall, kisses me. Hard. Somehow I manage to stretch my arm out and knock on the glass. It's like fireworks are exploding inside me. Seriously, this boy can kiss. My body eases into his when someone clears their throat behind us.

Jake releases me and I gasp for air. My face is flushed and for some reason, it's hard to breathe. The man before us frowns and shakes his head. His name tag reads *Glen, Resort Manager*.

"This section is for the resort staff only," Glen explains to us. "If you would please head back to the guest area."

"Our apologies," Jake says. "We are here for our honeymoon and got a little lost as you can see."

"Yes, well." The man clears his throat, obviously flustered at Jake's words while I try to smooth down my shirt and hair. "Congratulations to you both. If you'll excuse me then."

I hold my breath until he steps inside a room that reads 'Maintenance.'

"What was that?" I round on Jake.

"What?"

"That kiss? I thought we agreed to be serious."

"You never nixed the no kissing rule, so I figured…"

"Is he gone?" Javier pops his head out of the door. At our nods, he says, "Come on. I found something."

The two of us duck into the dark room and trail after Javier to the back desk where the glow from a computer screen illuminates the corner of the room.

"I did a search for names under contacts," Javier says. "You were right, Jake. Technically this resort is owned by Paradise Entertainment, and Zhang Lau is their chairwoman. But according to the records, she frequents this resort more than any others. Ironically it's the only one that's not a casino."

"Did you find an address where we might find Lau?" I ask.

"I hadn't gotten that far," Javier says. "I was kind of hoping Jake here could help us out with that."

"Let me take a look." Jake slides into the chair and starts tapping away at the keyboard.

He pulls up a stream of deleted emails between the head manager and Lau. As he scrolls down the list, one of the emails catches my attention.

"Open that one," I say, pointing.

Jake clicks on the email labeled "Therapy Conference." Right away a name catches my eye. "That's Dr. Reasner from California. He's a competitor of my dad's. Was ticked off when Dad sent in the patent for the Dreamscape."

"So what is he doing over here in Asia?" Jake says.

"What if he's the one behind all of this?" Javier asks. "He could've hired someone to kidnap your father so your dad would hand over the coding for the Dreamscape."

"Dr. Reasner?" I scratch my head. "He's a weasel, that's for sure. I could see him hiring someone to kidnap people or steal millions of dollars. That said, the guy can barely button his jacket."

A noise in the hall catches our attention. Jake turns off the monitor on the computer while I hold my breath. The three of us duck behind the desk and wait in silence. Nothing happens. Finally, I dare to peek over the edge of the desk.

"No one is there," I whisper.

Jake leans back in the chair and turns the monitor back on. The glow casts his face with a ghostly blue.

"Regardless," Javier says. "We should keep him on our suspect list."

"One thing we can do," Jake says. "Find out where these suspects are located. Their contact information is here in this one email. If that phone number comes from a phone that they carry around with them, we can trace them by their IP addresses."

"You can do that?" I ask.

"Yep." He types IPFingerprints.com into the computer and then copies Dr. Reasner's phone number into the search button. "It would be easier if I had my computer which was stolen, but I can get a general idea from this. And if you give me a few minutes, I'll log into my cloud account. I've got better software there."

I hunker down in the darkness beside Jake, gazing back and forth from his face bathed in blue to the computer screen. Sitting here, I feel helpless, so I pull my phone out and click on my flashlight. File cabinets line the back wall like watchmen. Perhaps the hotel kept some of the files from the Therapy Conference.

I open drawer after drawer, trying to make sense of the system that it's in place. My only consolation is that everything is written in English. Finally, I make a discovery that sends my heart beating. It's labeled *Conferences*. Inside, I flip through the faded manila folders until I come across one labeled: "Therapy Conference: Where the Mind Meets Matters."

The attendance lists ten scientists and psychologists in the field of mind therapy. I only recognize Dr. Reasner's and Dr. Woo's names. I have two of Dr. Woo's books at home. He's got some good theories on brain development that have always fascinated me. I sit cross-legged on the floor, trying to figure out why these people would be here at this particular resort.

"There has to be a connection between this conference," I mutter, "and Dad's disappearance. That just seems like too big of a coincidence, don't you think?"

"Makes sense," Javier says.

"Okay," Jake finally says, leaning back in the chair. "So if they're carrying the phone that is listed on this email, Dr. Reasner is in Hong Kong right now, your Dr. Woo is in Beijing, and our Mr. Bosu is still in Dhaka, Bangladesh."

I sit up. "Bosu is on that email?"

"Naw," Jake says. "I just got his phone number while he was hanging out at our sleepover. Thought it was better to check just in case."

"So that leaves us Hong Kong and Beijing." Javier rubs his face in frustration. "Nothing like two cities being incredibly far from each other."

"What about Ms. Lau, the owner of this resort?" I say. "Have we found anything on her yet?"

"That's what I'm looking up now."

A shadow blocks off the hall light, causing me to freeze. It's a figure strolling by the front of the glass walls. Yikes. I bet it's the resort manager, Glen. He pauses at the door, squinting as if trying to see into the room.

"Duck!" I whisper-yell. "The manager is right outside of the door!"

Jake pushes the monitor's off button, throwing us back into darkness, and we sink behind the desk as the door handle giggles. The whites of Javier's eyes break through the darkness. He waves us to follow him. Crawling across the linoleum floor, we squeeze into the small space between the wall and the last file cabinet. My heart pounds. If Glen inspects this side of the room with a flashlight or decides to flick on the lights, we are doomed.

Especially if he makes a phone call to the owner.

The door cracks open and I hold my breath as the manager steps into the room. I peer around the side of the cabinet. His eyes pan across the desk where we were working only seconds ago. I cross my fingers that he'll see nothing is there and leave, but instead, he darts into the room and pokes his head under the desk. The file folder I had been reviewing lies inches from his foot.

*Don't see the folder!* I mentally scream.

My heart stops when he reaches down and picks it up, opening the flap and scanning through the contents. I wait for him to turn the computer on or even to look just to the right a few inches and see the three of us huddled against the wall.

I clutch Jake's hand.

And hold my breath.

But then he tosses the folder back onto the desk, rubs his forehead like he's got a headache, and then moves back to the door. After a quick turn of the lock from the inside, he clicks the door shut.

I lean back against the wall, letting out a long breath. "That was close."

"What haven't we done that hasn't been close?" Jake mutters. "But I've got some good news. We got ourselves an address for Paradise Entertainment. I think it's their main headquarters, which means there's a good chance Lau will be there, too."

I gasp. "You did?"

"Yep." He lifts up his phone where he's taken a screenshot of the address. "Macau, China. It's on the mainland, close to Hong Kong. Not far from where your dear Dr. Reasner is hanging out."

The three of us manage to escape the room and decide to meet up on the beach, heading there separately just in case we're being watched. It feels a little extreme, but Javier was insistent. I take the round-about way to the shoreline, forgoing the path, and instead, cutting around through the wooded area behind the bungalows. Every creak, crunch of dead leaves, and shadow has my heart skittering.

I tell myself that I'm just being silly, my nerves on edge from everything that has happened the last few days, but as I weave around the tall palms, I can't deny that feeling that someone is following me.

I duck into the folds of shadows behind one of the palms and lean my back against the rough bark to wait. I crane my ears for any sound. If I can make sure I'm not being followed, then I know my imagination is getting the best of me, but if I am being trailed, I need to know.

The wooded area remains quiet other than the chirping of cicadas and the laughter of hotel guests hanging out by the pool not far away. Through the moonlight area, the pool and torches cast a glow into the air. I allow my body to relax, chuckling to myself at how paranoid I've become when I hear the crunch of footsteps across the pine-needled ground.

My ears ring and my body stiffens. Someone is near. Within a few steps of me, in fact. I dare to peek around the tree trunk and spy the dark form crouching by a set of bushes, waiting. Could this lurker just be a perverted hotel guest or is he connected with the kidnapping and heist?

The instinct to run, and run fast overpowers me, but rational thought holds me in check. I'm not a natural runner. What if I'm not fast enough? My eyes sweep the ground, searching for something to protect myself with. There is nothing about other than a few twigs, pebbles, and coconuts.

Suddenly, my stalker springs to life, eating up the distance between the bushes and my tree in a few terrifying seconds. I hear myself screech and I claw at the ground for something to protect myself. My nails scrape across a coconut, and I snatch it up.

The shadow looms before me, reaching for my body. In the moonlight, I catch the brief outlines of a man's face. Light skin, crooked nose, a scruff of a beard. I don't hesitate, but smash the coconut against his head, shoving all my might into the blow. The man grunts and staggers backward. I bear the coconut down on his head once more and he crumbles into a heap.

The moment I'm free, I take off through the grounds, sprinting and wheezing from the run as I search for Javier and Jake.

A set of wooden lounges are on the beach where two dark shapes sit. That has to be them. I keep running, gasping for air as I careen up to the chairs.

"You're okay," I say, hunched over, panting.

They both jump up, startled.

"Hey," Jake says, but when I collapse into the sand beside his chair, he springs to my side. "What's wrong? Are you okay?"

"A man." I gasp for more air. "Followed me. Attacked."

"Where?" Javier grabs my shoulders and looks around as if to protect me. There's a slight shake of his hands.

I've never seen Javier lose his cool, no matter what we've seen or experienced in the Dreamscape.

"I was in the wooded section over here. Not sure if it was just some creeper or someone who is tied to Dad's kidnapping. I smashed a coconut on his head. I think I knocked him out."

"It was stupid of me to let you walk alone here," Javier mutters. "What was I thinking? From now on, we need to be more careful.

"Especially you, Aria," Jake says, frowning. "I think they're targeting you. Did he hurt you?"

My body still shivers in horror from the experience. "No. I'm okay, just freaked out."

"We should find him," Jake says. "We can't let him get away and tell anyone about us."

Pretty much everything inside of me definitely does not want to go back into the woods, but Jake's right. This guy could be more dangerous than I'm realizing.

"Did he have a gun?" Javier asks.

"I don't know," I say. "But he tried to tackle me rather than shoot so I'm guessing maybe not."

The three of us creep back into the woods with me leading the way. I find the guy lying on the ground where I left him. Javier crouches at his side and checks his pockets.

"No gun," Javier says. "And his pockets are completely empty."

"Who do you think he is?" Jake asks. "Does he look familiar to either of you?"

I shake my head. "I've never seen him in my life."

"We need to take him with us," Javier says.

"What are we going to do with him?" I ask.

"We'll take him to my room." Javier grabs the guy's shoulders while Jake takes the legs. "It's the bungalow right behind yours."

"This carrying bodies around is starting to get old," Jake mutters.

"People are going to get suspicious when they see us

carrying him around," I point out as I hold up his midsection.

Javier shrugs. "We'll walk fast."

By the time we are on the walkway right near Javier's bungalow, we are all out of breath. We set the passed-out man on the ground for a moment.

"You sure got him good," Jake says.

I follow Jake's eyes to the gash on the stalker's forehead. The blood has dried, a black slash trailing across his forehead and down his face.

"He does kind of look like he belongs in a haunted house," I mumble.

A couple ambles past, arm in arm as if they're out on a romantic stroll. But upon passing us as we heft the intruder back up, the woman stops and gasps.

"What happened to him?" she says.

"Aw." Javier grunts as he adjusts the body. "Drank a little too much at the tiki bar down the beach and hit his head. He'll be fine other than a slammer of a headache in the morning."

"Oh, dear," the woman says, which spurs the three of us to grab the guy back up and hurry even faster to Javier's room.

Once we enter the bungalow, a little smaller than Jake's and mine, we drop the guy on the floor. Javier works quickly to rip up one of his shirts and gags my stalker. Then he procures a long tasseled rope.

"From the curtains?" Jake asks, eyebrows raised.

"Yep," Javier says. "Got to use our resources, right?"

Once the man is secured, Javier inserts a dose of Temazepam. "That should keep him out of it for a while. At least until tomorrow morning. Then I'll give him a second dose before we head out of here. Hopefully, we'll be out of the country by then with a cold trail at our heels. I'd say we could enter his dreams, but we've already entered four times in the last week. That's more than we've ever done before and too risky."

"Yeah, the last time was rough on my system as well," I add.

"We've got all the information we need," Jake says. "No reason to push things. Plus, I'd like to run a diagnostic on Dr. Hale's laptop. Check for its vulnerability to virus or malware."

"Absolutely." Javier passes him the computer. "Just don't do anything to risk Aria's safety. This isn't a video game, you know. These criminals are professionals."

"And so are we." A rush of anger floods through me. "We might not be thieves or professional killers, but we've got skills. That's what we need to focus on."

"Skills in sleeping and dreaming?" Javier scoffs. "Some skills."

"Don't forget we've got Jake," I point out.

"Just call me Batman." Jake settles down on one of the seats, opening the laptop, but his face is paler than usual.

"Right and a computer nerd," Javier says, gloomily. "The dream team."

I glower at him because I hate how right he is. "What do you guys suggest?"

"Looks like Ms. Lau's main office is at Casino Kam Pek Paradise," Jake says.

"Then we go there." I pull out my phone to look up flights. As I do, I notice messages from Mom, Tony, and Sun. I tell myself I'll read them later. "We need to get there as soon as possible. I'm going to look up flights out of here."

"And do what?" Javier says. "Waltz in there and say 'Hello, we think you kidnapped Dr. Hale and maybe even stolen 81 million dollars, too. Hand the doctor and the money over.'"

I don't answer. I turn off my phone in frustration and face the window looking out into the ocean. The dark waves crash and then rush onto the shoreline. He's right, isn't he? Who am I kidding?

"How is it that after all we've done and experienced we're held up at this point in the game?" I say, bitterly. "If we could just find Zhang Lau and put her to sleep."

"You want to enter her dreams?" Jake's eyes widen. "That doesn't sound like a great idea. I mean, I'm sure she's heavily guarded. And if we do get a hold of her, we'll just get one shot. And there's no guarantee that she'll dream about your dad or the heist either. Right?"

"We've been entering the Dreamscape more than our allotted time," Javier adds. "It's dangerous and not healthy for our brains. I think it's time to contact the federal investigation team back home."

"You want us to call the feds after everything we've done?" I ask. "And tell them what? That we got solid evidence from breaking and entering people's minds and resorts? They'll lock us up in prison."

"Wait a second." Jake squints at the computer screen. "Do either of you like to gamble?"

I cock my head to the side, trying to read Jake's expression. "I'm a scientist. I deal with hard evidence and results. So no, not really."

He leans forward and pats the lounge cushion in front of him. "Now it's my turn for wild ideas."

"I'm listening." I plop down in front of him.

"I don't like this already," Javier mutters.

# THIRTY-EIGHT

# A FANTASY

Jake and I head back to our bungalow, promising to meet Javier at the ferry tomorrow morning. The next flight out of Manilla leaves tomorrow night and it will take nearly a full day of travel to get there. Selfishly, I don't want to leave Boracay. It's almost as if being here has been an escape from reality. If only I could stay here, spending MaxLife's money and forget about everything that happened, believing that Dad is safe back at home and Jake's dad isn't being accused of a crime he never committed.

Inside our room, I charge up my phone using the transformer we bought at the airport. Then I sag onto the soft bed and lean against the fluffy pillows. I pull up the message from Mom.

*Mom: Where are you? Sun called and said you left for*

*the Philippines? I need you to get home now. The feds have said these people are extremely dangerous. Call me.*

*Me: Hey! I'm fine. We found another lead. I can't turn back now. I'm headed to China. Should be home in a few days. Don't worry. Don't be mad.*

Jake's voice rises, pulling my attention to where he's talking to his dad on the phone. He's pacing the room, rubbing his free hand through his hair as he talks.

"Can't one of your guys track the SWIFT codes?" Jake asks. "It can't be that hard. No, it's gone. I um, dropped it in Bangladesh. Killed the hard drive. I just need enough money for a new computer and a flight. Dad!"

He pauses and glances over to where I'm curled up against the pillows of the bed. "Listen, it should just be a few more days. I'm close."

Another pause and then, "A lot closer than any of those idiots who work for you. If you'd just listened to me —" He listens for a moment. "Okay, you're right. I shouldn't have done that. They know? How did they know it was me? Unless you told them."

I focus back on my phone, trying to ignore his dad's yelling muffled voice that carries to where I'm sitting. I open the messages from Sun and Tony.

*Sun: Tell me you're ok. Worried.*

*Tony: Any breakthroughs?*

I sigh and then despite myself and Javier's warning to not tell them anything start texting.

*Me: Yes. We are headed to Macau. Flying into Hong*

*Kong. Tomorrow. Should be there by tomorrow night or the morning after.*

*Sun: Not cool. Macau is a seedy area.*

*Me: Lau's headquarters are there.*

*Sun: OMG*

*Tony: Come home*

*Me: Miss u guys*

*Sun: Do u have to go?*

*Me: Yep*

*Sun: You make me so mad*

*Me:*

*Sun: !!!!***#&####*

Seeing Sun's last text makes me laugh. It's her version of swearing. I turn my phone off and lean back against the pillows, suddenly feeling achy and unsure about everything. What if they're right? I roll my eyes, chuckling. Who am I fooling? They *are* right. This idea of ours is stupid. Ludicrous.

Jake hangs up and tosses his phone onto the chair, clearly frustrated.

"Didn't go well?" I ask.

"It's fine. Other than the fact my dad believes in his incompetent employees rather than me. And he told the feds about you guys going into my dreams to get the codes." He plops down on the bed beside me, staring up at the ceiling. "Were you laughing?"

"Just at how ridiculous it sounds that we can actually outwit Zhang Lau and get my dad back and recover the Federal Bank's money. Tony and Sun think it's not safe."

Jake turns on his side so he's facing me. "If you want to back out, I'm okay with that," he says. "You know I want to nail these people for what they've done and clear my family and my name, but I don't want to put you in jeopardy. It's not worth the risk."

"Thanks." I reach out for his hand and trace the lines on it. "Your plan is a good one though. I just hope the three of us can pull it off. Actually, it's not that. I know you and Javier can, it's me. The last time I went into the Dreamscape, I started thinking about my mom when I heard Bach. And well, I freaked out. I'm—"

"Smart, brave, capable," he says, and my eyes search his. There's truth to them, sincerity. "Beautiful."

He takes a strand of my hair in his fingers and pushes it out of my face. I catch my breath, remembering how he did that in his dream. He shifts closer to me and suddenly it's just his presence in the room, filling up every crevice, taking away all of my fears and insecurities.

His fingers trail down the side of my face and then across my shoulder. My skin responds to his touch, burning as if it's on fire. My breathing intensifies as he kisses my bare shoulder, his lips so soft that every part of my body craves for him. To hold him tight. To realize that there's more to Jake than being there to fix everything.

Another kiss on my neck, and slowly, his lips trail up to

meet mine. Then I'm reaching for him, my fingers tangling in his hair. Outside, the ocean waves crash, creating a rhythm of magic and passion, and we become lost in each other's arms. This moment. It's wilder than any dream I've ever entered.

This reality is more fantastic than any fantasy I could conjure.

MORNING COMES TOO QUICKLY. The alarm from my phone clashes against the cry of seagulls outside and distant laughter from beachgoers. I sit up in bed, sheets tangled about me. Jake is already awake, eating rambutan fruit and staring out the window. He's not wearing a shirt this morning and I find myself blushing when he turns and catches me gazing at the line of muscles along his back. The sheets hang loose around the lounge where he slept last night.

"Rough night?" he asks. "You cried out in your dreams. I sat by you a few times, but I've heard you shouldn't wake someone from their dreams."

"Yeah." I laugh faintly at his joke and run my hands through my hair, trying to tame the mass of curls, but finally, give up. "I guess I did have a few nightmares. But even still, I don't want to leave. I guess I'm kind of scared of what lies before us."

"I know. I feel the same."

It's a relief admitting the truth and hearing him agree. "What we're about to do feels uncertain, wrong even."

"No." He leans against the wall, strands of hair falling in his face. "What they've done is wrong and they asked for this. We've got to stop them before they hurt someone else."

We pack up the little belongings we have and head outside in the morning light. The soothing sunbeams soak into my skin as my feet shuffle across the sand-packed path.

"Do you realize we haven't even been here for twenty-four hours?" I say with a sigh.

"It's a shame." He gives me a mischievous side glance. "I could really get used to this."

I think about last night. Being with Jake made me forget everything that has happened so far, but then it was almost like a fantasy in the end. I wonder if this is a relationship that will last or if it's only the passion of the moment.

As planned, we don't cross paths with Javier until we arrive at the airport where we find him standing in line at security.

"I can't believe we're traveling to another country again," I say, wearily dragging my suitcase behind me. "If only we could've found our answers here in the Philippines. I'm so tired of traveling."

"Join the club." Jake's got dark circles under his eyes.

From the looks of him, he didn't get much sleep last night. "I'm so messed up. I don't know what is day or night."

On the flight, we don't have seats together since we booked the last available ones. As I stow my suitcase into the compartment above me, I memorize where Javier and Jake are sitting. After everything that has happened, being alone makes me feel exposed and vulnerable. It's only a two-hour flight so I tell myself that nothing could happen in that short amount of time.

Once in the air, the stewardess passes out drinks and pretzels. I pop open my bag and nearly consume all of its contents at once, kicking myself for not eating breakfast.

My thoughts are interrupted by a man shuffling past me. It's his side glance that stops me from chewing. Did I just imagine that he was staring at me more than necessary? I swallow my pretzels and stow the rest away, suddenly my appetite has vanished. I wait a few seconds before glancing over my shoulder to check on the man, but he's just settling into one of the window seats and pulling out a magazine.

For the next hour, I'm so distracted that I can't rest. So I pull out Dad's watch and put it in one hand and then pull off Grams' emerald ring and hold it in my other.

Seeing both of these, it's like a part of them is with me on this insane journey. I lean my head back and let out a long breath, trying to pull up one of my favorite quotes in my head.

*Fear brings two choices. Forget everything and run or face everything and rise.*

I tell myself to stay calm and decide to get a little sleep before we arrive in Hong Kong. I'm half asleep when I get that prickly sensation someone is watching me again. My eyes pop open and a tingling feeling crawls along the back of my neck. I sit straighter and look around me, trying to make sense of that sound, but no one looks out of the ordinary other than me and my hyper sense of being watched.

I'm so tired. I'm sure it's just my paranoid brain making stuff up.

# THIRTY-NINE

# PARANOIA KEEPS YOU ALIVE

## HONG KONG, CHINA

Once we land and exit the plane, I spot the man again. He doesn't even glance my way. Which makes sense. He's just a passenger on the plane and now headed to wherever he was planning on going. That's it. Nothing more.

"What's wrong?" Javier asks when we meet up in the terminal. I guess he knows me well enough to sense me worried.

"It's nothing," I say. "I'm just tired, hungry, and completely paranoid."

"You have every right to be paranoid after what you've been through," Jake says softly.

The three of us head out to the curb to order a taxi when a voice calls my name. "Aria!"

I turn around to find Sun's brother. "Danny? What are you doing here?"

"Sun sent me to keep an eye on you." He strolls

toward us wearing his designer suit jacket flapping around him in the wind. His black hair is perfectly sculpted, and he looks like a model unlike the three of us, travel-weary and haggard.

"How did Sun know we would be here?" Jake asks.

"I might have mentioned our flight plans," I say.

"She's waiting for you back at the hotel," Danny adds. "Along with Tony."

"What?" My eyes bug out.

Jake whistles. "I thought they weren't going to get involved."

"We agreed this was too dangerous," I tell Danny, thinking of the guy who was waiting for me in the hotel woods. "You need to take them back to Florida and stay safe."

"Sun said you'd say that." Danny rolls his eyes. "Trust me, I agree with you 100%. But she also said you can't do this without them."

Javier sighs and shakes his head, muttering in Spanish under his breath. I try to think of some comeback, but the reality is, Sun is right. We do need them.

"Stop fighting and just get in the car." Danny waves us to follow him.

I'm too tired to argue so I trudge after him to his car. I toss my bag into the trunk, but as I'm about to slip into the backseat, I spot that same guy from the airplane. He's got a cigarette in his hand, leaning against one of the outer walls in the dark shadows. I wouldn't have seen him except another car's headlights swerved in to park at the curb and beamed its lights directly at him.

Our eyes meet. He tosses his cigarette to the ground and stamps on it before taking off down the sidewalk, hands in his pockets.

"Javier," I ask as our car zips away from the airport. "How long did you say our Boracay stalker would be asleep?"

Javier checks his watch. "I'm guessing he'd have woken about two hours ago. There's no way he could have followed us and caught that flight."

*Unless he is working with someone.* Still, if he wanted to capture or stop us, he'd have done it by now. Right?

"You okay?" Jake touches me on the arm.

"We're here in China," I say. "That much closer to my dad. So yeah, I'm great."

---

THE FIRST THING I do when I see Sun is yell at her.

"How could you come here?" I drop my bags, clamping my fists against my hips. "You were supposed to stay home where it's safe."

"Come and give me a hug." Sun grins. "My family is from Hong Kong. This is like my second home. Besides, I can't have you come here without taking you shopping."

I step into her arms and tears edge at the corner of my eyes.

"Nice place," Javier says as Jake and he roll their suitcases into the suite.

"Look at you three," Sun says. "You're in worse condition than the lizards my cat drags in. This is what happens when you fly commercial. We should've stayed with you the whole time. I told Danny that, and finally, he listened."

"I couldn't say no after she told me you were going to Macau." Danny throws himself onto one of the plush couches. "This is our old stomping ground. My uncle owns the Shanghai Tang department stores. And then Sun explained to me the stakes involved and how the feds were doing nothing and getting nowhere. I realized maybe your mission wasn't such a bad one."

"And the fact that we're after Zhang Lau," Sun adds. "She's been stealing from Daddy and his company for years."

"Woah!" Tony waltzes into the room, wearing a bathrobe and holding a towel. "Look what the cat dragged in!"

"Tony!" I smile as he gives each of us a high-five. "Is your mom okay with you being here?"

"Sure, sure," Tony says vaguely, which means no, not really. I frown. "I mean, how could I pass up a trip to Hong Kong, am I not right?"

I laugh, shaking my head.

"Glad you're back with us," Jake says. "What's up with the robe? You having a spa day?"

"Had myself a dip in that wicked pool they've got

here," Tony says. "Oh, and I ordered some food. A spread of all my favorites. Figured my people would be starved."

"You figured right, bro." Jake sets down his bags and sinks into one of the soft chairs. "Airplane pretzels just don't cut it. You saved my life."

It's weird to see Jake and Danny here with the rest of the team. Actually, it's more like our team of four has somehow expanded to six.

As they talk, I take in the penthouse suite. It's extravagant, but it's also large enough for all of us to be in one place together. I wander to the far wall, which is completely glass and overlooks the city of Hong Kong. The bustling city glistens with a million lights while dark mountains spike up, ringing the entire metropolis.

Sun gives me a quick tour of the suite, which has three bedrooms, a living room, a small kitchen, and a dining room.

"You can sleep with me." Sun snatches up my bag and leads me into the room just ahead. "And then the boys can fight over the other two rooms."

The room she's picked for us feels fresh and modern with gray walls and abstract paintings over each of the double beds. A flat-screen TV hangs over a dresser set and there's an adjoining bathroom. Sheer curtains are drawn over the window, but when I pull them back, I discover another stunning view of the city.

"Something happened in the Philippines, didn't it?" Sun perches on the edge of the bed.

"Yeah." I drop the curtain back and turn toward her. "Some guy tried to attack me in the woods. I hit him with a coconut."

"A coconut? Seriously?"

I laugh, thinking about it now. "We put him to sleep and then left him tied and gagged in the forest before we left."

"Serves the creep right for trying to hurt you."

"I want to believe he was just a random stalker, but I doubt it. Other than that it was pretty calm. At least, no cars blowing up."

"You know I wasn't asking about that."

I open my suitcase and begin going through the few things I have. "Thanks again for lending me your clothes."

"Jake and you," Sun continues, ignoring my attempts of avoidance. "I see how you two look at each other."

"I don't know. I'm not sure if what's between us is just this connection to the heist and kidnapping or if it's a fling. Or—"

"It's something more."

"Yeah. It's just that I promised myself not to get involved with boys. Career first. They just slow you down, distract you, hurt you, use you."

She gives me a knowing look. I know she's remembering that time when I thought Jerome was seriously into me. Ninth grade. He invited me to the prom, and I, of course, being the enthralled, clueless underclassman was sucked into his charm. Turns out he had been hoping to be the first guy to score on me. Freshman girls equal fresh victories. I haven't thought about or dated a guy since.

"Girl, not all boys are scumbags. And there's more to life than having a successful career. That's just one part. Besides, I know plenty of people who have a great love life and a successful career. Take me for example."

"You and Nathan aren't even together anymore. And I wouldn't call Blake the blind date a success."

"They just weren't right for me, that's all," she proclaims breezily. "All I'm saying is a career won't fill the part of your heart that love will."

Someone whistles from the main room, interrupting us.

"It's here!" Tony cries from the main room. Then he whistles. "You've got to try out these spring rolls."

When Sun and I join the others at the long dining room table, Tony pops the rest of the roll into his mouth. "Forget what I said about the spring rolls being good. They're awful. I'll sacrifice myself and eat 'em all for the greater good."

"How thoughtful of you, Tony." Sun wrenches the spring roll tray from him and pops one in her mouth.

A spread has been laid out for us on the dining room table by the hotel's staff. The smells of steamed rice, sweet and sour pork, and fried chicken waft into the air. My mouth waters and my stomach growls so loud we all laugh.

"Javier says you guys have a plan," Tony says, piling his plate with noodles.

Jake nods, puts down the drumstick, and licks his fingers. He takes the long strip of paper lining off the food cart and, moving the dishes out of his way, slaps it in the center of the table. With a pen, he begins to sketch out the plan.

"I'm envisioning we break down our plan into categories: needs, locations, risks, and players. With six of us, we have a lot more options than with just three people."

*Needs*

- *Computer*
- *Costume for Aria*
- *Dreamscape*

*Location*

- *Casino Kam Pek Paradise*
- *Nearby location within long-range connection*

*Players*

- *Aria, Sun, Tony, Javier, and Jake*
- *Danny—escape vehicle and driver*

"What? I'm the driver?" Danny doesn't look too impressed. "I've got skills, too."

"I'll also need your help finding a computer that will meet our needs," Jake tells him. "You know this town better than anyone. Also, I need you to find us the travel plans. Plus, we need someone who can help with interpreting. I don't speak Mandarin. Does anyone else?"

"I speak a little," Sun says. "But I'm rusty."

The rest of us shake our heads. I twirl my noodles with my chopsticks, reviewing the plan in my head.

"But what exactly are we going to do?" Sun asks impatiently.

"This is stage one," I explain. "Our target is Zhang Lau. We're going to find her and force her to tell us where my dad is."

"You mean you want to do this in the Dreamscape again." Sun frowns. "I don't like it."

"It's the only way," I say.

"And while you all are having sweet dreams with Zhang," Jake says. "I'm going to sneak into her server and try to determine where the money went."

We spend the rest of the evening planning out our positions and roles. Jake and Javier get into an argument over our entry point and how we will get behind the security barriers while Tony insists I should stay behind because I'm too emotionally involved.

Finally, at 3 a.m., we part to get some sleep, promising to finish our work the next day. I'm about to stumble to my room when I notice Jake hunched over a computer Danny lent him, the glow from the screen lighting up his face.

"You should get some sleep," I say. "The brain needs rest to work properly."

He leans back and rubs his face with both hands. "Just found out something I wished I hadn't."

"What?" I sit beside him, resting my hand on his shoulder.

"There's something I haven't told you about when I hacked into the Federal Reserve."

I bite my lip. "Okay."

"I was mad at my dad. Mad that he wasn't paying me any attention, wouldn't take my computer skills seriously, wouldn't take my advice. So I was complaining to my best friend, Larry, about it all. You know him. He's in our Calculus class."

I frown and shake my head.

"The thing is, he actually gave me the idea to hack into the Federal Reserve. He even helped me out. He's really into the Dark Web and got me involved in a group there and stuff."

"You think he's a part of all this?"

"Honestly, the thought never crossed my mind until one of my friends on the Dark Web—the person goes by NightLife—just messaged me saying Larry was paid by an anonymous donor to dare me to hack into Dad's system at the Federal Reserve and get all of his codes."

"Paid?"

"Paid $10,000 if I did it and was successful." He hangs his head into his hands. Then he looks at me. His eyes are red. "I don't have many friends, Aria. Like real live friends. They're all on the internet. My parents are so busy with their lives I hardly even see them. And here I find out my one friend, who I thought was *real*, the one I've known since 5<sup>th</sup> grade just sold me out for 10 g's."

"I'm so sorry, Jake." I brush the long strands of hair out of his eyes.

"Aria." He takes my hands and tugs me closer to him. "You are the most real thing I've ever had in my life. And tomorrow, I'm afraid I'm going to lose you. What if there's more to all of this than we think? We should be dead. They had so many chances, but we're still alive. Do you think that's a coincidence?"

"Did you forget the bomb?" I point out. "They nearly killed all of us if you hadn't gotten us out of the van with only seconds to spare."

"Unless the food delivered to your room was supposed to knock you out, keep you from getting into that van. And I know this sounds paranoid, but what if the guy who has been helping me this whole time on the Dark Web has been working for Lau. And the guy that attacked you in the woods could've easily killed you with a silencer. But he didn't. It was like he was just trying to grab you. The more I think about it, the more I'm wondering if we haven't been lucky. That we're being led into a trap."

"A trap? We've put ourselves into this position, not Lau. Besides, I can't *not* do this, Jake. I have to find my dad. And the team needs me. Without me, they aren't as effective in the Dreamscape. You have to understand I need to see this to the end. No matter what."

"I don't think we should go tomorrow."

"I have to go. I have no other choice."

"There's always a choice, Aria."

Then he turns back to his laptop. I feel him pulling into himself, withdrawing from me. The boy who held me last night, warm and alive, suddenly feels cold and isolated as if he's retreated into the code that fills the screen before him.

FORTY

## TO DREAMS AND AWAKENING

When I wake the next morning, the sounds and rustling of my teammates force me to toss aside my covers. Sun's bed is empty, but made up, not a wrinkle in sight. I forgot what a morning person she is. I pull out my phone and look on my inspirational quotes app to read today's quote.

*It's in our trials that true strength is found.*

I screen-shot the quote, and then after taking a quick shower, shuffle my way into the living room. No one is there except Jake, staring out the window, a glass of orange juice in his hand. When he spots me, he pauses and smiles.

"Hey, sleepyhead," he says.

"Is everyone gone?" I pick up a croissant from the room service cart where there's a platter of an assortment of breads and fruit along with coffee and juices.

"Danny and Javier went to pick up supplies and Sun went shopping. Tony left to scout out the casino."

"You didn't go?" I perch myself on the edge of the couch.

"Naw." Jake sits beside me. "Figured you might need some company when you woke up. Plus, Javier says that the less you and I are out in the open, the better."

"So we're prisoners now?"

"I'll just be happy when Danny gets back with a new computer for me. I need to test out this new malware I'm playing with. Besides, I didn't want to download anything on the Dreamscape laptop in case it would mess it up."

"Having withdrawals?" I tease.

He lightly touches my face. Goosebumps trickle up my arm at his touch. "Yes. In more ways than one."

That look in his eyes, soft and yet intense, takes my breath away. The boy I am falling for hard is back and standing before me. What is this relationship we have? I have no idea. He leans in, but laughter outside of the door pulls us apart. The door flies open, and Danny and Javier come barreling in, arms full of packages and bags. Jake leaps off the couch to meet them.

"Got your computer," Danny says. "You weren't kidding. That sucker wasn't cheap, but it's a beauty."

"Don't worry," Jake says. "It'll be worth it. I'll make sure my dad transfers you the money. What about the rest of the list?"

"Wasn't easy to find." Javier begins unloading equipment on the table. "Especially the sound transmitter. But your computer, the earphones, coms, and ropes were no-brainers."

While Jake turns on his new computer and begins downloading his files saved on the cloud, I pull out the notes for the mission and log what we've done into the MaxLife's Dreamscape's laptop. Once I'm finished, I join Javier and together we work on linking the coms to Jake's computer.

Hours pass before Sun comes waltzing into the room, hands full of shopping bags. I glance at the clock, 2 p.m.

"Where have you been?" I ask her.

She plops three bags at my feet. "Shopping for you."

Danny frowns. "I thought you were supposed to get an outfit, not a wardrobe."

"Fashion should never be limited." Sun straightens her hair and kicks off her heels.

Speaking of fashion, Sun is dressed to the nines wearing a tight black pantsuit with a teal blouse beneath her jacket and a thick, rope necklace that accents against her flawless skin. "How are we doing on the prep?"

"Tony isn't back yet," Javier says and moves over to the window to look down at the street below as if that will help bring him back faster. "Let's hope he's okay and hasn't been recognized as part of our team."

"He'll be fine." I dig through the bags. "He's smart. Just as long as he doesn't pass by a music retailer. Then we're sunk."

"We should get moving soon," Jake says. "I'll need time to get into position. But I think I've got everything loaded and prepped on this baby."

"What about the Dreamscape?" Sun asks, coming to peek at the MaxLife computer.

"It's ready." I pull out a blonde wig and a teeny-tiny skirt from the bag. "What is this?"

"Your outfit," Sun says, not bothering to glance away from the computer screen. "I think you could pass for a blonde with your skin tone. And isn't that skirt adorable?"

I hold it up to my body. "Is it really a skirt? Hard to tell."

"You'll look great in it," Jake says.

"I'll look like an idiot," I say. "And a bimbo."

"That's the goal." Sun withdraws a giant pink purse from one of the shopping bags at my feet. She tucks two Dreamscape masks in the inside pocket. "There, you're all set now. You better change soon. We've got to get going."

I'm about to head to the bedroom with my scanty amount of clothing when the door opens and Tony steps into the room. He's got a set of earbuds on and his head bounces to whatever music he's got playing.

"How's it going, people!" he says, waving his hand and pulling out one earpiece. "Took me longer than expected. Got lost a few times."

"Glad you're back," Javier says. "We were getting worried."

While Tony loads up the photos from his phone onto

Jake's computer and the two discuss potential headquarter locations, I duck into the bedroom to change into the clothes Sun got me. The skirt is pink with white polka dots across it and the shirt is a tank top with pink sequins. I'm strapping the tiny heels on when Sun comes into the room.

"Look at you!" Sun nods approvingly. "You look fabulous. Now come here. Let me help you with that wig."

I tuck my hair into a hair net and then Sun slips the short, blonde wig over my head. Next, she drags me to the chair by the window and pulls out her makeup kit. With perfect efficiency, she applies my make-up and fake eyelashes.

"There." She stands, pulls me to my feet, and gives me a good look-over. "You look perfect."

The person in the mirror looks nothing like me. So much so that I'm hardly able to convince myself it's really me I'm looking at.

"You're amazing," I say.

"Why thank you!"

"I don't even look like me."

"Sure you do. It's you, just a jazzed-up version. Now have you been practicing your lines and accent?"

I dig through my jeans that I threw on the bed. Inside my pocket are the lines we wrote as a group. "I don't know if I can pull this off," I say.

"Don't be ridiculous. Of course, you can. And if you ever question yourself, pretend you're in the Dreamscape where anything goes."

I think about the times in the Dreamscapes when my hair has changed color or I'm wearing something totally different than before. "It feels different this time. More real."

"I know." Sun's face grows serious. "It is real this time. And if you don't want to do this, just say the word. None of us are making you."

"I have to." I pull out my dad's watch, rubbing my fingers over its cracked surface. "For my dad."

"Here." She takes off the necklace she's wearing and uses one of the still attached watch band links as an eye, she threads her necklace through a link in the watch so its face hangs from the chain like a necklace. Then she slips it over my head, and I tuck it beneath my outfit.

"Thanks," I whisper. "It's perfect."

Finally, we head back into the main room, or in my case, more like wobble on my towering heels, and find that the others have packed up all of the equipment. Tony is wolfing down one of the pieces of pizza we saved for him while Jake chugs down a Coke.

I pull out two more Cokes from the frig and hold them out to Jake. "For good luck," I say.

"I won't say no to a Coke." He takes them, grinning.

"I think we're all set then," Javier says, but he doesn't move.

I get it. It's almost like the moment we move, the wheels of this mouse trap we've created will start churning and there will be no going back. The uncertainty of our success hangs over us like a flickering lightbulb, any minute it will blink out and thrust us into darkness. Our luck has held on this far, but Jake's doubts whether it was luck or our enemies' pure design that we're still alive lingers at the back of my mind. Could he be right? That everything we've done has been orchestrated by Lau?

"It's 6 p.m.," Danny says. "The cars are ready."

"To dreams," I say and hold out my fist.

The others bring their fists to mine and repeat my words, "To dreams."

Then Tony adds, "And awakening."

FORTY-ONE

UNDERCOVER

MACAU, CHINA

Those words release us from the lock holding us back and spur us to action. We head out of the suite without another word. As we ride the elevator, no one speaks. Sun shifts the Dreamscape computer from one hand to the other. Tony sticks both earbuds into his ears, instantly bobbing his head to the music. Jake's hand reaches out for mine, and for this brief ride, we hold hands as if clinging to each other by a mere thread because the truth is we don't know how this is all going to go down.

The doors to the elevator slide open and our team strides out into the bustling lobby. Jake's hand slips out of mine and he nods once before veering left with Tony and Sun. Meanwhile, Danny, Tony, and I bolt straight out of the hotel where Danny gives the concierge his name. A car pulls up to the curb and a bellhop opens the doors for us.

The sun is just dipping below the rounded mountain

tops as we take off on the left side of the road, merging into the lane with heavier traffic.

"You trust this driver?" Tony asks, fidgeting with the wires of his headphones.

"Absolutely," Danny says.

Danny's confidence relaxes me, and I try to focus on taking in the beautiful city rather than the task we are about to do. Hong Kong is an eclectic mix of modern buses and cars along with bikers and rickshaws. Glass skyscrapers tower on either side of the road, their windows glittering golden from the sun's final rays. Large banners hang on street posts and against walls, announcing the Lunar holiday celebrations.

Our car swerves down to the port of the bay. Danny explains that's where we will take the ferry to the other side of the city. Along the sides of the bay, red lanterns dangle from long strings, casting off a light glow in the growing darkness. Vendors have set up their wares and food stalls along the river's edge, already calling out to the crowds of people working their way to stroll along the banks. I spy children laughing as they race each other, flying dragon kites while others watch and cheer for the dragon parade.

Soon we make our way to the IFC Towers in the Shun Tak Center where we park and then head to the Hong Kong Ferry Terminal where we board the high-speed Turbo boat.

"This boat is incredibly fast," Danny explains. "Worth

every penny for the fifty-five minutes it'll take to get there. Before we take off, you need to check out the view of the city at night from this vantage point."

As we head up onto the ferry's second level, Tony whistles. "This is incredible!"

He's right. Through the windows, the buildings glisten along the shoreline, scattering all the way up to the base of the mountains. Then above the city line, the mountains stand dark against the purple sky as if giants are guarding the city. A junk sails beside our ferry, the jagged red flags highlighted against the last tentacles of sunset.

"It's all so lovely," I tell Danny. "I can see why you come back here often."

He smiles. "It's not bad if I must say so myself. I grew up on the other side of the harbor. Sun doesn't remember much of when we lived in Hong Kong, but we still have the apartment here to stay at when we come to visit my father or deal with business operations."

We sit in our arranged seats, which remind me of an airplane seat. Once I clip in my seatbelt, I review my lines, what I'll do tonight, and imagine how the events will play out, deliberating over the various outcomes. Most importantly, I envision finding Dad and rescuing him. I dig into my purse and pull out the quote that I chose for tonight:

*The way to know the future is to create it yourself.*

I sigh, wishing I could believe my quote. There's still so much uncertainty. After all, we don't have any idea of where they could be holding Dad. Danny didn't think they would be holding him at the Casino Kam Pek. The sickening reality is that Dad might not even be in this county! I stare out the window. Thousand upon ten thousands of buildings spread out within my eyesight. Here I am, so close, but seeing this huge city, it feels like an impossible task.

Once our high-speed ferry reaches the Outer Harbor Terminal, we hail a taxi and head deeper into Macau. My nerves are fried by the time we enter mainland China, and I check my purse for like the hundredth time to make sure I've got all my supplies.

"You good?" Worry fills Tony's face, knitting his forehead. "You sure it has to be this way?"

"I can't think of a better idea," I say. "You?"

He shakes his head and I attach the comlink behind my ear while Tony and Danny do the same. I decide to test my com.

"Alpha to Echo," I say into the air. I wait, anxious.

After everything that has happened, I can't depend on anything going right. I can only hope the other half of our team, whom we named Echo, is okay.

"Echo reading," Jake's voice comes through my ear. My heart thrills at hearing his voice, which feels so close and near to me. "We are in position and ready when you are."

"Good to hear your voice," I say.

"Right back at you," Jake says, and I can hear a smile in his voice.

"Hey, you two," Sun says. "No flirting during the mission."

Our car pulls up to Casino Kam Pek Paradise and an attendant in a tuxedo strides to my door and opens it. I step out, trying to keep my balance. The bright, flashing lights of the drop-off area momentarily blind me as I step onto a crimson-red carpet. Fortunately, Danny slides to my side and holds my elbow for support. Tony remains in the car where he'll be dropped off at the service entrance.

"You good?" Danny asks me.

I nod and we ascend the stairs. Pop music pumps out of the speakers and attendants dressed in black suits with crimson lapels whisk open the doors for the two of us.

"We're in," I say into my com.

The security at this place is as intense as Danny had warned us it would be. Not only do we have to walk through the full-body scanner, but we're also searched again by their security team.

"You weren't joking when you said they were thorough," I mutter to Danny as we finally step out of the security check-in and into the hallway.

"Let's just hope the security isn't as strict for staff," Danny mutters. "Or Sun's going to run into issues."

My heartbeat thumps against my eardrums. "You think she'll be okay?"

"Don't worry about her." He pats my arm as he escorts me across the gleaming golden floor into a huge ballroom. Then he grins. "She's gotten away with murder her whole life."

Massive chandeliers dangle from a bright blue ceiling.

Golden sheets engraved with ornate geometric designs plate the walls. A haze of cigarette smoke fills the grand ballroom along with the smell of alcohol. Slot machines are lined up in neat rows, nearly all occupied.

In my ear, I hear Tony's voice, "I'm in. Heading to the security wing."

"Copy that," Jake says.

Meanwhile, I cling to Danny's arm as we enter a room where a poker game has just finished. The tray ceiling is lower here, making the room feel more constricting. I glance about nervously. My nerves scream to hide in case someone suspects me for the fraud that I am.

One of the men at the table pushes out of his padded chair and storms out of the room. I stiffen as he nearly shoves me aside to get out. My first instinct is to slide into the corner of the room and study the situation, but tonight that's not my role.

Unlike in our Dreamscape, I need to be noticed. My fingers shake as I reach for the chain where Dad's watch hangs. I can do this.

"Gosh!" I practically yell. My voice sounds a bit shaky. I clear my throat, forcing confidence into it. "This looks like gobs of fun. I bet it's super easy."

Then I charge through the few bystanders and plop down into one of the chairs at the table. This earns me a couple of glances and whispers. My back stiffens at the looks, but I pretend not to notice. Instead, I drum my fingers on the table.

"Let's get the party started." I whip out my lipstick and slather on another layer of red. "What's taking y'all so long? I'm ready to win!"

"If anyone can do it, it's you." Danny rushes to my side like a dotting boyfriend, patting my shoulder. Then he switches to Mandarin and says something to the two Chinese men sitting at my table. The man with a blue tie man laughs while the other with a mustache frowns, a look of annoyance crossing his face.

Danny pats my hand encouragingly again and backs away from the table, but his eye is twitching. *Great.* My heart sinks. *He's nervous.*

Another man joins us. He looks Middle Eastern with deep dark eyes. He gives me a tight nod. I, in turn, flash him a smirk and then pop a piece of gum in my mouth and start chomping loudly. This awards me a few disgusted looks, but no one says anything as the dealer moves to the table and reviews the rules of the game. I'm hoping that to them I'm just an annoying American girl.

"This is going to be such fun," I say loudly while twirling a blonde curl. Might as well take the blonde hair girl stereotype to the extreme. "I'm feeling lucky tonight!"

"Madame," the dealer says gravely. "Please keep your voice down should you not wish to be disqualified."

"Sure." I smack my gun, batting my lashes at him. "Not a problem, handsome."

The dealer deals the deck, flicking them to each of us with perfect ease. Even still, it's hard to concentrate on anything other than the pounding of my heart. As I pick up my cards, I try to remember how I'm supposed to play this game. Jake reviewed the basics with me back at the hotel room. I lost to him every time.

Tony's voice pops into my ear. "Echo, the device is rock solid. You should be able to hack into their surveillance system. Holler if you have any problems, bro."

"Copy that," Jake says.

Suddenly it's my turn, and I freeze. I study my cards. A pair of eights stare back at me, but are those good? I remember Jake said two of the same cards are good, but he also said don't bid on anything less than a face card. Luckily, a server waltzes into the room, interrupting my thoughts.

"Excuse me, miss," the lady says in a thick Mandarin accent. "I have a gift for you from a man in the next room."

I look up to find Sun staring down at me wearing the waiting staff's uniforms and a cute blue wig. Leave it to her to look gorgeous even in a uniform. One of her eyebrows lifts expectantly as if challenging me to do a better job performing my role. On her tray rests a thick braided silver rope and hanging from its end is a giant blue gem.

She did it! She got through security.

"Oh!" I shriek, snatching up the piece of jewelry. "It's gor-gee-ous!" I lean back and call Danny. "Darlin', did you see this gift I got? This is exactly what I was talking about earlier. Being treated like a lay-dee, that's what."

Danny frowns and crosses his arms as I secure the necklace around my neck, beaming. A smirk crosses Sun's face as she follows my gaze to Danny. He glares at Sun, which only makes her smirk grow wider. Then she spins on her heels and vanishes out the door.

Her voice pops over the com. "Package delivered."

"Accessing," Jake says.

"Your turn to bid, Madame," the dealer tells me, clearly annoyed that the game has stopped because of me.

I swallow and stare back at my cards. Was I supposed to try to get a flush? Or was it a house? I can't even remember the terms. What should I bid? My head hurts. Why couldn't this be a game on brain development or an analysis of human response systems? I'd totally nail that.

I pull up the corners of each of my cards again like Jake said to do so he could see them through the hacked tournament cameras that were installed in the table.

"My bid is," I pause, waiting for Jake to speak into the com. Where is he? Did our com system go down?

Finally, a crackle of noise comes through followed by, "Your cards aren't great," Jake says. "Raise ten."

I shift in my seat, trying to figure out which chips I should throw out. Some have dollar amounts on them, but the gold ones don't. I decide the dollar amounts are too scary so I choose the unmarked ones.

"How about ten of these cute little yellow chips?" I finally throw out the figure to the table, hoping my mic is working so the team can hear me. Then I push ten of the solid gold chips out in front of me. "What do you say, boys?"

Blue Tie leans back in his seat, clearly distressed by my announcement. Mustache Guy appears unfazed while the Middle Easterner really looks at me for the first time.

*Well,* I think smugly. *At least I've gotten everyone's attention.*

"Are you out of your mind?" It's Jake's voice, emerging through the crackle. I jerk and nearly fall out of my chair, surprised by his urgency. "You just put out 100,000 dollars. I meant 10 hundred dollar chips! We haven't even seen the flop yet."

"Madame, are you okay?" the dealer asks me.

"Oh, yes, sweetums," I say. "Just excited, that's all. This game is so thrill-ee-ng, isn't it?"

The only responses I get are a few dark looks. Most of the table folds and mutters under their breath, but the Middle Easterner calls my bet, glaring at me the whole time. The dealer lays three cards in the middle of the table. Two sevens and a four. I have no clue if those are good or not.

"Okay," Jake says. "I'm finally in their system and I can see everyone else's cards now, too."

"Finally," I mutter.

"Excuse me?" the dealer asks.

"Finally." I clear my throat. "I get my chance to win."

"Aria, you've got nothing. The Middle Easterner has the hand to win. A full house, sevens over fours. The only way you can win is if another eight pops up or you get four of a kind, which you probably won't get. Just tap the table to check unless someone else bids. If he does, fold, and next time I'll walk you through the rest of the hands. We can still win that money back."

Okay, I can do that. Except I need to win and win big, don't I? The Middle Easterner bets another $1000. Ouch!

The dealer looks at me and politely asks me for my play. Jake says I'm supposed to fold, but a niggling tickles the back corner of my mind. It's the twitch of the Middle Easterner's right eye as if he's not sure what to do. Maybe this game isn't as much about skill, but more about reading people.

"I'll raise five more." I lift my head and give the Middle Easterner a knowing look. Then I push five more gold into the center.

Just as I suspected, his face blanches and he loosens the top button on his collared shirt. I stare hard at him, daring him to fold. His eye twitches again, and he tosses his cards down, saying, "Fold. Stupid American. Why don't you go play the slots?"

I look around. My competitors groan and sigh.

"Take your winnings," the dealer says. "You've won this round. Two hundred thousand plus change."

Two hundred thousand dollars? The giant pit in my stomach opens and all my emotions drop into it. That was way more than I can handle. I thought it would be a hundred, or even a few thousand. But hundreds of thousands? That's insane! What had I been thinking? What if I had lost? No wonder Jake was freaking out.

"I won?" I croak. I'm so shocked that I drop my pretenses for a moment. Somehow I recover, lift my chin and glance over at Danny. "Whoopee! See, sugar cakes? I told you this game was easy."

Danny doesn't look so good. His face is a bit green as if this game is more than he had gambled for. After all, I'm playing with his money, but kudos to him because he nods and tries to give me a shaky smile.

"That's my girl," he says.

I remain in my seat for the next round. This time, I rely on Jake to lead me through each hand, since he's able to see everyone's cards thanks to his access to the security system. By the end of the hour, I've got a massive pile acquired. I do a little jig in my chair, waving my hands.

"Look at me!" I say. "I'm win-ee-ng. Can you believe how lucky I am?"

"This is ridiculous!" Mustache guy throws his cards on the table. "There is no way this bimbo could possibly win so many rounds. It's almost as if she's cheating!"

A murmur from the spectators around us fills the air. The Middle Easterner nods as does Blue Tie.

# FORTY-THREE
# CAUGHT

I gasp, pressing my hand to my throat. "Did you call me a bimbo? How could you say such a thing? That's utterly slanderous."

Mustache Guy knocks his chair to the floor in his hurry to leave the table, pushes through the throng of spectators, and storms away. A set of security guards stream into the room, their faces grave. I wave at them, "Hey boys, what are you up to? I'm the luckiest girl in the whole world, wouldn't you say?"

"Excuse me," one of the guards says in English, obviously for my benefit. "If you could stand, please?"

"Whatever for?" I smack on my gum and frown.

"Just taking precautions," the guard says. "If you'll just stand and remain still for a moment while I do a quick security check on you."

"But we did that back at the entrance, sweetums," I titter as I rise up.

He pulls out a wand with a metal bar on it. I steady my nerves as he begins trailing it up and down my body.

"What is the meaning of this?" I wave my hands about. "Get that *thing* away from me. I'm not to be treated like an animal or criminal. I'm special! I'm lucky!"

As the wand runs over my chest where the necklace hangs, a screeching beep fills the air. Instantly, two security guards rush to grab either arm. My two opponents gape up at me, obviously shocked at the turn of events.

"Let me go, you filthy scoundrels," I yell.

But they don't bother giving me details or consider my words. I glance over my shoulder at Danny, reaching for him.

"Darling," I call. "Forget all of those mean things I said about you. Help me!"

"I'll be right here, waiting for you," Danny says as if he's still seriously upset. I fight against the two men holding me as they drag me out of the poker room into a long white hallway with freshly painted walls and shiny, white floors.

"Where are you taking me?" I ask.

"Just need to ask you a few questions," the head of security says. "Then you can leave and never return to any of our casinos."

I'm taken into a small room where I'm offered a seat at a metal table. The guards hold a discussion in Mandarin, pointing to my necklace, and then pulling up a video feed of me playing. While they are distracted, I withdraw two earpieces and pop them into my ears.

One calls on his walkie, notifying someone about the situation. Finally, they appear to come to an agreement, nodding and growing quiet.

"Who gave you that necklace?" the leader asks me.

I touch the necklace. "Isn't it gor-e-gous?" I declare brightly. "A secret admirer gave it to me. I have no idea who. Isn't that romantic?"

The guards don't look convinced.

"How is it possible you won every hand?" one man presses. "The odds of you winning every hand are impossible."

"I'm luck-ee," I say. "You saw me back there."

"Take off that necklace. We must look at it."

I press my hand over the necklace protectively, looking aghast. "Whatever for?"

Suddenly the door flies open and a tall woman strides in, flanked by two security guards. She has ivory skin and straight black hair that bounces fluidly against her hips. Her dark eyes glisten coldly as she assesses me. Goose-bumps trail up my arms and the act I've been playing is sucked out of me.

"It's her," Javier announces into my com. "You did it! You pulled her out."

"Remember, her name is Zhang Lau," Sun adds. "Let her talk and see if you can get any information out of her."

"*This* is the girl?" Lau's red lips curl. "What is this? A joke from my competitor?"

They say something to Lau in Mandarin and then she turns to me.

"My security guards believe your necklace has a camera within it that is letting you share your cards with someone else at a remote site. Is this true?"

"Of course not!" I say, indignantly. "It was a gift."

I cross my fingers, hoping the necklace will be the decoy rather than them realizing that we've hacked into their surveillance system.

"But can a mere camera in a necklace see all the players' cards in the room?" she wonders aloud, tapping her finger to her chin. *Crap. She's smart.* "I doubt it. She must have access to the security system. Give the necklace to my men for inspection. If it's clean, then we will not turn you over to the authorities and you can be on your way."

I unclasp the necklace and hand it over. While the men are busy studying the necklace, I turn on my noise-canceling earplugs. Instantly, the room falls into absolute silence.

The men place the necklace into Lau's palm. Her lips move, but I don't hear anything she's saying. Instead, I wait, clutching the sides of my armchair, praying Javier and Jake can transmit the Sound Oasis through the necklace and put everyone in the room asleep.

This is all a huge risk. After all, I don't have any Temazepam on me.

The necklace is the first to fall, clattering to the ground. One by one the guards crumple along with Lau. I rise from my chair, assessing the whole situation and making sure the group has passed out. Then I peek outside to discover Sun and Jake lingering in the hall.

"Jake?" I pull out my earplugs, confused. "You're supposed to be manning the computer operations."

"I was. But I couldn't stay away. Besides, this is too dangerous for Tony. If someone is going to go down in all of this, I don't want it to be him. This isn't his fight. It's ours. So we switched positions."

I want to argue with him, but he's absolutely right.

We slip inside the room, plugging in our earplugs as we enter so we won't be affected by the Sleep Oasis that's being broadcast into the room from the necklace. Right away, Jake and Sun slap handcuffs around the wrists of each guard while I lock the door. Then I drag the chair against it just in case.

While Sun whips out the laptop with the Dreamscape, I withdraw the two sleeping masks I've got tucked inside my hip purse. First, I slip one on Ms. Lau and then I lay on the ground beside her. Ugh, lying on the hard, cold tile floor is a far cry from my comfy pod back at MaxLife. Jake joins me on the floor, shifting uncomfortably. He pulls out a sleep mask of his own.

My eyes widen, and I shake my head in a furious *no*.

What is he thinking? He hasn't even been trained to be in the Dreamscape.

He just smiles and lifts his thumb as if to tell me it's all good, but it's not. Going into the Dreamscape without a sleep pod is brutal. Going in with no training without a sleep pod is dangerous.

My heart races a million miles a minute at what we're going to do as Sun gives us the thumbs-up. Jake grabs my hand and squeezes me as if to tell me this is going to be alright. Then he slips on his mask and takes out his earplugs.

"No!" Angrily, I take out my plugs, saying, "Jake. Don't do this."

"Our fight..." Jake falls silent, a smile curling on his lips.

The ringing pierces my ears. The last thing I notice is Sun slipping my mask on as I drift into the world of dreams.

## FORTY-FOUR
## DEADLY DREAMS

The room fades away and I'm floating, lilting music filling my ears. Pink petals fall over my face, soft and sweet-smelling. More than anything, I just want to continue lying here in the green grass and forget about the madness of these last few days. But then something niggles at my brain.

*Get up. You have a job to do.*

So with a sigh, I rise to my feet. One of these days I just want to enter a Dreamscape and have some fun. I'm standing in a field dotted with yellow flowers on top of a mountain peak, a light breeze wafting across my face. A crumbling Chinese temple is off to my right. Multi-colored lanterns sway on a thick rope attached from one end of the ruins to a gnarled oak.

A stone path catches my attention and I decide to

follow it. As I hike, I spot a woman standing by a spring not far down the path. She's lifting a ladle of sparkling water to her lips. She has thick dark hair sweeping against her lower back. That has to be Zhang Lau.

I scan the area for Jake. I almost laugh when I spy him crouched behind a row of bushes. He is blinking rapidly and rubbing his eyes.

"Hey, Jake." I touch his shoulder. "Can you see and hear me?"

"I'm having a hard time seeing you, but your red hair helps." He rubs his head and tries to stand. He wobbles a bit like he's on a rocking boat. "Man, I don't know if I can stand. Does the ground always roll like this?"

"Only for a second or two. It'll settle soon. I have to admit, it is weird having you in the Dreamscape."

He holds my arm for support. "Maybe this wasn't a good idea. I might slow you down."

"It was a horrible idea. But you'll get the hang of it. Stay here until you feel stronger. Just be sure to keep the dreamer, that's Lau, in sight at all times or you'll be kicked out of the Dreamscape. Got it?"

He nods, his face turning pale green. Still, knowing he's here strengthens my resolve. I march up the path to face off with Lau. She's got her back to me and is still drinking from the water.

"Excuse me, Ms. Lau," I say. "Can you show me where Dr. Hale is located?"

She spins around and upon seeing me, her eyes widen in shock. She drops her ladle and takes off running. *Great.* I spooked her.

Then I realize where she's headed. Straight for the cliff.

That is so my luck. I start racing after her and Jake joins me at my side.

"She's going to jump," Jake says, panting heavily.

"I hate it when they do this."

Lau halts at the edge of the cliff where clouds drift around her feet. She glances up to a crag to our left. There's a group of people standing there holding guns. They aim at her. I grab Jake's arm and push him behind a tree. No need for us to be caught in the crossfire. Sure enough, the air fills with the sound of gunfire. Bullets pepper the ground, kicking up dirt and rocks in the vicinity of where Lau is perched on.

"What should we do?" Jake says.

"If we don't move closer to her and she moves, she'll be out of our range, and we'll be kicked out of the dream. That said, I've never been in a person's dream where bullets were flying."

"Can those bullets hurt us?"

"It's all mental. If you believe they are fake, then they are fake. But if your brain believes you've been shot, your body is going to act like it has."

I bite my lip, trying to decide what to do. There's no

guarantee we'll get another chance at getting inside her dream to find Dad's location. Even now, back at the casino, the rest of security could be investigating why the guards haven't answered their radios, or worse still, they could find us all passed out sleeping on the floor. We have Sun watching over us, but there's no guarantee how long she can keep us safe.

"Tell me where my dad is," I yell at her.

She turns and frowns as if confused by my being here. And then she turns away from us and jumps off the cliff.

"Did she really jump?" Jake asks.

"Come on! The gunmen have vanished." I grab his hand and we race to the edge of the cliff. But as I peer over the edge, it looks like a thousand-foot drop, plunging into a sprawling city below.

"I'm thinking I'd prefer the gunfire," Jake says.

"No kidding." I glance behind me. If we don't jump in the next three seconds, we're going to fade. "Don't think. Just jump. We can't risk waiting."

"Right." Jake's voice shakes. He doesn't believe me.

Every muscle in my body screams at me to turn around.

"How about on three?" Jake suggests. "One—"

There isn't time to wait. I squeeze his hand tightly and leap off the cliff. Jake follows.

And I scream as I plunge through tendrils of clouds, heading straight for a line of skyscrapers. The world shifts and a dark hole yawns open directly below us. Lau sinks into the hole and slowly inch by inch the gap begins to close shut.

"We're going to miss it!" I scream.

I twist my body so I'm in a diving position, face first, arms reaching for the darkness. Jake mimics me and we plunge toward the sliver of black remaining.

The brightness of the day vanishes, and darkness consumes me. I made it through the transition. I reach out for Jake and find his solid form beside me. He clasps hold of my hand so we won't get lost.

Then the dream transforms and suddenly, we're standing on solid pavement in the center of a city. A mist coats the street, and it's filled with city-goers rushing about, intent on getting to their destination. The sounds of beeping and people yelling push through the silence.

"Where are we?" I wonder.

"I think we're still in Macau." Jake points ahead. "Look. There's the Casino Kam Pek Paradise."

He's right. At the end of the street, the flashing lights of the casino cut through the mist. People are running up the steps of the casino, holding wads of money and handing it to attendants before entering. I spin in a circle, searching the throngs for the president.

"She's gone," Jake says. "We lost her."

"No. She has to be somewhere close by for us to still be in the dream." I notice that the one end of the street where the casino rests hangs in a fuzzy haze as if it's on the verge of fading. Meanwhile, the other end is sharper and clearer.

"She's headed that way." I nod to the clear stretch to our right.

We take off in a sprint, weaving in and out of people, trying to keep up with Lau until we nearly catch up with her. I smash into one person, but they don't seem to notice me, instead they merely move forward, faces blurred. I hurdle a crate filled with vegetables and duck around a cart selling umbrellas with Jake right at my heels. Slowly, we are gaining on her, but it's not enough and I have to know the truth before she wakes up.

"Where is he?" I scream at her. "What did you do with my dad, Dr. Hale?"

"What?" Lau faces me, suddenly alarmed. "Your father is Dr. Hale?"

The dream skews into disarray. The sky presses down on me and the pavement at my feet buckles. I wobble, trying to remain upright. This is why it's risky to talk to the dreamers. Sometimes it can disrupt everything and even wake the dreamer.

Suddenly the ground at my feet drops away and with a

scream, I fall. My fingers scrape over the pavement until I catch the jagged edge of the sidewalk. My feet dangle over nothingness. She stamps her heel on my knuckles and I cry out in pain. Then she strides away, laughing hysterically. Meanwhile, Jake runs over to me and helps me crawl out.

"Are you okay?" he asks.

I don't bother responding but chase after Lau. Blasts of fire block our path, throwing us backward. I cover my hands over my face to ward off the intense heat. The area behind us is fading away and that's when I realize we're about to get kicked out of the dream.

"She's getting away," I say.

"Then we have to keep moving and catch up with her," Jake says. "The dream is fading."

"Which means we have to go through the fire." I breathe in deeply, trying to force my terror under my control. "It'll be okay. It's not real."

"Woah. You sure this is a good idea?"

"You have to believe it's not real," I explain, but it's more for myself than him. "Like what we did jumping off the cliff. You stay and fade. I'll see you when I wake up."

Then, pumping my arms, I sprint into the flames, ignoring the heat and the screaming sensation of burning as flames lick my skin.

After I stumble out on the other side of the fire, I glance down at myself. The burning sensation has vanished and even my clothes don't look charred. Jake emerges at my side, hunched over, panting.

"That was beyond weird," he says.

"I told you to stay behind," I lecture, worry tightening my chest.

But there isn't time to ponder all of this though because Lau is already striding into a restaurant. We rush after her, but the moment we step inside, everyone in the restaurant turns to stare at us. The clatter of silverware evaporates and the music that once was playing vanishes. The tables are lined with linen and candles are on top of them, flickering long shadows across the faces of the guests.

"Everyone is staring at us," Jake whispers. "It's super creepy."

"No kidding."

I stalk toward Lau who is sitting at one of the tables on a raised platform. As I grow closer, the tables around me vanish so it's just Lau and myself. Reigning my fury within so I can think and act sensibly, I sit at the table and clasp my hands before me. It won't do Dad any good for me to lose my cool at this stage.

"Tell me what you've done with my father," I say.

"I sold him." She lifts her chopsticks and takes a delicate bite of a wiggling octopus. "He's quite valuable, you know."

My heart sinks. "Sold him? Whatever for?"

"I heard you were quite smart," she says. "Apparently the rumors were wrong."

"Where is he?" I pound my fist on the table.

Nothing even moves or makes a sound. She takes another bite of food. "You two are rather annoying."

"What about the money?" Jake adds, coming to my side. "You need to return that. We've caught you. I entered your accounts and discovered an uncomfortable amount of funds deposited into them. If you don't wire the money back tonight, I'll leak out what you've done. Your casinos will be put out of business and you'll lose more than you could've gained."

Lau laughs. Beside me Jake falls to the ground, grabbing his stomach, his face wrenched in agony.

"What are you doing to him?" I leap to his side, holding his body to mine. "Stop this!"

Instantly Jake's body goes rigid as if he's frozen.

I snatch her plate of octopus away. "Tell me who you sold my father to," I demand.

"Never!" she screams.

But as her words echo around us, it's as if her thoughts betray her, and we're whisked away once again, this time we're standing inside an old warehouse. The hallway rises up around us appears to be forgotten, littered with garbage. The walls are pocked and painted with graffiti. An opening at the far end catches my attention. A wedge of white light spills into the hall as if beckoning me to look inside.

"Don't go in there." Lau suddenly blocks my path. "You will not like what's in that room."

I glance around. Jake isn't with me, I realize. I just hope he wakes up with a clear mind and with no headaches. Lau doesn't move. I know I won't get far without fading if she doesn't come with me, so I grab a hold of her and push her down the hall.

Tackling the dreamer or kidnapping them in their own dream would be an automatic disciplinary action at MaxLife. But we're not at MaxLife. We're in a thief and kidnapper's dream. I drag her down the hall. She claws and resists me. Her fist smashes into my cheek and the impact sends me flying backward and smashing into the wall. Searing pain wracks through me.

"It's not real," I tell myself. Pain trickles through my body, but I climb back to my feet.

Her eyes widen and she comes at me again. This time with some type of wild Kung Fu kick. Her foot smashes into my stomach and then another foot snaps across my face, whipping my neck sideways. My neck bone snaps and I crumble to the ground. There's a wetness dripping down my cheek. I wipe it off with the back of my hand.

My hand is smeared with blood. I frown. I'm bleeding. How is that possible? I've never bled in a dream before unless this is what Lau wants.

She backs away, a smug look on her face. I watch, useless, as she preps to kick me again. Gritting my teeth, I roll to the left and race toward the open doorway. But as I do, a line of guards holding massive machine guns form a barricade in front of me.

What is this? I've never experienced a dream where the dreamer was actively trying to kill me.

"Shoot her!" Lau screams from behind me.

Bullets blast across the small space between the door and me. Explosions of pain erupt all across my body as the bullets hit my chest, leg, arm, neck. Everywhere. My body is pushed back from the force of the bullets, and I fall to the ground.

"This is not real," I tell myself, aching and panting. "Because if it was, there's no way I'd still be alive."

I drag my battered body back to standing and begin hobbling down the hall. Deliberately, I block out the guards and their guns from my mind and focus on the door. I just need a peek inside to see if Dad is in there.

Bullets shoot past me. The walls erupt, sending plaster, wood, and concrete raining down on my body like snowflakes. Lau is screaming something in Mandarin.

I keep walking.

The moment my foot crosses the door's threshold, the world shifts once again. I'm in a laboratory. I recognize what looks like makeshift sleep pods, but these aren't as fancy as those we have at MaxLife, just a gurney with a hard shell to block out the light.

Every gurney has people sleeping on them, motionless. Unlike the simple heart monitors that we have, these people have all sorts of wires connected to them that snake about the room to one large computer.

I don't see Lau. Which is odd. She has to be nearby for me to still be in her dream. I'm so confused.

A man wearing a lab coat turns around from a computer monitor. His wild gray hair sticks out like he stuck his finger in a socket. It's when he picks up a tablet and begins making notes that I recognize him.

Dr. Reasner.

Dad's competitor. I had underestimated him back at the resort when I actually should have listened to all of those alerts that first went off in my head about Reasner. From the looks of things, he is trying to mimic Dad's work.

Then sitting in a chair beside Reasner is a girl with long red hair. She lifts her head and stares directly at me. My legs buckle because the girl is me, sitting there, handcuffed to the seat. I'm wearing a sensory cap just like the one Dad used to put on my head when I was twelve. Lights blink around the perimeter of the cap, which tells me this mad scientist is downloading my brain construction onto his computer.

"Run!" my chained self yells at me.

I'm so startled. So confused that my feet balk. Where do I go? What should I do?

"Where's Dad?" I ask.

"It's a trap!" myself says again.

The ground at my feet pixilates. The room vanishes piece by piece until darkness reigns.

When I blink my eyes open, the room before me swims. My head pounds like someone has smashed me with a brick. Every muscle in my body aches almost as if I really did get into a fight. I suppose I shouldn't be surprised. Entering the Dreamscape outside of our regulated sleeping pods back at MaxLife protected me from most side effects.

Still, I've never felt this awful before.

Groaning, I move to sit up, trying to regain my vision. Except my body won't seem to move, which sends me into a disorientated spin. I close my eyes again and breathe deeply to calm myself like we're taught to do.

"She's coming around," a voice I don't recognize says.

"Excellent." This voice is higher, excited.

The conversation forces me to open my eyes again. The room blurs, but I'm finally able to gather that I'm not in the holding room in the casino anymore. The walls are a mix of concrete and distressed wood. Three figures in white lab coats stand not far off from where I sit, observing me. Their faces are fuzzy.

A sinking sensation drops into the pit of my stomach. Either I never left the dream and I'm still lost in it, a likely probability, or I've been kidnapped and taken to the laboratory that I saw in the dream. My temples throb so hard, it's hard to even think clearly.

"Where," I pause. My voice is raspy and my lips are swollen. I lick my cracked lips. I must have bit down on it during my dream. That happened once to Tony. Maybe that's why I experienced myself bleeding in the dream. I clear my throat again and try to speak. "Where am I?"

"Good evening, Aria," the shorter one says. "We are so pleased you've come to join us. We believe you are the key to all of our issues and your arrival couldn't have been timelier."

I shake my head, trying to lift the fog out of my thoughts.

"Don't worry," the other man says who oddly looks a lot like Dad's new assistant, Dr. Cage. "The sleeping drugs we gave you should wear off soon. The headache and blurred vision will pass. Ever since I realized your dad wasn't able to help me as I thought he could, I've been sending my men out, searching for you."

"My dad," I croak, and my heartbeat kicks up. "Where is he?"

"Your father?" The shorter man steps closer.

With him so close, I recognize him instantly. Dr. Reasner. He's got shaggy gray hair that looks untamed, reminding me of a mangy dog that hasn't gotten a bath in some time. A beard grows from his chin, hanging wild and forgotten. Dark circles ring his eyes and wrinkles crease his face. A faded blue tie dangles from his neck, half-knotted and tucked beneath his white lab jacket.

The emblem on the jacket catches my attention. Memory Retract Corporation. What could that be? Does he have his own Dreamscape that's similar to Dad's?

No, that's not it, I realize as everything becomes crystal clear. "You're trying to steal my dad's work, aren't you?" I confront him. "Because you're not smart enough to think of your own ideas, you have to steal someone else's."

Then I turn to Dr. Cage. "And you were my dad's new assistant. You totally betrayed him. You betrayed us all."

Dr. Cage beams as if I've just paid him the best compliment.

"You're as smart as I remembered you being," Dr. Reasner says. "I've been working on the human brain and memory recall for some time now. I like to think of your father and me as pioneers in the race to cure mental illness and memory loss."

My vision has now fully repaired itself. This is the exact room as the one in the dream. It looks like we're in a large warehouse. My eyes peer around Dr. Reasner for any evidence of my dad.

"But your father failed to see the true potential of our research," Dr. Reasner continues. "Why stop at bridging memory gaps when we could explore so much more? Why simply heal a damaged mind when we can improve the brain? Here we have within our grasp the opportunity to expand the potentials that the brain can accomplish. The potential is monumental and for everyone, not relegated to merely the old and weak."

I twist my hands, testing the handcuffs, and inwardly curse. This guy is either delusional or completely driven by fame and money. Either way, I need to get out of here ASAP.

Reasner continues, "My trusted assistant, Dr. Cage, got a job at MaxLife. Meanwhile, we gave Jake Hale pills to think he had severe headaches. Then we conned one of his friends to dare Jake to get the SWIFT codes. Of course, he accepted the dare as we guessed he would be able to see and access the codes."

"It's interesting that you have to bribe and cheat to get results," I note.

"It was a gamble on our part, but it paid off. Once he saw the codes, we orchestrated for you and your team to snoop into Jake Hale's brain until you found the SWIFT codes for us. So maybe I should be thanking you for all of your hard work in making this happen."

I spit at Dr. Reasner, but he doesn't seem to notice. Instead, he begins to pace the room, clearly enamored by himself.

"Did you ever realize, Aria that there's the possibility to use the confidences of the mind to reveal government secrets and plotting schemes," he asks. "Consider how in one mind travel, we can abolish interrogations permanently. No more torture or conjectures. Instead, we can merely gain entrance into an enemy's brain, determine their secrets, and BOOM! We win."

"You're sick." I grip the edges of the armrest so hard my knuckles whiten. "What you suggest is against everything MaxLife stands for."

"Ingenious. Revolutionary." He chuckles to himself. "The great master scientists of their time were often ridiculed for their brilliant, and yet, peculiar ideas. Take Galileo or Gregor Johann Mendel, for instance. Totally unappreciated and misunderstood during their time, but are now hailed as masters of science."

"My father told me you were ambitious," I say, "but you didn't have the conscience to accomplish your crazy philosophies. He was completely right."

"Your father is a great man," Dr. Reasner says. "But he lacks vision and ambition to make him truly great. He was too obsessed with healing his mother that he couldn't see the potential his work had. Still doesn't."

"Don't you dare speak about my grams!" I push against my restraints, and that's when I realize my feet are shackled into clamps as well. "Why have you bound me? Why am I here?"

"It was fortunate that Zhang Lau and I crossed paths

not long ago at a conference." Dr. Reasner taps his fingers together, creating a tent with them. "She wanted money. I wanted your father. It was the perfect plan. And as you can see, it worked. Until you and your friends got involved, but then I'm a believer in Fate. And Fate has brought you to me."

I search the still bodies on the gurneys, trying to figure out if any of those people are my friends. A pair of loafers catches my eye at the end of the line. Did Jake wear loafers? I can't remember. I wish I'd paid more attention.

"Well, your plan failed," I say. "Because the American government is on our side. Now that I've gone missing, they'll be here in no time."

"I doubt that." Dr. Reasner points to a van parked at the other end of the warehouse. "As you can see, we're a movable lab. We travel anywhere we want. By the time your government gets through all of their red tape to believe a girl has been kidnapped at a casino—crazy story, by the way—all evidence of your existence will have vanished. We snatched you and your boyfriend at the casino. Your other friends have no idea where you are now."

My heart soars realizing Sun must have somehow gotten away. Plus, he doesn't know about Javier and Tony. The Dreamscape would have shown my friends a visual of this warehouse. But who would ever be able to pick out or recognize this place?

The odds are extremely thin. My stomach twists and I

feel like I could throw up. Dr. Reasner is right. He outsmarted us.

"But why bother bringing us here?" I ask.

"You, my dear," Dr. Reasner says, "are the key that I was missing all along. It wasn't until three days ago I figured it out. When I heard my men had practically blown you up in the van when they were just supposed to kidnap you, I nearly lost my mind. You have no idea the relief I felt when I received the report you were unharmed and on your way to Boracay."

"How thoughtful of you," I say sarcastically.

"Bring out her father," Reasner commands. "It's time to make history!"

Two large security guards wearing all black who probably served as bouncers in their previous lives escort a man out of a room at the far end.

"Dad!" I scream. I can't stop the tears that spring to my eyes at seeing him.

His graying brown hair is disheveled, and his dirt-smudged clothes hang from his body. I cringe seeing how much weight he's lost. His right eye, rimmed with a dark blue bruise, is squeezed shut. My heart tightens, and it's hard to breathe. But a small voice inside me reminds me that he's alive.

"Hello, Dr. Hale," Dr. Reasner says cheerily. "I hope you are feeling more cooperative this evening than in previous days."

Dad's one good eye falls on me. I expect to see joy and

hope on his face, but instead, his eyes and mouth widen in horror. The guards shove him into a chair beside the computer that Dr. Reasner is typing into, and then they clamp his hands and feet into place like they did with me.

"Aria," Dad says. "Are you okay? Did they hurt you?"

"I'm fine. I've been looking for you. I wasn't going to stop until I found you."

"You should've left this to the federal agents. These people are too dangerous."

I'm hurt by those words. Sure, he may be right. Okay, so he *is* right. But in my mind, I imagined this incredible reunion where I had rescued him and he threw his arms around me in a fierce embrace, thanking me.

"Whatever happens with this lunatic," Dad says, interrupting my thoughts. "I'm proud of you. Leave it to you to find me when the feds couldn't."

I want to tell him everything. How the police wouldn't believe me. How we chased him down through the hints the dreams gave us. But that would just give Dr. Lunatic more horrible ideas of how to use the Dreamscape, so I clamp my mouth shut.

"What a lovely family reunion!" Dr. Reasner says. "So Aria, let me give you an update on what's been happening. Your father kindly gave me the schematics for the Dreamscape he created. Brilliant stuff, really. But the bizarre thing is that every time a team enters a dream, they get kicked out. Or die." He sighs at that. "Those were unfortunate causalities."

"Are you serious?" I'm aghast. "You let people die in the Dreamscape?"

"He didn't have the right connections between his Dreamscape and his Dream Walkers," Dad explains wearily. "I couldn't stand watching so many scientists go in only to die so I gave him the missing coding. Plus, he threatened to kill you and your mom."

"And I was very grateful for his shared information," Dr. Reasner adds. "Thanks to your father we have the Dreamscape. I thought all of my troubles were solved. But I was the fool, trusting your father to be of true assistance. We couldn't keep our Dream Walkers in the dreams. They kept getting kicked out, staying within the dreams for only seconds at most."

My heart sinks and I lean backward. He's having the same problem we had. So that's why they kidnapped me rather than killed me. Ever since I started entering the Dreamscapes, we began making progress, and no one got kicked out of the dreams.

And that's when the pieces of a puzzle that I never knew existed snapped into place. My head swivels and I stare at Dad as the truth unfolds before me. Why hadn't I seen it before?

All those times when Dad and I worked together to create the Dreamscape fly through my mind. It was *my* mind that he used as a prototype. It was *my* mind that he studied and downloaded the data from. Without me, no one could enter the Dreamscape for longer than a few minutes because the entire program had been built around my brain. He had made adjustments in the team's sleep pods to help, but those had been short-term fixes.

Dad's eyes are so sad. He closes them and hangs his head.

"I'm sorry, Aria," Dad says. "I never thought my vision of helping people with memory loss would lead you here. I never wanted this for you."

"No." I shake my head. "Don't be. I wanted to help Grams just as much as you did. I wanted the Dreamscape to work, too. This is just as much about my goals as yours."

"Yes," Dr. Reasner says and with a touch of a button pulls up a halo-vision of a brain. It rotates through the air before us. "Apparently your father used your brain as the prototype. He developed his entire work and Dreamscape around it."

My mind flashes back to when I wore the headset as I ran through the backyard when I ate my favorite ice cream —chocolate marshmallow—and even when I opened my birthday presents. The Dreamscape had been my invention, too, in a way. It had been my idea to wear the headset when I slept and when Grams and I'd sit on those late nights to watch her favorite movie, *A Kiss Before Midnight*. I suppose on some subconscious level, I've always known the Dreamscape and I were connected. But seeing it before me, hearing Dad admit it and Dr. Reasner explain it, overwhelms me.

"You, Aria," Dr. Reasner says, "are the alpha and the

key to the Dreamscape. No one can control it like you can."

My gaze pivots to Dad. It's not that I don't believe Reasner, I just need to hear it from him. "Is that true, Dad?"

"I never meant for that to happen," Dad explains wearily. "But when you first went into the Dreamscape and it worked—it finally worked!—I suspected it. Over the past two months, I've been testing my theory and reached the conclusion that yes, you can control the dreams. That's why you've been able to manipulate the Dreamers so well."

"Which means until I can fix this system glitch of you having to be in the Dreamscape for it to work," Dr. Reasner explains. "You get to work for me now."

I glare at him. "You kidnap my father and me and want us to help you?"

"Trust me." Reasner's lips curl into something that resembles a smile. "This is not an ideal situation for me either. But it is a necessary means to an end. Plus, I have my ways of enticement."

At the snap of Reasner's fingers, the security guards press a key against my chair and the locks on my wrists and ankles pop open. I pull my arms away and start massaging my aching muscles when they heft me up and drag me across the room to a gurney. My heart sinks. He's going to make me go into the dream.

"Dad!" He's always been there for me, stood up for

me, but I know my words are futile. There is nothing my father can do for me now. I'm on my own.

"Don't do this, Reasner!" Dad grips the edges of his chair, straining at his constraints until his veins are bulging. "She's just a kid. There has to be a better way."

"I have to make sure my theory on her being the alpha is true," Dr. Reasner says. "This won't take long and then we'll know for sure."

As they strap me onto the gurney, Dr. Reasner comes to my side. Sweat trickles down the sides of his face and his eyes are bright as if light by an inner fire. How different he appears from the lethargic photo in the conference flyer.

"Now listen carefully," he tells me eagerly. "This is your task. Go into the dream and have your hacker boyfriend show you how he's able to hack into the Federal Reserve site. Once he has the codes, you'll prove to me you are being helpful."

My boyfriend? Then it hits me. Jake! My eyes dart over to the gurney with the loafers. That has to be him. Guilt tugs at me. When he's dreaming, he won't even know it's not real. My mind flies, trying desperately to find a way out of this.

"I'm sure the feds have amped up their firewalls after everything that happened," I say. "He won't know anything that can help you."

"Are you saying he's useless?" Dr. Reasner points to Jake. "I don't keep anything useless around. It just creates clutter. And then there's your father. I'll even consider releasing him if you cooperate."

*Crap.* It's like walking through a minefield. One misstep and you're dead.

"Maybe not," I hedge. "I might be able to get him to show me something useful. But before I do anything, I want you to give my dad an ice pack for his eye and some food."

"Ah, a negotiator. Impressive." He nods to one of the assistants who runs off to do his bidding. "There. Happy now?"

"Happy? Oh, I'm just full of laughs today."

Then an attendant slips a dream mask over my eyes. This one isn't as silky or comfortable as ours at MaxLife, which gives me pause because I know that one miscalculation in the Dreamscape, one malfunctioning wire can really screw with your brain. I dig my nails into my palm, trying to not think of the ramifications of what I'm about to do. My only hope is that Dr. Looney has done his homework and we all don't die.

The music that streams in through my ears isn't as relaxing as anything we have in our system at MaxLife. I think of Sun and the others. Do they know where we are? Are they looking for us right now? Maybe if I can fight these sounds, I can stay awake.

But my mind begins to drift, and I sink into the world of dreams.

## FORTY-SEVEN
## DREAM OR REALITY?

The darkness shifts around me as mist tendrils weave around my legs, sending chills across my body. I shiver, rubbing my bare arms as I squint into the murky light. My feet are bare as well and rocks and roots dig into my soles as I creep forward. Trees stretch out, gnarled and twisted as if blocking my path, and vines tangle around my hair. This strange forest feels alive.

Panic seizes me and I break into a run, trying to avoid the sharp rocks that cut into the soles of my feet.

And then I stop.

*Wait. This isn't real, is it?* It feels like a dream.

And if I'm in the dream, then the dreamer can't be far. Priority number one in the mission is the dreamer.

But who was the dreamer again? It's there, on the tip of my mind as if I should know this. A low rumble fills the forest along with the shifting of branches being pushed aside. I freeze, listening as my heart kicks up into a gallop. Which direction had that come from?

"This is not real," I whisper to myself. But the damp air smells of decay and rot. The shifting shadows and the hollowness in the pit of my stomach make it hard to convince myself otherwise.

Slowly, I continue trekking through the strange forest, creeping on the balls of my feet. Just ahead a growl rumbles like distant thunder and I freeze. The ground before me shimmers and then a massive dark form rises up out of the mist. It unravels, stretching out a long neck and a head that's a mix of a dinosaur and snake. Slanted green snake-like eyes stare unblinking at me. I stumble backward.

"This is a dream," I say out loud. But why does it feel so real?

The creature opens a massive mouth, wider than a lion's, revealing jagged razor teeth. It releases a loud screech that causes my own teeth to shake.

I run.

Over fallen branches, staggering through the brush, ripping my body free of the vines snaking around my core, desperate to wrap around me and choke me to death.

"Hey!" a deep voice calls.

I crash into the arms of a man. Jake! I throw my arms around him.

"You're safe." I cling to him. "You're here. But why are you out in this forest?"

I'm so confused, but there isn't time to process my thoughts. The trees behind us shift and there's that deep growling sound again.

"It's the Receptor," Jake says grimly. "We need to go."

"Receptor? What is that?"

But I'm not sticking around to chat about it, so I don't argue with him as he grabs my hand, and we take off running again until we reach an open clearing where a horse is tied up to a post.

"You ride horses?" I rub my forehead in confusion.

"Sure do." Jake mounts the horse and holds his hand out to help me up. "At least, in this land I do. This is the realm that I created for my game, Battle for Eternity. What do you think?"

I allow him to pull me up onto the horse just as that horrible beast barrels out of the forest, green eyes piercing the darkness, and a thick, sludge-like black slime pours out of its mouth.

"Gross. Next time you brainstorm ideas, I want to be involved." I wrap my arms around his waist and press my cheek to his back. "This place isn't exactly vacationing at Bora Bora."

The horse leaps forward and we break into a full gallop. Wind gushes over us and we ride fast and hard. I glance over my shoulder, sure the beast wouldn't be able to keep up.

I was wrong.

"It's gaining on us!" I yell.

"Hold on tight and don't let him touch you. His claws hold poison within them."

"How reassuring."

The Receptor eats up the distance between us at a harrowing speed. As Jake veers the horse into another forest, I clutch my arms tighter around Jake's torso, but there's no way to stop the beast's speed. The rotting scent engulfs me, sending my stomach into contortions and making me want to throw up. Then its obsidian claws swipe through the air and scrape across my back.

Searing pain wracks through my body and rivers of fire courses across my skin. I cry out and nearly lose my hold on Jake.

"Aria!" Jake reaches for me and secures me tighter against him. "What happened?"

"Claws... ripped... my back."

Jake doesn't respond, but it seems as if the horse runs faster.

Warm liquid—blood—seeps against my shirt and drips down my back, pooling onto the horse where I'm sitting. *Poison*, Jake had said. Does that mean I'm going to die? I lean my head against his back and close my eyes.

*Wait. This isn't real. This is just a dream.* How could I have forgotten that?

I lift my head, telling my mind the pain doesn't exist,

and yet, the pain remains, burning and smoldering my skin. There was another dream I bled in...

My mind clears and suddenly I start remembering things outside of Jake's world. I had bled when Lau hit me in her dream. When I woke up, I had actually been bleeding in real life, probably from biting my lip.

Could I really be bleeding in real life? I recall how Dad said Reasner had gone through so many bodies. Had Dr. Reasner not sequenced the Dreamscape properly? Or is Dr. Reasner's Dreamscape more sinister? Maybe it replicates reality so well that it tricks all the Dream Walker's brains that we are living a reality?

I squeeze Jake tighter for reassurance.

The boughs of the oaks pull back, opening up a narrow path for us as if it knows he is the creator. Soon our horse storms out of the forest where shafts of sunlight poke through thick clouds, lighting the plain stretching out before us. We cross the wide expanse filled with yellow flowers that swipe at my legs as we ride. Jagged snow-capped mountains rise up in the distance and I remember where I've seen these images before. They were hanging on the walls of his pool house back in Florida.

Suddenly, an icy chill wracks through my body and I draw myself even closer to Jake. "I think the poison really works. I'm not feeling good."

"I'm going to get you the cure. Hang in there." Except his voice doesn't hold its usual confidence.

The ground shifts below us, rumbling. The earth

crumples below the horse's hooves and a massive fissure opens up in the ground, growing into a larger crack.

"Watch out!" I warn.

But the horse races blindly into the crack and we fall. My grip on Jake loosens and I scream, flailing my arms about, trying to hold onto Jake or the horse, something, only to plummet into the deep darkness below us.

FORTY-EIGHT
SURVIVAL

I grit my teeth against the pain, telling myself it's not real, and focus on following Jake through the black hole. Before I realize it, my feet are sinking into soft sand. The air is full of brine and the sound of waves crashing overwhelms my senses. I blink hard, trying to adjust my vision. Soon a purple-hued sunset fingers across the horizon. I'm at a beach and the view is literally breathtaking.

I sink to my knees, expecting the pain from the Receptor's marks to still be raging through me, but the pain has vanished as if it never existed. The fall or the transition must have refocused my brain from the supposed poison to the danger of falling.

But where is Jake?

I rise back up and spin until I spy him sitting on a lounge, typing frantically on his computer. This place looks familiar. It's an unsettling feeling since I've never actually been to the same place as one of our dreamers. The memories rush back to me. It's the Surfside Resort and Spa.

Except I'm here to save my dad, I remind myself. And I'm supposed to get Jake to do something. Or maybe that's not it at all. I ball my hands into fists, frustrated with my inability to think clearly in this Dreamscape.

"Jake." I hurry to him.

"Hey, you." His computer vanishes and he holds out his hands.

"No healing ointment for me?" I tease.

He frowns, clearly confused, which tells me that his brain has already forgotten the last dream segment. The overwhelming urge to be near him overcomes me. I sink into his lap, straddling him on the lounge. His arms wrap around me and I feel so safe, the worries of the world forgotten. Our lips meet and he kisses me deeply. My hands comb through his hair while he runs his palms over my body, giving me goosebumps.

"I don't ever want to leave," I whisper into his ear.

"I could stay here forever."

This drags me back to reality and I slide off him remembering Carol who got lost in a dream and how we were worried her mind would never leave the dream. I blink, desperately trying to focus on why I was here again.

My dad.

Jake and my friends.

Captured. It was Dr. Reasner who sent me into this dream to see if Jake was worth keeping around. I have to get Dr. Reasner the codes to prove we're all worth keeping.

"What is it?" Jake asks.

Lightly, I caress the side of Jake's face. How much can I tell him without throwing him out of the dream? Except Reasner's Dreamscape replicates reality so well that even I keep finding it hard to even believe this is a dream and not reality.

"Dr. Reasner wants you to give him a code that will get him into the Federal Reserve's system."

Jake frowns, clearly not happy with this. "And you want me to give him this?" He shifts, studying me. "Are you one of his spies?"

"No! He needs the codes so he can see how useful you are. If you're not useful, he'll kill you. We have to prove to him that we aren't dispensable."

"He's crazy, you know. Like certifiable. I know this sounds weird, but I don't know if I can trust you. Or even myself. Wait a second." He looks around, sitting up. "Is this a dream?"

The breeze kicks up into a heavy wind and the waves grow larger, crashing against the surf and spraying us. This isn't good. I need to keep Jake in this Dreamscape.

"Yes." I tense and my brain flies, trying to solve this. "This is the Dreamscape like the ones we've entered before. Dr. Reasner sent us both here and even now he can see what we see through the video feed. His crew might even have someone that can lip read."

"That's reassuring."

"They have captured us and my dad, too. Somehow we've got to figure out a way to give him what he wants and still stay alive."

He frowns, rubbing the side of his face, thinking. "Okay. But how?"

"I know this seems weird, but this Dreamscape feels too real to me. Almost like you can't ever escape."

"Which means the coding for this Dreamscape is slightly different."

"Exactly," I note. "And also, there haven't been opportunities for fading, and look at how long we are sitting here and chatting. It's like it's real."

"Perhaps they've created a simulation that adds to the boundaries the Dreamer has imagined. These technicians on the outside could then control when Dream Walkers leave or don't leave, which means no fading for you."

"And that a person could experience death and believe it. Theoretically, if a mind believes it's dying, it will die."

"That's morbid," he says.

"Reasner has created something very wrong here. It's no wonder he's having a hard time finding Dream Walkers. He keeps killing them because he won't allow them to fade."

"He's probably testing the coding."

"Or how strong the human brain can be." I stare out at the ocean and an idea forms in my mind. "I have a plan."

"Uh-oh." He lifts his eyebrows skeptically.

"It's a wild, dangerous, and probably very bad idea. But it's something."

I take his hand, and holding his palm close to my chest, I finger-write my message. This way the people watching the Dreamscape won't be able to figure out what I'm saying to him by lip-reading or listening to me.

"Yeah," he says. "That could work. It should work if I can prep it correctly."

Movement from the corner of my vision shifts my focus away from Jake. Three figures dressed in white button-down shirts and white shorts, wearing dark shades stride down the beach, heading directly to us. There's something odd about the way they walk, the way their hair is perfectly slicked back, and their undivided focus on Jake and me.

"Those are Dream Walkers." I rise to my feet.

"You sure? Because they look very official."

I take Jake's hand and pull him toward me. "Don't you see it? They look too clear. Their images aren't as blurred around the edges like they would be in a real dream. I think...Reasner didn't like my writing trick."

Instead of running away, Jake steps toward the strangers, hands in his pockets, relaxed. "Hey. Can I—"

But the man in the center interrupts Jake and looks at

me, saying, "Dr. Reasner says he's not happy with your actions."

"I'm trying to get Reasner his codes," I explain.

The man doesn't even hesitate. He withdrawals a gun, aims it at me, and before I can even think, he shoots.

## FORTY-NINE
## SHOT

My body buckles backward as pain explodes in my stomach. The figures before me blur as my knees collapse from under me. I fall into the soft sand as I reach for the wound, trying to hold back the pain.

"Aria!" Jake screams, falling to my side. His arms wrap around me. "We need to get you out of here. Can you fade? You need to fade."

My hands are covered in blood. It gushes out of my stomach, oozing down to soak my cut-off jeans. This is just a dream, I tell myself over and over. And yet the blood continues, and the pain is unbearable.

"What's going on?" I choke out the words, horrified. "This isn't supposed to happen."

"Dr. Reasner wanted me to pass on the message that you've been shot in reality and now you are dreaming of it." The guy lowers his gun and focuses on Jake. "She will bleed to death unless you give us the codes."

"You'll get your damn codes." Jake grits his teeth and helps me to my feet.

My breathing comes out in gasps. I blink, pushing the thoughts of the blood and pain away. A black Audi R-8 car appears beside us on the beach. Jake throws open a door and practically shoves me inside. The moment the door slams shut, the men reach out for Jake, but he slips through their hands like liquid and appears in the driver's seat.

"This is still my dream," he reminds them.

The engine revs and the tires kick up plumes of sand. The men's clothing switch to sleek black jumpsuits just as we take off down the beach at a hair-raising speed. I glance out the back window. Our pursuers are riding motorcycles, chasing us down.

"Holy crap," I say.

"Does this happen often in dreams?" Jake grips the steering wheel like he's about to rip it out. "Dream Walkers coming into a person's dreams and killing people."

"Never," I say. "Reasner's Dreamscape has somehow morphed Dad's system into something completely different."

I lean my head against the headrest, trying to figure out how Reasner's Dreamscape must work. A glance at my stomach tells me the bleeding has slowed. What does that mean? I don't even know.

"Do you think they really shot me in real life?" I ask. "Actually, don't answer that. It's too much to deal with. Right now, we need to focus on surviving and finding a way to destroy Dr. Reasner."

"We'll find a way." Jake's lips press together, and he grips the steering wheel so tightly, his knuckles whiten.

"Go there." I point to a gaping black hole ahead of us. "Either it will take us to a different dream segment, or we'll fade. Regardless, it will be harder for the suits to chase us."

Jake guns the accelerator and we careen into its abyss.

The car flies airborne. The feeling of weightlessness flips my stomach. The sensations in this Dreamscape mimic reality perfectly and that terrifies me. If I hadn't been a trained Dream Walker, I'd believe this place was real.

The car bounces onto a winding mountain road. My neck whips sideways and then my body slams forward from the impact. I scream in pain as the seat belt presses against my gunshot wound. The car shudders but Jake grips the clutch tight and slams on the gas.

In this part of the dream, the sky holds a husky blue, clouds scudding above as if racing from a storm. Jake speeds around sharp bends and corners while I clutch the door handle with one hand and my stomach with the other.

"We're almost there," Jake says.

I'm too weak and overwhelmed to bother asking where

*there* is. Except the road dead-ends at the rock cliff of a mountain.

"It's a dead-end," I say.

Grimly, Jake eyes his rear-view mirror.

"What is it?" I follow Jake's gaze.

As if emerging through nothingness, the motorcycle gang slices out of thin air and lands on the road behind us, trailing us in full-speed pursuit. "They didn't transition with us so they must have been kicked out and sent back in. That's a fast reentry. Those riders can't be feeling great right now."

When I turn back around, I realize Jake hasn't slowed down. He's racing toward the rock wall at an alarming speed.

"You're going to crash," I yell. "You've got to slow down. We can't leave this dream without the codes."

He grins over at me. "I've got this one covered."

"Jake! Slow down!"

I grip the sides of my seat, screaming. Seconds before we slam into the rockface, it splits down the center like elevator doors, and we race through the opening. Then the rock doors slide closed behind us with a boom, the sound ricocheting through the massive rock tunnel we're now zooming through.

Jake cheers like he just hit the next level in a video game. "Take that suckers!" he yells.

"That was not funny." I glare at him. "You nearly gave me a heart attack. Wait a sec. What is this? The Bat

Cave?" I grin through my pain. "Admit it. You dream about being Batman."

His lips curve up into a smile. "Don't tell anyone."

The car zooms to the end of the tunnel where Jake parks. Once the engine is off, the doors pop open, and I ease out. Blackness washes over my vision forcing me to lean against the side of the car. I look down. Still bleeding.

Jake rushes to me with a first aid kit. He wraps a bandage around my body and offers me a pill.

"That's going to help?" I chuckle, but I swallow the pill anyway. "I'm going to imagine that you've given me a special healing drug that gives me unlimited powers."

"Let me carry you," Jake offers and lifts me into his arms.

I don't resist, allowing myself to sink against his chest as he steps inside an elevator. Surprisingly, the elevator hurtles down into what feels like the deep recesses of the earth.

"Where are we going?" I ask.

"You've been here before," he says as the doors swoosh open. "It will take a while for the Dream Walkers to find us and then get in. My security traps should keep them busy for now."

I wonder if he's forgotten that this is a dream again, but I decide it might be better to not say anything.

The world before us lies in darkness and above spans an emerald-riddled sky. Or at least I think they are stars until Jake sets me down.

"Computer codes," I realize when I spot the boxes with green numbers floating in them. "The last time I was here was when you dreamed about the SWIFT codes."

I slip my hand into his and look into his face, glowing emerald in the code light.

"Did you develop all of these codes?" At his nod, I say, "It's amazing."

"There's one I want to show you." His face twists in pain. "It's a risk though."

My throat tightens because I think I know what he means to do. I don't speak, afraid of my words, so I simply nod. We wind our way around the maze of boxes until we reach one code that rises up like a spiral. Unlike the others that are green, this one burns fiery red. Its numbers stream up like flames eager to consume and destroy.

*A virus.* "Is that the one you started working on in Bangladesh?"

"I figured it's always best to be prepared. When I realized the Dreamscape wasn't totally secure, and my computer was stolen, I knew MaxLife needed to have it is own security measures set in place. So I created a dormant virus that could be activated by imputing the numbers."

"Will it work?"

"Remember when I told you that the virus would have to be inserted into the program?" he asks. I nod. "Except, for this virus to work, it would have to be the alpha that made it happen."

"What are you saying?"

"You would have to be in the program," he says. "Your mind acts like a key. Since you're connected to the server, you could release it."

"Would we survive?"

"Probably." He grimaces. "Maybe. I don't know what kind of brain damage it could incur or how it may affect your memories."

"It could affect you as well, couldn't it?"

He swallows and nods. "Reasner isn't going to let me walk free. I'm a dead man, regardless. Might as well go out fighting. But you don't have to do this unless you want to."

My skin has grown cold, so cold as if I've lost too much blood. It's becoming hard to think properly.

"This code was developed because of me. Because Dad and I wanted to help others," I say. "But if Dr. Reasner uses it for what he intends, it could hurt many people. I can't live with that. These past few days have shown me what can be done in people's dreams and it's terrifying. Knowing something I helped create could in fact destroy or be wielded as a weapon is not what I signed up for."

A buzzing sound fills the air.

"What's that?" Jake asks.

"They're trying to wake us up." I grip Jake's hands. "Focus on me. We're going to stay in this dream and unleash the virus. We're going to stop this madness. Together."

A cracking sound above pulls our attention upward.

The ceiling splinters, and then it's as if the sky shatters. Glass showers over us, and ropes drop to the ground, followed by people slithering down them to the floor. Suddenly, we're surrounded, their guns pointed at Jake and me.

"Jake!" I say. "Imagine some kind of barriers for us."

But my words are futile.

Bullets fly. One hits my leg and another slams into my arm. I cry out, spinning around, trying to figure out what to do. Back in Florida we never had people shooting at us. No one trained me for this. Beside me, Jake drops to his knees. I grab his hand, trying to pull him back to his feet.

"We have to do this!" Terror races through me. "Now."

Groaning, he shakes his head, blood pooling all around him. My whole body trembles in shock. This isn't happening. This can't be happening.

"It's a dream!" I scream at him, gripping his hands as tightly as possible. "You have to tell your mind that it's only a dream."

"Take the code in your hands," he whispers. "And read it out as the numbers pass by you."

The men advance on us, one step at a time. There's fear and wariness in their eyes as if they guess my intentions.

I study the spiral. "Five-four-two-eight," I read out.

"Stop!" one of the men says. I turn to face him and recognize that wild hair and scruffy beard anywhere. Dr. Reasner. If he entered the dream, he must be scared or desperate. Or both. "Don't say another word or read another number. Otherwise, we will kill your father."

The ground Jake and I are standing on begins to rise. It's like we're riding a platform now. I look down at Jake lying on the ground. His jaw is slack, and his eyes are vacant from concentration. He's causing the platform to rise, taking us out of harm's way, but it's too much for him. He's holding his hand over his chest, any second now he'll collapse.

"You need to focus on staying alive," I tell him.

"This is my dream, and I can do what I want to." He growls but clamps his eyes shut.

The men start shooting again. One of them manages to leap on top of the platform. He tackles me, throwing me onto the floor. The number sequence slips out of my hand.

"No!" I cry. "What was that number sequence?"

"Five-nine-one," Jake says, grunting.

"Five-nine—." I roll onto my butt and slam both feet against the man's back, sending him overboard. His screams fill my ears and I dare a peek below. "One."

Below all the codes in the cavern spiral up out of their boxes and switch to a bright, blinding crimson. The men below cover their faces and cry out.

"Keep reading off the code!" Jake says. "We need to execute the virus immediately."

My hands tremble and my knees weaken. I've suffered too many bullets to even be standing, but the one in my stomach is worse than ever. I've lost so much blood. The floor is slick with it.

It takes every ounce of my willpower to stand back up and pick the code back up. The numbers stream out of my palms as I read them like crimson ribbons. They flood the room, touching everything in its fiery glow.

"It's working," Jake encourages.

The codes liquefy and drip to the floor, forming a sea of lava. It bubbles up and then rises, easing up the walls and melting them. Fissures break apart the rock walls and the world crumbles around us. Red numbers rain over us like fiery snow. And even through it all, our platform continues to rise until we break free of the shattered ceiling into the air.

As I read off the last of the numbers, the floor of the pedestal falls away so it's just Jake holding me and we're floating in the center of the madness. As I say the final number, I wrap my arms around him, staring into his eyes.

"It's done," he says. "The virus has infected the system."

"This may be just a dream," I say. "But whatever happens next, I want you to know everything that we've done together and every feeling I've felt has been real."

His arms wrap around me tighter as flaming codes swirl around us.

But all I feel, and all I know, are his lips on mine. The realness of him and his love consumes my core.

# FIFTY

# A LOST MIND

I blink my eyes, but I can't see anything. I can't move. Am I alive? Dead? A new thought erupts through the others. Perhaps I've lost my mind, or worse, my mind is lost in the destroyed Reasner's Dreamscape forever.

Panic floods my body and I scream.

That's when I feel something. Hands? The pressure on my wrists loosens, and suddenly I feel my hands drop. The darkness vanishes, replaced by blinding light.

"Aria!" That voice belongs to Sun. As my vision solidifies, I see her face is wet, I think she's crying, and a bandage is wrapped around her head. "I'm so sorry. At the casino, I tried to stop them. Tell me you can hear me. Tell me you're okay."

"I'm okay." My words are thick as sludge.

"She's okay!" Sun announces.

"Jake—" My heart pounds as I remember the two of us

surrounded in fiery code. I push myself to sit and the room swims before my eyes. "I have to make sure he's okay."

"Javier is with him," she says. "But he hasn't responded yet."

"No." A sob escapes me. I push myself off the gurney, only to collapse to the ground. "What's wrong with me?"

"It's the Dreamscape." She rushes to my side and holds my arms. "Reasner's coding tricked your mind into thinking what has happened to you in the dream is real. Your mind still thinks you got shot. How does your stomach feel?"

"They didn't shoot me?" Numbly, I touch my stomach and expect to see blood oozing out of a gaping wound. But there's none. I blink a few times, willing my mind to believe my eyes. "It still hurts. What about Jake? Is he okay?"

She nods sympathetically. "Your dad is trying to see if he's still caught in the Dreamscape."

It's then I focus my attention on what's happening in the room. Dream Walkers are still lying on their gurneys, unresponsive. Javier stands over Jake's body while Dad is at the computer, typing away furiously while Tony is tying up Dr. Reasner who's also hooked up to the Dreamscape. Guards are lying on the ground, passed out and tied up.

"What happened?" I ask. "How did you find us?"

"I have a confession," Sun says. "Don't be mad. The outfit I gave you had a tracker sewn inside the hem of your skirt. That's the real reason why it took me so long to shop."

She says shop while making quotes in the air. "Back at the casino when you were in Lau's dream, Reasner arrived and had his men take you and Jake. They hit me over the head and left me to take the fall for everything. Thankfully, Danny got me out before the police arrived."

"I'm so glad you're okay."

"We followed your tracker here and then used the Sound Oasis to put this whole crew to sleep. Then we injected them with Temazepam for good measure, tied them up, and woke you up."

"Jake used his mind to get me to enter a virus into the Dreamscape," I explain." Did it work?"

"You did great, baby girl."

I turn around to face Dad at my side. He looks horrible, but he's alive. I start crying, and he wraps his arms around me and also starts crying.

"Reasner's Dreamscape has been destroyed," he says. "You're lucky your mind wasn't damaged with it. But I'm worried about Jake."

"Take me to him," I say.

With his help, I stagger over to Jake and sag onto the gurney beside him. He's so still and too pale.

"Is he alive?" My voice trembles.

Javier points to the brain and heart monitor Jake's attached to. "Seems as if he is. Either he's in deep shock or his brain just hasn't found its way home yet."

"When you went missing at MaxLife, I was so scared I'd never see you again." I cling to Dad. "Then in Jake's dream, Reasner's men told me they were going to shoot you."

"Aria," Dad says. "I'm so sorry. For all of this. You like this boy, don't you?"

Tears spring back to my eyes as I nod. "We have to find a way to get him back."

"We will," Dad says. "We will."

"Listen," Danny interrupts. "I don't mean to be a spoiler, but we need to get out of here and fast. I don't know who else might know about this location, but it's not worth sticking around and waiting."

"But what about Jake?" I say. "We can't pull him off the system until he wakes up."

Everyone stares at me, silent. I see it in their faces. They believe he's gone. Braindead. I shake my head, saying, "No. No, no, no."

Then I turn back to Jake and hold his hand, praying and begging for him to come back to me. "Don't give up," I tell him. "Come back to me."

"I'm going to keep trying," Dad says. "I will stay and do what I can."

Meanwhile, the others step away and begin making preparations to leave.

"We have to destroy everything," Javier tells the group. "There can be nothing remaining that could help another developer reinvent this."

"Maybe he just needs a few more minutes." Sun lightly touches my arm. "He might wake up before we have to leave."

"I'm not leaving him." I look down the line of gurneys where the bodies of the other Dream Walkers lie. "What about them?"

"The last one just lost brain waves," Sun says. "Jake is the only one hanging in there. Maybe it's a sign he'll survive."

Sweat has slicked Jake's hair to his face. His body feels warm and alive against my skin. Somehow I must find a way to reach him. But how?

"Jake," I whisper into his ear. "Please. You have to come back. For me. We have to finish this together. Remember, it's only a dream. Please wake up."

I lay my face against his chest, listening to his heartbeat. A steady thump. Then I move my face to hover over his and kiss him, holding his hands in mine. It's the first time I've ever kissed him when his body hasn't responded to me.

I press my forehead to his, waiting, hoping. And then it happens. A beep pings on the monitor and a spike shoots up on his brain monitor.

"Was that him?" Dad asks from the mainframe computer. At my nod, he says, "Whatever you are doing, keep doing it. He has a chance."

My heart skips and I curl up beside Jake and continue whispering in his ear.

"We've got company!" Tony says from where he's overlooking the window. "It's Lau and her cronies."

"We have to go now!" Danny says. "They've got guns."

Javier and Tony rush to turn over the portable tables holding all the equipment and barricade the door to the warehouse with them.

"We have to get out of here!" Sun is insistent, pulling me from Jake's side.

I shake my head. "I'm not leaving without him."

"We can't pull him off the mainframe," Dad warns. "That will cut his brain's ties from his body. He has to wake on his own."

"He stays," I say. "Then I stay. You all go without me."

"Guess we're all staying then," Tony says, dismally.

"Fine," Sun says in a way that sounds anything but fine. "I'll load up Dr. Reasner's van, but we might have to take Jake with us before he wakes up. And take these." She hands me a pair of earplugs. "Put them in when I give you the signal."

"Got it." I pocket them.

I hate putting the rest of the team in danger, but there's no way I can leave Jake. If it wasn't for him, Dr. Reasner would have the data for the Dreamscape and the ability to look into any person's brain and study their innermost secrets and use it as a weapon. I can't live with myself knowing I left him.

A pounding at the large wooden slider door pulls our attention to Zhang Lau and her guards. Frantically, Sun and Danny load items into the van while Dad and Javier remain at the computer, frantically trying out different systems. Tony stands in front of the door, holding a machine gun, but between his shaking arms and pacing, I'm not sure how capable he would be using it.

I doubt he could actually bring himself to use it.

I kiss Jake on the forehead and then snatch up one of the discarded guns, rushing to stand at Tony's side.

"This is so wrong," Tony says. "I'm a scientist and musician. I don't even know how to shoot this thing."

"Me either." My actions prove my words as I fumble over how to hold the gun. "But at least it will give them pause."

The pounding continues. The bolts on the door buckle and then pop off, one by one. My pulse pounds in my temples. I glance back at Jake, still sound asleep.

"Still sleeping?" Tony asks me. At my nod, I hear him mutter, "Damn."

With a groan, the door cracks and smashes flat to the ground, kicking up dust in its wake. Tony and I brace ourselves, holding our weapons before us.

FIFTY-ONE
NIGHT FLASH

Five security guards rush into the room but halt upon seeing Tony and me.

"Don't move," Tony yells. "Or you die!"

Lau strides in next, nose wrinkling at the dust. "What have we here?" she asks, surveying the scene before her.

"Dr. Reasner's experiment failed," I say. "And we're on our way out."

"Way out?" she says. "Hardly. You know far too much to be allowed to leave."

"We can either resolve this peacefully and everyone lives," I say. "Or we don't."

"Such a negotiator!" Lau states sarcastically. Then she nods to the man beside her, saying something in Chinese.

"I wouldn't do that." Sun steps out from behind the van and crosses her arms. "My uncle is Ma Yuzhu and if word got out on the street that it was, in fact, *you* who stole the \$81 million, things wouldn't go so well for you, now would it?"

Lau snarls. "You can't prove anything."

"Actually we can," a scraggly voice says behind us. My heart dives and then soars. It's a voice I've fallen in love with.

"Jake!" I practically drop my gun, but then remember to hold it at one of the security guards. Instead, I backtrack to Jake's gurney as he's ripping off his monitors and blood pressure wrap. "You're okay! Tell me you're okay."

I grab his hand as he grunts and sits up, blinking rapidly. His pupils are dilated and there is not an ounce of color on his face, but he appears right in his mind.

"Aria." His voice is hoarse. "Did it work?"

"Yes." I want to toss the gun onto the ground, cup my hands around his face and kiss him hard, but now is hardly the time. "It really did. I wasn't sure if you would wake up though."

"Me either. I kept running through this maze." He swings his feet over the edge of the gurney, but when his feet won't hold him, he resorts to sitting. "But then I heard your voice. I followed it out."

I bite my bottom lip to keep myself from falling apart and crying. I need to get my act together because we're not out of the situation yet. Jake focuses his attention back on Lau, helping himself stay upright using the medical stand.

"We've traced it." He pulls out a phone from a pocket hidden under the cuff of his dress pants and holds it up showing off some type of programming app. "After you stole those SWIFT codes from my brain, I was so ticked off that I designed a new program. It's called Tracker. Think of it like a digital fingerprint.

"Everything that you've done using those SWIFT codes has left behind a mark leading directly back to you. Tracker searches through the data until it identifies those fingerprints. It's all right here on my phone."

"Impossible," Lau says.

"How do you think we found you?" he asks.

I frown. He never mentioned designing this program. Plus, we found her by hacking into people's dreams to hunt her down. Lau presses her lips together and her security guards glance worriedly at her as if seeking guidance.

"All it takes is for me to push SEND." Jake lifts his phone into the air as if to prove his point. "Then all of my research and data will go directly to the Federal Reserve."

"I love the sound of the *ocean waves*," Sun interrupts meaningfully.

"What has that to do with anything?" Lau snaps at Sun.

"It means you can accept our deal." I discreetly withdraw my earplugs from my pocket. "Or you will regret you hadn't."

Lau clenches her fists. "What's the deal?"

"Let us go quietly and we won't send the feds Jake's data," I say. "They can slowly figure out the truth on their own through formal investigations."

"You take me for a fool," Lau scoffs. "I didn't build this empire without brains. Most people wouldn't even have the brilliance of understanding how to pull off a heist like I had. They wouldn't even know what to do with a million dollars or even how to hide them and that's where you underestimate me. In fact, my plan is greater than even Dr. Reasner."

"So I take it that means no," I say, dryly.

"You, boy, seemed like you might be a valuable person that I would want to keep alive." Lau turns to Jake, ignoring me. "But now I'm thinking you're just an annoyance. Kill—"

I don't hear anything else she says, because Sun has touched her ears, signaling for the rest of us to turn on our earplugs, which we do.

Except Lau is prepared. She smiles at us and holds earplugs of her own, waving them at us before putting them in along with the rest of her group.

*Crap.*

Sun frowns and her hands falter on the button. What can we do now? We're at a standstill. And that's when my eyes land on the black bag of the supplies we brought from MaxLife back home. The NightFlash is sticking out of the side.

We have only tested the NightFlash a few times since the Sound Oasis always works so well and is an easier transition into the Dreamscape.

It emits a series of pulsing blue light flashes that target

the parasympathetic branch of the nervous system. Basically, it triggers the part of the nervous system that slows down the heart and puts a person to sleep.

"Distract them," I mouth to Sun. She nods and starts reemphasizing why Lau should leave us alone.

Meanwhile, I creep over to the bag and snatch up the long bar. I'm not sure where the bag with sunglasses is located, but I don't have time to look for it. The rest of the team is watching me, and the moment I nod to them, they clamp their eyes closed. I just hope Jake thinks to do the same thing.

Sun turns on the Oasis and I flick on the NightFlash, clamping my eyes shut the moment the blue light begins to pulse through the room. Blindly, I dig through the bag until my hand closes over a soft bag that has the sunglasses in it. I manage to put on the glasses, allowing me to open my eyes again.

Lau and all her crew are now lying on the ground while my team has their hands over their eyes. Quickly, I distribute the glasses and Sun turns off the Sound Oasis, which allows us to talk again.

"Tie up Lau and her guards," Dad says. "Then we'll get out of here."

"All her security men had earplugs in," Javier says after checking the guards. "They were prepared."

"How could they have known?" Tony says.

"They learned their lesson at the casino," I say.

"Then I guess it's a good thing we were more prepared," Sun says. "Nice work, Aria."

"Can someone tell me what just happened?" Jake asks.

"It's called a NightFlash," I explain. "It works in a very similar fashion as the Sound Oasis, but it doesn't last as long, so let's hurry and get to the van."

"Wait," Jake says. "Let me stop recording."

He pauses to push the stop button on his phone and grins.

"You were bluffing with Lau, weren't you?" I ask. "You never created an app called Tracker."

"Guilty," He grins. "But I did record Lau confessing to the whole thing. Never underestimate the simple camera feature on your phone."

The flight back to Florida on Danny's jet is blissfully uneventful. Before we flew out, Jake called up his dad and sent off the video file of the conversation with Lau in the warehouse.

"It'll speed up the process of procuring the money," Jake explains as we settle in for the long flight. "He says he'll pass it on to the feds. If all goes well, he'll be released of all charges."

I squeeze Jake's hand. "You know it's weird, but it feels like I've known you for a lifetime."

"And just think." He winks at me. "All you've seen is my cranky, jet-lagged side. Wait until we get back and I can show you my true skills and finesse."

I punch his arm.

It's like a burden has been lifted off my shoulders. Dad sits in the seat in front of me, sipping seltzer water while

Danny passes out his favorite dumpling soup. I withdraw Dad's watch from around my neck, turning it over in my hands once before holding it out to Dad.

"I found it on the floor of the lab the night they took you." I drop the watch into his palm. "It got a little beaten up, but it still tells time. I know this sounds weird, but I just kept telling myself that as long as it was working, you were still alive."

Dad stares at the stars swirling in an endless circle. A single tear trickles down his face. Then he grabs my hands in his, gripping me tightly. "You are so brave. I have to admit, I was mad when you showed up." He chuckles lightly at this. "But you did well. I owe you everything."

"Does that mean you'll pay for my college of choice?" I grin mischievously at him.

He laughs louder then. "Yes, any college you want. And I want you to keep the watch. As a reminder of what you can do when you believe in it."

He then slides the chain back over my head. It settles neatly on my chest as if it belongs there.

"Mom won't be upset?" I ask. "You giving away her gift."

"No," he says. "I'm sure she'll just be glad to see us both alive and healthy when we get home."

"What did your mom say when you told her everything?" Jake asks.

"She could hardly speak, she was crying so hard," I twist the chain through my fingers. "But it was a good cry."

"By the way," Jake says. "My dad said I'm pretty much grounded until I graduate, but I was thinking maybe you could come over and I could show you Battle for Eternity in the comfort of a lounge chair rather than being chased through the forest in my dreams."

"Are you asking me out on a date, Jake Sutherland?"

"Yeah. I just might be."

IT'S a cool evening as I drive with my convertible top down over to Jake's house. I soak in the feeling of freedom as the wind cuts across my face. The air smells of orange blossoms and a hint of the sea. When I pull up to Jake's house, he's waiting for me, sitting on the back of his mom's car.

"Your mom doesn't mind you sitting on her car?" I ask as I step out onto the pavement.

"She'd kill me," he says. "Which is why your lips are sealed."

"That's going to cost you."

"Now that sounds like fun."

I roll my eyes, but I can't resist a smile. "So is it really ready?"

"It's got a few tweaks still, but it's pretty solid." He takes my hand and leads me to the pool house, which I aptly named the Bat Cave.

"Tell me you got rid of the Receptor." I cringe just thinking about the memory of that awful creature.

"The Receptor? Are you crazy? That beast is killer. He's one of my best creations."

"He still gives me nightmares."

"Exactly!" Jake opens the door and motions for me to step in first. "Which is why he can't be terminated."

The cool AC of the room washes over me as I step inside. Jake leads me around the cases of his superhero paraphernalia to a soft cushioned couch positioned in front of a massive computer screen. A snack table is set up to the right with Cokes chilling in an ice tub and a platter with an assortment of doughnuts.

"Doughnuts?" I say.

"From the King himself," he says. "They're your favorite, right?"

I'm impressed. And I'm not easily impressed. I didn't think he would remember that Donut King made my favorite doughnuts. Jake shifts on his feet, suddenly looking a little lost in his own place.

"Okay, Batman," I tease. "Show me the final product of your baby."

He grins, and when he does, I just want to wrap my arms around him and kiss him hard and forget the game altogether, but he flicks on the gaming center. The screen lights up, casting an image that looks exactly like the beach we stayed at in the Philippines. The halo projector beams from the ceiling, washing the gaming square that he's set up so that the area looks like it is the beach.

I step onto the gaming mat, and instantly it feels as if I'm transported across the world to Boracay Island. The image of my avatar pops up on the screen. I laugh at seeing the rendition of myself. I'm wearing a bikini top and a sarong, and my red hair is billowing around me just like it did in Mr. Bosu's dream. The sound of crashing waves fills the room and—

"Wait, is that the scent of the ocean?" I ask as he moves to join me.

He holds my hands in his, smiling. "I cheated a little. It's a sea-scented candle. So what do you think? Are you ready to try it out?"

"Maybe." I wrap my arms around his shoulders, drawing him closer. "After you give me that kiss you promised."

He kisses me then and I'm swept away into a dream that only exists in reality. After everything we've been through and experienced, for the first time in my life, I don't know what my plan is or what tomorrow will bring. Somehow that feels okay though.

"I feel like I'm dreaming," he whispers, his breath hot against my cheek. "It's all too good to be true."

"If this is a dream, let's never wake up."

# TAKE YOUR NEXT ADVENTURE WITH CHRISTINA FARLEY

The Dreamscape Series

**The Dream Hunt**: the sequel to *The Dream Heist* coming to stores on Nov, 14, 2023.

*Only the fearless survive.*

Plunge headfirst into the vivid landscapes of Peru and the dark, twisted realm of dreams in the action-packed thriller, The Dream Hunt, the anticipated sequel to The Dream Heist.

Aria Hale, a young and brilliant scientist, is ready to spend more time with her boyfriend and family. That is until she's kidnapped and taken to Peru. There she discovers a new enemy, one who has taken her father's Dreamscape program and altered it to unravel the very fabric of reality. With the help of her friends, Aria sets out on a perilous journey to destroy the programming. The hunt takes them through catacombs, the Amazon jungle, and into the heart of danger.

Aria must use her wits, courage, and technical prowess to save the world from a catastrophic event. But time is running out, and this new Dreamscape is more dangerous than even she could imagine. The hunt is on and only the fearless will survive.

The Immortal Bound Series

**The Immortal Secret:** Enter the world of immortals in this contemporary fantasy series.

*A sizzling romance of supernatural thrills, impossible choices, and heart-stopping adventure.*

Step into a world where immortals reign and power is everything. When Estrella is cast out from her immortal people, she's sent to live with mortals without her memories. As she struggles to uncover her true self, she meets two rivals for her heart. One wants to protect her from the past. Another wants her to embrace it. But soon she discovers her secret is more dangerous than she could ever imagine. A sizzling romance of supernatural thrills, impossible choices, and heart-stopping adventure.

**Start reading for free at**: https://www.amazon.com/kindle-vella/story/B0BC9DBV67

The Immortal Legend: The prequel novella to The Immortal Secret. (Available for free to newsletter subscribers. Go to www.ChristinaFarley.com to sign up.)

The Gilded Series

**The Gilded Series,** a bestselling contemporary fantasy series set in Korea.

Sixteen-year-old Jae Hwa Lee is a Korean-American girl with a black belt, a deadly proclivity with steel-tipped arrows, and a chip on her shoulder the size of Korea itself. When her widowed dad uproots her to Seoul from her home in L.A., Jae thinks her biggest challenges will be fitting into a new school and dealing with her dismissive Korean grandfather. Then she discovers that a Korean demi-god, Haemosu, has been stealing the soul of the oldest daughter of each generation in her family for centuries. And she's next.

But that's not Jae's only problem.

There's also Marc. Irresistible and charming, Marc threatens to break the barriers around Jae's heart. As the two grow closer, Jae must decide if she can trust him. But Marc has a secret of his own—one that could help Jae overturn the curse on her family for good. It turns out that Jae's been wrong about a lot of things: her grandfather is her greatest ally, even the tough girl can fall in love, and Korea might just be the home she's always been looking for.

Middle Grade Novels

**The Princess and the Page**: Get enchanted in this magical, fairytale mash-up set in France.

*A mystical middle-grade adventure about a pulls-no-punches princess and the power of her magical pen.*

A dark secret lurks in Keira's family. She comes from a long line of Word Weavers, who bring their stories to life when they use a magical pen. But for generations Word Weavers have been hunted for their power. That's why Keira is forbidden to write. When Keira discovers her grandma's Word Weaver pen and writes a story for the Girls' World fairy-tale contest, she starts to wonder if anyone ever truly lives happily ever after. Inspired by the life and times of Gabrielle d'Estrées, a real French princess who lived during the 1500s, The Princess and the Page follows the mystical journey of a modern-day "royal" who goes from having a pen in her hand to wishing for the world at her fingertips.

**Explore all Christina Farley's published works and forthcoming novels at**: www.ChristinaFarley.com

# AUTHOR NOTE

I hope you enjoyed *The Dream Heist* and traveling the world with me!

This story was born from two separate news articles. One was about a new dream therapy designed to help dementia patients' brains reconnect with their memories. This was a special interest to me because my grandmother was dealing with memory loss when I wrote this story and it was so hard to watch her struggle with that.

The other article was about an $81 million bank heist called The Bangladesh Bank Heist. I was completely riveted by that someone could steal so much money never leaving their home. So I thought, wouldn't it be fun to create a story based on these articles? So I did!

As you may have guessed, I also put many of my own personal travels and experiences into the story. As a world traveler, one of the things that brings me joy is sharing the world and my experiences with you!

If you loved *The Dream Heist*, check out its sequel, *The Dream Hunt*.

Thank you again for reading!
Christina

# ACKNOWLEDGMENTS

This book was so much fun to write, but the science and tech of it really pushed me as a writer! I am incredibly grateful to my MiG Writers critique group—Kate Fall, Andrea Mack, Debbie Ridpath Ohi, and Carmella VanVleet—for reading and helping me work out all the kinks in this story. We have been together as a group for over a decade and your friendship is priceless. I'm so grateful to be a part of such a talented circle of ladies.

This book wouldn't have reached the reader's hands if it hadn't been for Beth Revis, Megan Shepherd, Brook Hatchett, and Mindy McGinnis. I'm eternally grateful for your expertise, encouragement, and knowledge as I developed this project. What a journey!

A huge thank you to my ride-or-die ladies—Vivi Barnes and Amy Christine Parker. Words can't express how much I appreciate you both. I can't wait to hit the road with you for another book tour!

To Jessica Khoury for a stunning and riveting cover. I am in awe of your talent.

I must give a shout-out to my family for making this writing dream of mine possible. Mom, Dad, Julianne, David and Cassia, I wouldn't have wanted to take this writing journey without you!

I'm so thankful to God for giving me the ability to write stories and share them with others. Finally, thank you to my two boys, Caleb and Luke, and husband, Doug, for always encouraging me to follow my dreams. You three are my everything!

# ABOUT THE AUTHOR

Photo: Liga Photography

CHRISTINA FARLEY is the author of the bestselling Gilded series, THE PRINCESS AND THE PAGE, THE DREAM HEIST, and THE IMMORTAL SECRET. When not traveling the world or creating imaginary ones, she spends time with her family in Clermont, Florida with her husband and two sons where they are busy preparing for the next World Cup, baking cheesecakes, and raising a pet dragon that's in disguise as a cockatiel. Visit her at ChristinaFarley.com.